# Framed Deception

Rita Redswood

# Acknowledgements

Thank you very much to everyone who has given me support in the creation and editing of this book. It truly means a lot, and I greatly appreciate it.

<u>Chapter One: Sip</u>

*Delicate hands swept across the light creation. Eyes filled with an almost inhuman grace snapped the delicacy in half and watched the miniscule crumbs descend in the air to wooden floor.*

Dark brown lampshades dimmed the light from the lamps upon the oak tables, which were stained in a dark finishing polish. Bookshelves lined the right and left walls. A front window permitted the late afternoon rays to shine through, but a gold-colored shade blocked out some of the sunlight. That shade also prevented the customers from seeing the café's name on the window: Bread and Books. It was a simple name, but it portrayed the purpose of the shop well.

Inside, it was mostly quiet. There was the occasional flipping of book pages, the careful sip of one's drink and the sound of customers ordering. Among all of this, there was even the delicate sound of breaking off a piece of pastry. The crispiness of the buttery treat snapped in beautiful harmony among the atmosphere.

There were only so many tables in the café: eight to be exact and four on each side. Four tables seated two, and four permitted one customer each. The shop wasn't made for conversation, but an occasional quiet one did spring up every now and then about the books, food or drink in the establishment.

The small, brass bell chimed. A few customers peered up from their books. Some quickly turned back to their readings, having lost interest in the individual. Others stared for a little longer. They wanted to assess whether or not the customer understood the environment and what was expected of her. If she was a loud newcomer, she wouldn't last long in the shop. After all, not everyone saw the sign near the front door. *Please keep your voice down.*

None of them had to fear her presence, though. Some even recognized her. She was a regular at the shop, and she would come every other day in the late afternoon. A few knew her first name to be Elaine. Another even possessed knowledge of her last name: Margarit.

As the door closed behind her, her lush short, curly and dark brown locks bounced around her head due to her bob hair cut. A red bow was on the left side of her hair and restrained some of her strands in a perfect fashion. Dark brown eyes stared ahead and at the pastry display. Vibrant red lipstick painted her lips while the perfect amount of black eyeliner, eye shadow and mascara complemented her orbs.

Adorning her form was a simple, red blouse with ruffles around the collar and the hems of the sleeves. A black chiffon skirt flowed around her legs with an elegancy that most would never bother to possess. Red Jeannie pumps with small black bows decorated her feet and clicked lightly against the wood flooring. On her right shoulder rested a black leather purse.

Confidence rang in her step, and most couldn't keep their gaze on her for long. She did smile to a few individuals who she recognized along the way: Mr. Gregory and his wife, Mrs. Gregory. They were an elderly couple, and they came to the shop every Wednesday to share in their love of mystery novels. Sometimes, the pair would be heard reading softly to each other.

Passing by another familiar face, she dipped her head a bit in recognition. "Good afternoon, Kelly." She received the gesture in return before the young adult returned to her history text on Versailles and its founding. Kelly brushed back some strands of her black locks while her brown eyes took in the next paragraph of the book eagerly.

In the shop presently, there was one more individual who she had seen before. He always seemed to be in the shop when she was, but she thought it as not being odd. To her, he was another regular. The man lowered his book on the biography of Claude Monet and gave a gentle smile. She returned it before she reached the front counter.

"What will it be today, Elaine?" asked the owner, Frank, energetically. His glasses rested on his nose a little loosely, but he adjusted them as she inspected the display case. Both of them already knew what her drink order would be. "Wait." She glanced up to him. The man wore a friendly smile that fit his silver-white beard well. "I've got this thing that you'll love."

She chuckled as he moved over to the display case and pulled something out for her. Before she could even have a say on the matter, he set down a glass plate with a slice of tiramisu. "I've already had that before." An amused smile was on her lips.

"Exactly. Now, your usual with it?" He continued to bear his smile, already knowing that she was fine with the dessert.

"Yes. Thanks." She retrieved her black wallet and paid for the order before he set a fork on her plate. Facing away from her, he moved over to the espresso machine and worked on her cappuccino. Only his head of silver-white hair could be seen from her perspective.

Taking her treat, she placed it down upon the last table in the space. It was near to the back and close to the man reading the biography. Generally, she always sat at that table unless there was a seat closer to the front window. Her heels clicked against the wood before she stopped in front of one of the bookshelves.

Reaching back, her hand slipped behind the books and into the small space in the back. Her fingers grasped the smooth, worn binding of her desired read. The book slipped out from its hiding place, and her cherry lips upturned into a tiny smile. She returned to her seat as Frank was setting down her drink. "Enjoy, kiddo." Elaine laughed without a sound before she thanked him and flipped open the fiction novel.

While she sat, read and ate, she entered her own little world. Her typical happy persona faded by a smidgen, and it was only noticeable by a watchful eye. If one observed her closely, that person could tell that her mind faced darker troubles than what pastry to order in her favorite coffee shop.

Every day, she read the same book in the café. She hid it behind other books so that no one else could find it, and she thought that her action was secretive enough, but it was far from it. Everyone who knew her saw what she did, but they didn't comment on it. They let her be and never touched the book that she seemed to adore so much.

One of those individuals, though, understood that on some days she hadn't even read the book. She had flipped the pages mindlessly as thoughts about her situation filled her mind. Some days, she actually had read the text, but those had been becoming less and less. That person comprehended her behavior so well that he could even tell just by looking at the back of her. Her posture told him everything.

If she bent over too much and ate her dessert swiftly, she was reading, but if she sat up relatively straight and took miniscule, steady bites, then her mind was elsewhere. He had confirmed these thoughts when he had passed her by on his way to leave in the past. Always, he had left before her.

Today, she took thirty minutes to finish her cake, and she was sitting up straighter than yesterday. His book lowered by a fraction. That had been the longest time. Before, it had been twenty minutes maximum. Had she received a call before she had entered the café? The man's left foot tapped against his shin, and the light shone off of his polished black dress shoe.

News on that wretched man must've changed. Perhaps, it was in his favor, but he doubted it. No, she probably planned to visit her dearly beloved again that night. The thought sickened him, but he knew that he didn't have much longer to wait.

Still, he wished that she would choose a new book. That book was an indication that she always was thinking about that lover of hers. It was his favorite book, and it became hers once the accident had happened. A scowl touched his lips. If only she could realize how she was wasting her time sooner than later.

Not being able to stand his passive state towards her any longer and worried about her, he stood from his seat. She was at a two person table. Without asking, he pulled out the chair across from her. People glanced up from their reads, but when they saw her divert her eyes to him calmly, they returned to their books.

He didn't allow her to utter a word of questioning. "Are you alright?" he asked as though he didn't know the troubles in her life. His eyes held a gentle, caring glow, and his lips were formed in a concerned line. "Forgive me for prying, but you seem ... off."

Blinking, she tried to enter her usual state, but it was too late. She understood that and placed both of her hands over the book. A light sigh left her stunning, plump lips. "It's ..."

"It's not nothing." Her eyes widened a bit, and she gave him a more inquisitive stare. He perceived easily that she was stunned to have someone care about what was behind her daily mask. She was even more amazed that he saw through it, especially when they never had talked before.

Without another word, he retrieved her book from her and closed it. In its place, he left his. He sent a reassuring smile her way and deposited her text in its usual spot. The man didn't glance back to her. Rather, he left, but she remained seated. Shock ruled her countenance before she noticed a tiny piece of white paper sticking out from the biography.

Curious, she removed it. *Talk to me if you need to. I'll listen.* A number followed next.

## Chapter Two: Wait

*Artificial light illuminated the room and gave a deathly glow to the individual below it. Her eyes gazed upon the person, but another set of eyes watched her.*

Dark blue velvet heels clicked against the old, cracked tile, which needed to be mopped for the evening. Artificial lights cast shadows across the long halls. Many mint-colored doors were passed by. A nurse in pink scrubs walked past at a brisk pace. She was checking her watch, and a smile was on her lips. Probably, she was getting off of work.

Elaine gave her a small smile and received the gesture back, though; that smile faded quickly away. The number forty-four was coming up. That number created dread in her heart but also hope. A lengthy sigh escaped past her maroon-painted lips. She pushed a loose strand of hair behind her left ear. Maybe, tonight would be the night.

To distract herself, she slipped her left hand into her purse and removed the piece of paper. It had been a week since that man had left her his number, and she hadn't called him once. He still had come to the café and had given his usual smile to her, but she had trouble delivering her typical one back. Her nervousness probably had been painfully apparent.

Looking down at it, she furrowed her brow and pursed her lips. She didn't know what to do with it, but she didn't desire to dispose of it. Truthfully, she needed someone to talk to, and she didn't have coworkers; she worked from home as an editor for multiple online blogs. There had been no one that she could talk to face to face and have them simply listen until he had deposited his number in that book.

He was nearly a stranger, though. They had never talked to each other before last Wednesday, but she wondered how he had seen right through her. The man always had sat behind her. Had he been observing her that entire time? A chill ran up her spine, but she wasn't sure if it was unwelcome or not. Admittedly, it had been nice to find out that someone cared enough to look past her usual front. Her fingers dropped the paper back into her bag. Maybe later, she would call him.

Stopping, her body tensed. She stood directly in front of the door. Her hand reached out and grabbed the metal handle before she pulled on it. The large wooden door opened before she closed it gently behind her. Elaine's quiet behavior, though, was unnecessary. He wouldn't wake ... unless things took a turn for the better.

Heels tapping against the tile, she moved over one of the questionable chairs. She set her bag down on the plastic nightstand and seated herself on the worn-out pink cushion. The chair rocked a little with her weight, but she was used to the ancient chair's behavior. Her hands smoothed out the skirt of her short, dark blue dress before she adjusted the black belt around her waist.

Gently, she wrapped her hands around the man's left hand. A pained smile crossed her lips, and her thumbs rubbed circles into his skin. His eyes remained closed, and he didn't move against her touch. Her other hand reached over and brushed back smooth locks of his sandy brown hair. She wished that she could stare upon his stunning light green orbs, but that wouldn't be a possibility until he woke up. Elaine trailed her fingers along his face. Lightly, she chuckled at how his cheeks were somewhat chubby. They made him look adorable, though; in the past, it had made it hard at times to take him seriously.

Now, though, those cheeks had scars on them, but they were small in comparison to the rest of the marks on him from the car accident. She leaned over and kissed her lover's forehead. Her lips left a light stain of lipstick there, and she grabbed a tissue before she wiped it off. Before she removed her hand, her fingers lingered near his thin lips that somehow had managed to form a cute pout every now and then. That had been part of his so-called frustrated stare. Another quiet laugh left her, but it morphed into a near sob.

It had been months since the accident. Reginald had been driving to their apartment after work, but another car had run a red light and slammed right into his side of the car. The doctors had expected him to die, but he had pulled through to some degree. He had been in a coma since, but she was losing hope. None of hospital staff helped. They had administered to her words of sympathy, but she had heard the conversations behind closed doors. All of them expected him to pass soon, and that broke her heart.

Despite that, though, she forced herself to come to the hospital as much as she could to sit with him. Even with her dim amount of hope left, she told herself that she might get lucky one night. He might open his eyes for her.

A door opening behind her drew her from her thoughts. She sat more upright and glanced over her left shoulder. It was one of the nurses who took care of him. Her dirty blonde hair was done up in a bun, and her brown eyes revealed exhaustion. Gina smiled tiredly to Elaine while she walked over to her patient and performed her usual checkup on him.

"You really should take care of yourself more, Elaine." One of those sympathetic smiles was shot towards the younger woman. "This is wearing you out. You should go home and rest. It's late."

Elaine glanced towards the clock in the room. It was eight in the evening. Visiting hours would be over at nine. "I'll stay for the usual hour. It's not that late." A fake smile painted the lips of the twenty-two-year-old female. "Thank you, though. You're always so kind to me."

"Just let me know if you need anything." Her pink lips stretched into another smile, but it was smaller that time. The nurse's façade was disappearing. She made a few more checks before her eyes stayed on her clipboard for a few moments. Elaine didn't notice, though, that the nurse was glancing towards Reginald in actuality. When her eyes met Elaine's again, she stood a little straighter. "Have a good night, Ms. Margarit. Call if you need something." There was a more professional air around Gina, and her pronounced cheekbones aided that. Her pen tapped the clipboard once more before it clicked shut. Gina's work shoes squeaked slightly on the tile, and it made Elaine thankful for her heels.

Relaxing a little, the woman reached for her bag but stopped. Reginald's hand ... it twitched. Her heartbeat grew, and her hands wrapped around his tightly. "Reg, Reg," she called out softly, shaking his hand a little. No response greeted her, but she tried several more times. Nothing. Elaine's heart sunk, and she slouched over.

Maybe, she had imagined his hand moving. Beforehand, she had done something similar. She had thought that his eyes had opened a crack, but it had been nothing but tiredness affecting her. Her fingers rubbed the bridge of her nose as she tried to keep in her tears. A few slipped past and dropped onto the tile. Shifting her eyes back to him, she bit her bottom lip. How much longer would she have to wait? Or, would he forever be in his present state.

Needing to stand, she bent over and kissed him on the cheek before she wiped off the slight lipstick mark again. She would retrieve some coffee for the next hour. That would help keep her mind off of what just had happened. Elaine entered the hall and turned to her right and headed straight. Not too long after, she found the two coffee containers: one decaf and the other regular. In comparison to Frank's coffee, it was ... trash to be honest, but she couldn't complain too much. It was free, and it kept her mind on other things.

Grabbing a paper cup and putting a holder around it, she pressed the button on the regular and watched a few trickles enter her container. A frown covered her lips, and she wanted to collapse against the counter. She supposed that she could grab some milk or water from the patient fridge, but that wouldn't have the same effect.

"This is a surprise." Almost, she chucked the cup and jumped. A melodic, light laugh sounded next to her. Her eyes turned to her right and widened significantly. Before her was the man from the café. He was leaning against the wall, and a cup of steaming coffee was on the counter. She never had heard the decaf container being utilized, though. It bothered her even more that she never had heard him walk up to the spot.

"I won't keep you long, but I had seen you over here and thought to give you a suggestion." Still baffled by his sudden appearance, she didn't respond; she only continued to stare. He chuckled again before he pointed to her empty cup. "Go to the nurse's desk. They have some fresh coffee there and better cream than that powder stuff. It makes it a bit more bearable."

"Wh-why ..."

"Why am I here? I have a friend who I wanted to visit."

"Oh, I hope that they feel better soon." She didn't exactly sound sincere, but her mind still was processing him before her. It also was troubling her that he wasn't mentioning her lack of calling him at all. In fact, he was acting like he never had passed her his number.

"Thank you. I think that they will." He smiled ... a genuine smile. "I'm leaving soon, so you know what," he took her cup and handed her his, "have mine. I about had to wrestle the nurse for this. I'll see you at the shop?" Hesitantly, she nodded, and he smiled all the more. "Till then." The man walked off, and she stood in the hallway for a few minutes, shocked, before she returned to Reginald's room.

## Chapter Three: Meet

*A magazine, crisp and new, sat on the plastic, grey table. Two individuals were seated across from each other: one a woman and the other a man.*

After that night in the hospital, she had seen him like usual in the café, but she also realized that she never had received his name. He probably knew hers since Frank had used her name almost every time that she had ordered her drink and dessert. Despite that fact, she never had asked for his name.

The present day was the same, but she had initiated a meeting with him. He had been too mysterious for her not to, though; she had been safe about where. It was at a local fast food chain: Cropper's. She also picked the location that was the most crowded in the city. That way, several individuals would at least see them together.

Her plum purple strappy wedges carried her across the asphalt ground and towards the building. She pressed the lock button on her keys for her red mini cooper and heard the locking sound behind her. Elaine adjusted the plum-colored ribbon around the black collar of her black button-up dress.

Nerves ate at her as she grew closer to the establishment, but she forced her feet forward. She pulled out her phone and checked the last text message from him. *At five.* It certainly seemed curt, but his previous messages indicated that he was looking forward to the meeting. Maybe, it bothered her because it sounded almost like a demand.

It didn't help that she recalled how he seemingly had popped up out of nowhere at the hospital. She desired to question him on his friend, but that would be impolite and might cause her to be out of his favor. Right now, she wished for his company to both learn more about him and also to have someone to talk to about Reginald's situation that wasn't a doctor or nurse.

Taking a deep breath in and exhaling, she pushed on the door, and it wouldn't budge. Elaine blinked before she read the sign on the door. *Pull.* Nearly, she face-palmed out of embarrassment. She followed the sign and hoped that no one had taken notice.

A bell rang as she opened the door more, and a few glanced her way before they returned to their food, ordering or work. Her eyes glanced over the front seats, and she didn't find him. When her dark brown orbs stared to the back, she saw him flipping through a magazine, but she couldn't read the title due to her distance. He didn't look up either, nor had he been one of the individuals to shift their attention her way briefly.

Tightening her grip on her purse handle, she made her way over to him. Each step sounded louder in her ears until each was almost booming. Hopefully, she didn't appear as nervous as she felt. Besides her reasons from before about the man, there also was the simple detail that she never had met with another man outside of work after she had started to date Reginald. The whole thing was rather awkward for her, and she didn't wish to give the impression that she was searching for something more than a friendly ear. She hoped that he wasn't expecting something more either.

As soon as he had heard the bell, he had glanced up by a fraction so that she wouldn't notice. He had been leaning against the orange cushion and had his legs crossed. The magazine had been level just below his eyes so that it would appear that he was continuing to read. He had kept it that way even as she began to walk towards him. Every step of hers had been music to his ears, and it continued that way as she advanced all the nearer.

Each strand of her luscious locks bounced in rhythm to her steps. He didn't know how she kept her hair so perfect. After all, the curtains in her bathroom always had been closed. How she was dressed appealed to him too. The way the dress hugged her curves was perfect and made him ache to wrap his arms around her waist. It fueled the desire in him to rub rough circles into the skin of her hips. In actuality, it was like that every time he gazed upon her. Her style suited her splendidly.

When her movement stopped, he heard a light, delicate cough. Placing the magazine down, he smiled up to her and stood up. He loved how even when she wore heels he was taller than her by still quite a bit since he stood at six feet and six inches. "Please, take a seat." His arm indicated to the bench across from him.

Politely, she nodded her head in thanks and seated herself. "Thank you." She made herself comfortable, but he could practically spot her nerves shaking. How cute. He reseated himself as she folded her hands over her lap. "I would've called ..."

"Please," he held up his left hand slightly, "there's no need for that, Elaine." He chuckled in a friendly manner. "You hardly know me. I hadn't been expecting you to call me early."

Hesitantly, she nodded her head. "Well ... yes." Her lips tightened as though she was debating something, and it took all of his willpower not to stare at her maroon-painted lips. Dark brown orbs met his eyes. "I've been meaning to ask ... What's your name?"

Secretly, he watched her lips relax as pure curiosity filled her orbs. He pushed his magazine to the side, and her orbs followed the movement as expected. His fingers glided away from the cover, and he stood up from his seat once more. Puzzlement crept into her eyes, and a slight bit of worry soon joined it when he moved to beside her. "Edmund."

His right hand extended out to her, and she shook it lightly in return. He was tempted to place a kiss upon the back of her hand. Her beauty did deserve appreciation after all, but he resisted the urge so as not to frighten her off. "I'll go order us some food. What would you like?"

Reaching to her purse, which was now resting beside her, she shook her head. "I can pay for my own." She was about to put her purse back over her shoulder and get up before he placed a hand on her left shoulder. Elaine froze slightly at the action, and a chill ran over her, but it left a pleasant feeling behind.

"My treat. I had given you my number. It's only fair." His lips upturned into a kind smile, and she couldn't help but agree to his offer. "Good." He removed his hand. "Now, what would you like?"

Thinking over the menu swiftly in her head, she replied, "A smoothie and a cookie will be fine. I'll eat dinner later." He was ready to chuckle, and she noted the gleam of amusement in his orbs. "Is something funny?"

"Yes. Your tastes are cute. I was expecting you to order a coffee." His lips twitched a little before he did release a chuckle. That one sound brought a slight bit of heat to her cheeks. Her lips formed into a pout. "But, I understand." Slightly, she averted her eyes up to him. Almost, she was taken aback when she realized how much taller he was. Only then, did she really notice it, but she kept silent on the thought. "After coffee from our favorite café, I suppose that you wouldn't want to pay for a cup anywhere else."

Not being able to form words in that moment, she hummed in agreement. "I'll be back shortly. You're welcome to look at that magazine while you wait." He smiled to her one last time before he walked off. Her eyes followed him for a bit and considered how well he was dressed. A black suit jacket, which was open, matching pants and a black and plum striped dress shirt adorned him. Black dress shoes clicked lightly against the tiles. In color scheme, he ... matched her. That was ... odd.

Almost, he grinned. He practically could feel her eyes scanning over his form, so he slowed down his pace by a little so that she could enjoy the view for awhile longer. If only she could stare at him like that all of the time or with different feelings in mind than mere curiosity and confusion. She probably spotted that they were matching. To others in the restaurant, they most likely appeared as a couple, which was what he wanted.

Edmund heard the sliding of paper amidst the other noise of the place. She had to be dragging the magazine over to her. He desired to find out which painting she liked the most out of the magazine. His home required a new one, and he wished for her input on the subject.  Reaching the front, he stood in line and sighted her upright form. Her fragile fingers turned the cover page, and he drew his eyes away from her in satisfaction.

Elaine examined each page, but she wondered why he had a magazine about the interior of one's home. Was he planning on redesigning his home? The items in the magazine were awfully expensive, and her lips even parted at the ridiculousness of some of the costs. Maybe, he was using it for ideas. Her eyes paused on one of the pages, though.

On the wall of the room in the picture she saw a stunning painting. She didn't know who the artist was, but it was difficult to look away. Various pastel flowers grew high into the artwork and tried to hide the mountain range and lake ahead of them. Grey clouds coated the sky. It looked like an ideal retreat, which her mind probably needed from all of her visits to the hospital. Perhaps when Reginald woke up, they could visit a place like that.

"Ah, that suits you." Almost, she jumped until she recognized his voice. "What do you think of it?"

Not looking up at him, she eased into her seat again and smiled to herself. "It's peaceful. I would like to visit a place like that one day." Unbeknownst to her, he smirked and knew that he could arrange that.

## Chapter Four: Pass

*Dark brown orbs stared over the chilled hand as the line went flat. Crystalline tears dripped onto the tiles, and glass-like fingers soon covered the watery source.*


The conversation with Edmund had taken an unexpected turn since they hadn't discussed at all what had been troubling her for so long. Rather, they had conversed over the magazine more and the various paintings within it. She, though, always had found that one painting to be the most spectacular. Their meeting had become one that had been lighthearted and peaceful.

She had left the Cropper's feeling refreshed and a bit better about things. Edmund had seemed to enjoy their time together too, and she wondered if he would join her at her table next time at Bread and Books. Elaine wouldn't mind that in the slightest. They wouldn't be able to talk like they had done that day, but they could chat quietly here and there. A smile touched her lips at the thought.

Early next morning, however, she heard her phone ringing. She shifted in her sleep and grumbled a bit at the noise, but it persisted. Irritated, she blinked open her eyes tiredly. Her dark brown locks were in disarray, and the left strap on her olive green nightgown was slipped off of her shoulder.

Sitting up, she yawned and fixed the strap before she reached over to her phone. Instantly, her eyes widened at the number. Her orbs checked the time and noted that it was four in the morning. A pit in her stomach formed. She answered and hurriedly asked, "What happened?! Is he okay?!"

Hesitation was on the other line before the nurse finally responded, "Ms. Margarit, he's in critical condition ..." Immediately, Elaine hung up and raced out of bed. She didn't even bother changing out of her nightgown. The woman threw on a red coat and buttoned it hurriedly before she slipped on black pumps and rushed out of the apartment.

On the drive there, she didn't care that she was going twenty over the speed limit. All that mattered was getting to the hospital. Thankfully, she never got caught. Otherwise, she might've lost it. She slammed on her breaks in the parking lot and threw open the car door. Quickly, she locked it and sped off towards her boyfriend.

People gave her looks on the way, but she didn't care one bit. To her, everyone was but a mannequin that needed to be pushed out of her path. She didn't have to shove past anyone, though, because they understood the expression on her face and how she presently carried herself. It was easy to tell that she had received dreadful news.

Standing in front of forty-four, she saw the door wide open. A doctor and multiple nurses were in the room. She heard the word *clear* and saw Reginald's body jolt up a bit. Things remained in the red. Elaine stood by the doorway and felt the world melt away from her. "We're losing him!" Her heart seemed to stop, and her head felt dizzy. *Clear.* The beeping sound in the room faded, and her legs steadily carried her into the room.

Noticing her, the doctor looked over, and his eyes held sympathy. She barely glanced at him. Elaine stopped close to Reginald's bed. Droplets splashed onto the tile, but she didn't note the sound. Rather, she kept hearing *clear* over and over again. The woman was so distant from the world that she didn't notice the nurse Gina cry and leave the room.

Gently as though he would morph into dust, she wrapped her hands around his left one. Already, the warmth from it was fading, but she held on all the tighter. Her eyes stared to his closed ones, and her heart seemed to snap into two. The *if only* game began to play in her head, and her legs nearly collapsed under her. Shakily, she leaned down and placed a kiss on his cold lips.

Hands rested on her shoulders, but she didn't register who they belonged to. All she realized was that she was being moved from her lover. Her head shook, and she muttered, "Please stop." Such a plea, though, went unheard as she was led further and further from the room. The door shut. Sobs escaped her, and they refused to pause.

Before she knew how, she found herself on a mauve-colored chair. A clock ticked by in the background, and forms passed in front and behind her. They all looked like shadows. None of them meant anything to her. She only wished that Reginald would walk out from the mix, but no such luck occurred.

Leaning forward, she rested her face in her hands. More cries parted from her as she desired to curl up into a ball and cry herself into eternal sleep. At one point, someone talked to her. She thought that it was the doctor, but she didn't check to make sure. Elaine felt a hand squeeze her left shoulder, but she didn't peer up at the individual.

Time was forgotten by her until she registered that someone sat down beside her. Gradually, she lowered her hands. Her puffy eyelids blinked shut before they reopened, and her red, tired eyes noticed that it was six in the morning. She blinked again and faced her right. A gentle, calming smile greeted her. For a second, she thought that it was Reginald until she noted the characteristics of the person.

"Ed-Edmund?" Confusion dominated her orbs as her exhausted mind tried to make sense of his presence there.

"I'm here to visit my friend again. I saw you on the way." He loosened his olive green tie. "And, you looked like you needed some company." No words left her. Her eyes fixated on the tie's color as though he hadn't said anything. "Or, do you want me to leave you alone?"

At the mention of being alone, she sat upright and shook her head. Her hands folded on her lap, and she didn't meet his eyes. He kept silent, but she understood that he probably was waiting for her to speak. She tightened her fingers' grip on each other. Reluctance entered her orbs, but she had to ask. Maybe, it would be selfish, but her mind required such neediness in that moment. "... W-would you mi-mi-mind taking m-me h-home ... n-now?"

His eyes lit up, but she didn't notice. She was off again in her own world. Edmund didn't mind in the slightest, but he held back his smirk. Finally, that foul fool had died. It broke his heart that she was in such a state, but he could fix that. It might take time, but he could give her that. There was no rush.

"I'm sure that my friend wouldn't mind." He stood up from the chair and held out his right hand to her. Her eyes met his, and he loved that he could see pure gratitude in her dazzling orbs. She placed her hand in his, and he lifted her up. Practically, she collided into him, but his hands held her upper arms securely and reassuringly. Before he could move a step forward, she pressed into him more.

Both of her hands tightened around his black suit jacket. He rested a hand on the back of her head and another on her back. Edmund relished the embrace, and he could smell the honeysuckle fragrance of her hair. How he wanted to administer kisses to it daily. The male breathed in her scent and was transported into his own world until she pulled away from him a bit.

Disappointment hid in the shadows of his orbs, but he met her gaze nonetheless. "Are you ready to head out?" He received a slight nod from her. She appeared ready to break down again, which made him all the more tempted to carry her out of the building.

Gina passed them by but didn't glance to either. Her eyes were red and puffy too. Elaine didn't spot her, but Edmund did. His orbs darkened a bit as a smirk tried to control his lips. It took all of his strength to hold it back. That woman's choices, though, would bring his lovely Elaine into his arms all the more, but he still despised her immensely.

Focusing back on his interest, he guided her carefully out of the hospital. She didn't mind the slow pace. In fact, she decreased it even more. "Have you ever lost anyone?" she questioned as she stared blankly ahead. He supposed that she would've asked anyone if they had given her their open ears, but he was happy that it was him.

"Yes. My parents had died when I had been three. My aunt had taken me in afterwards."

"Oh, I'm ..."

"Elaine, don't be sorry. There's no need for you to be. Let's just focus on you right now and what you need." His hand squeezed hers in a comforting manner. Slightly, a small smile touched her lips, but it quickly vanished. "I can take the day off from work mostly. I'll only need to answer a few calls here and there unless you mind." She shook her head and held onto his hand tighter.

Moving closer to him, she almost was hugging his right arm. His heart skipped a beat. "I don't. Thank you." Barely, he could hear her, but her response caused him to smile and nod in thanks. "I might need you for the whole day." Again, her voice was as quiet as a mouse's, but it was pure rhapsody to his ears.

"That's fine. Have you eaten breakfast?" She shook her head. "Then, I'll make you some. You shouldn't do too much today after all." Her head nodded in agreement. "We'll take your car to your home. I'll pick up mine from here tomorrow." Another nod was his answer. It was like she was a living doll. How beautiful, though, he preferred to call her his treasure.

## Chapter Five: Bite

*A tall figure stood over the stove while the other sat at a small, round table. Off to the side, the toaster beeped and popped out the toast.*

After they had left the hospital, she had remained quiet. Edmund hadn't seemed to mind, and he had been considerate not to turn the radio on either. When they had arrived at her shared ... her apartment, she had no recollection of actually getting out of the car and ascending the steps. She only had remembered standing in her room and finding that the door had been closed behind her.

Now, she stepped forward until she slipped off her coat and hung it on the hanger. Her feet slipped out of her heels, and she kicked them back into the closet. Every action of hers felt like she was moving at the pace of a turtle, but part of her energy was going towards not breaking down into tears again. Not only that but also her mind was exhausted from all of it. She wanted to sleep, but she could hear Edmund moving around in her kitchen.

He was being kind enough to make breakfast, so she would wait until later. Then again, it sounded like he was staying for the whole day, but she didn't mind. If anything, she was relieved for the company and for the fact that she wouldn't have to take care of herself that day too much.

Elaine removed her nightgown and folded it onto the bathroom counter. She didn't glance into the mirror; she didn't wish to view her face after crying, or she would cry all the more. Her feet dragged across the carpet before she removed a red pleated skirt, which went to her knees, and a white blouse with chiffon sleeves. After she changed into them, she slipped on some black fuzzy slippers and opened her room door gradually.

A yawn escaped her lips before her fingers traveled from covering her mouth to running through her hair. They got stuck almost instantly. Tiredly, she pulled some strands of hair to the front of her. Normally, she would've quickly run back into the bathroom to fix them, but she shrugged and removed her fingers. Later, she could repair her hair.

Continuing down the short hallway, she stopped. Her eyes glanced up to a framed picture, and her heart sunk lower into her chest. She closed her eyes and forced her head away. It had been an image of Reginald and her on a picnic in the mountains. A bubbling stream had been in the background, and trees had given them their own private grove.

Catching footsteps, she reopened her eyes. A black button-up met her eyes before her orbs stared at the olive green tie again. "I'm almost done with breakfast. Why don't you sit at the table and wait?" His voice was soft and smooth. It reminded her of the velvety texture of quality chocolate.

Instead of answering him, however, she reached up and loosened his tie until she slipped it from his neck. Her fingers ghosted across the skin of his neck in the process, and she thought for a moment that she saw him shiver. She brushed it aside and lowered her hands to in front of her before she held it back out to him.

Looking up, her eyes met his. "You should be comfortable. Make yourself at home." A kind smile greeted his lips, but she didn't note the overjoyed look in his orbs. "It's the least I can do for you helping me."

His hands reached out and took his tie back. He draped it over his right shoulder and stepped aside for her to pass. Their gazes broke, but he was tempted to grab her hand and guide her for the rest of the way. Edmund, however, abstained from the action and followed behind her. Noting that her hair remained uncombed, he made a note to help her with it later, though; it did cause him to smirk. It was as though they had shared a night together. If only that was the reality. In the future, he would guarantee that; he would get her to accept him.

Moving around her, he pulled out the chair for her, and she seated herself quietly. Her hands grabbed one of the oranges on the table, and she idly passed it from hand to hand before her thumbs glided over the smooth peel. The faint scent of the orange reached her nose and woke her up from her daze by a little bit but not enough to halt her present actions.

Behind her, she heard the spatula scraping across the pan. It smelled like eggs were being cooked, but she didn't turn around to check. Maybe, peppers were in the mixture too and even some potatoes. Whatever it was, it did cause her stomach to growl lightly. A faint bit of heat touched her cheeks at the noise, especially when she heard Edmund release a chuckle.

A loud beep, however, startled her. She sat upright in her chair and scanned the room for the source before her eyes landed on the toaster. Two pieces of toast were perfectly baked. Butter and grape jam were next to the machine.

Edmund shifted the pan to a cool burner and turned off the active one before he headed over to the toast and prepared it for the meal. "What do you want to drink?" His question knocked her out of her tiredness a little bit more. She set down the orange and placed it back in the glass bowl.

"Tea please." Her eyes traveled to him, and her right index finger pointed upwards even though he wasn't looking to her. "There should be some lavender and mint teabags in the cupboard above the toaster." She received a slight nod from him.

Pushing the plates aside, he reached up and retrieved two teabags before he searched the other cupboards. Elaine had an inkling of what he was trying to locate. She pushed her chair back and stood up. Edmund seemed to face her at the speed of lightning. "You can keep sitting."

"It's fine. I'm used to preparing things for my breakfast." She smiled to him lightly. "This is a treat for me, but I can still help." The weariness in her eyes remained present, and he gazed at her in concern. "Even before ... Well, I always had cooked for Reginald." A pained chuckle escaped her. "He often had burned food, so I just had relieved him from cooking."

Tears started to form again. She wiped them with the backs of her hands. "But, he had on occasion brought dinner home. He always had made those so special." Her hands traveled up to her face, and she covered her eyes. "I-I-I'm sorry. I ..."

Hands rested on her shoulders and pulled her forward. She pushed her head into him and continued her crying. "Don't apologize. You don't have to." Her hands shifted from her face to his shirt before her arms wrapped around him securely. Elaine's fingers gripped at his black suit jacket. His heart swelled, and he smirked to himself. Already, she was growing dependent on his comfort. How delightful.

"The ... T-he ..." She coughed quietly, and she pushed against him. Her head hung down, but he saw her tears all the same. He couldn't wait until he saw her cry tears of joy for him. That would certainly be a spectacular day. "The measuring cups and tea pots are in the cupboard above the one with the teabags," she mentioned as though it hurt to speak.

"Okay, thank you. Go sit down." A calming smile decorated his lips. Her eyes focused on it. For a moment, she thought that she spot it upturning into a smirk. It caught her off guard, and she didn't note that a frown began to appear on hers. "Is something wrong, Elaine?"

That snapped her out of her stare. She shook her head and turned away from him. "No, it's nothing," she practically whispered. Elaine retook her seat and slipped her feet in and out of her slippers as she waited. The simple action occupied her mind and kept her from any confusing and/or dark thoughts.

Within time, food and drink sat on the table. Edmund seated himself to her right and handed her a fork and napkin. She thanked him before her eyes stayed on him a little longer. He was about to eat before he paused and met her gorgeous eyes. "Do you need something?"

"No, but you can take off your jacket." Her fork pointed to the clothing item delicately. It was as though he could break the fork from her grasp like it was nothing more than a strand of hay. "Like I had said, make yourself at home. Its ... Its only me now." The second sentence barely was above more than a squeak. It was as though she hadn't even said anything. Elaine stared down, and her eyes seemed distant.

"Open." Confused, she averted her orbs back to him only to discover her fork hovering in front of her face with a bite of eggs, potatoes and peppers on it. When had he even grabbed her fork from her? She certainly hadn't felt that move of his.

Caught off guard, she couldn't prevent a light dose of heat from entering her cheeks. She gave him a questioning look, but he didn't reposition the fork. Like a snail, she leaned forward and ate the bite. Elaine distanced herself from the utensil and chewed. A tiny smile crept upon her lips. After she swallowed, she held her right hand up to her lips in shock. "That had tasted amazing."

After he handed her fork back to her, he sat up straight and smirked in complete elation. "Thank you. I'll be making lunch and dinner too." He slid off his jacket and placed it on the back of the chair along with his tie.

"Really?!" she asked almost too excitedly.

Laughing, he nodded. "I'm here for the day and night, and you need to relax. It's no problem." He would stay even longer if she later requested it. Working away from his office was quite easy after all. A genuine smile graced her lips before she began to eat more. Edmund would never forget that smile.

## Chapter Six: Confuse

*Standing at the doorway, two figures stared: one acting odd and the other bearing puzzlement. A heart ached for one of the figures to be someone else.*

A week had gone by since Reginald's passing, and Elaine had been managing to perform her job again. She didn't have a smile on her lips, though, even if she did enjoy it. Things still had been depressing if her mind thought about anything too much. Since her job had remained at home and in the same place where Reginald had used to live, the quiet had gotten to her at times.

Edmund had been sweet enough to drop in if she had called him and had kept her company. They had watched a movie, or he had cooked for her. He hadn't stayed as long as he had right after Reginald's death, but he had remained there for a few hours on each visit. With confidence, she had been able to call him a dear friend by the end of that week.

On the day of the funeral, however, she tried to abstain from calling him the instant that she woke up, but she couldn't resist the temptation. She had grown accustomed to his comfort if she needed someone by her side. The line on the other end rang and rang, but no one answered. Eventually, it went to voicemail. *This is Edmund. Please leave your name and message. I'll get back to you hopefully soon.*

"Edmund, this is Elaine ..." She had to take a break as the realization of Reginald's body being buried hit her hard again. The same thing had happened last night several times. Taking a deep breath, she exhaled. "Th-The funeral is today." Her hand started to shake. Before she could stop herself, her thumb slipped from nerves, and she hung up.

Staring at her phone, she cursed herself for the action. She released a rough sigh. "I hope that he understands," she grumbled before she tossed her phone onto her bed. Elaine slipped off her satin, navy blue nightgown and removed a few articles of clothing from her closet. When she was done changing, her black chiffon skirt, black-ruffled, short-sleeved blouse and black pumps adorned her form.

Heading into the bathroom, she tossed her nightgown into the hamper before she grabbed her brush and worked on her messy bed head. In the middle of detangling a massive knot, her phone began to ring. She glanced between the brush stuck in her hair and the device before she hurried over. The hairbrush remained in her hair, and she winced as it tugged a little too much for comfort.

Checking the phone number, she noticed that it was unrecognizable. Hesitant, she answered. "Hello? Who is this?"

"Elaine, it's Edmund."

Relieved, she asked, "Why are you using a different number? Did something happen to your phone?"

"It's charging at the moment at my apartment. I'm using my work phone right now, so I don't have long to talk."

"Wait, then how did you get my message?" Confusion dominated her voice, and she seated herself down on her bed. Her free hand worked on removing the brush from her dark brown locks.

"I didn't." Her brows furrowed in puzzlement. "I figured that I would call to let you know that I can't make it to the funeral with you." She felt her heart sink, but she understood. Edmund didn't even know Reginald, and he had his own job to worry about. "But, give me the location of the post-funeral reception. If I can't make that, I'll try to pick you up at least." By a little bit, she smiled at his consideration. "You're not driving there, correct?"

She hummed lightly. "I'm going with his parents, but you don't have to go out of your way just to pick me up. I'm sure that his parents won't mind bringing me back home." A part of her, though, was hoping that he would insist. His company really was soothing to a point that was unexplainable presently.

"I'll pick you up. Now, where will I be heading?"

Almost, she could see the smile on his lips. "The Fields. It's that ..."

"The all-organic restaurant in the middle of the city." She hummed in response, though; she wished that he would stop cutting her off, but it seemed to be a frequent habit of his. He probably even had noted how it had irked her some in the past, but his knowing smiles had erased any anger that she had felt. "And, the time?"

"Five pm is the start. Seven is the end."

"Okay, I need to go. Till then." Before she could get another word in, he hung up. A pout formed on her lips, but it didn't last long. It morphed into a smile. At least, she would have his company on the way back. She hoped that he wasn't going too out of his way, but that led her to wonder where he lived. Maybe, he was close by.

Hanging up herself, she placed her phone back onto her bed and went back to the task of her hair. When she finished, her hair shone under the light in her bathroom, and her curly bangs were brushed to the side a bit. Her makeup was more subtle than usual. A cool toned red matte lipstick decorated her lips, and her smoky eye look was lighter.

In the mirror, she gave herself a miniscule smile to prep herself for what would come ahead. Part of her wondered why she even had bothered with makeup since she suspected that she would cry early into the funeral. It wouldn't help that everyone around her would be emotional too.

Hearing a knock on the door, she exited her bathroom and grabbed her phone and purse. She made sure that everything was off in the place before she opened the door. To her surprise, it wasn't Reginald's parents outside. Her body froze out of pure perplexity. "G-G-Gina?" Her eyes squinted, and she wondered if she was imagining things. "Umm ..."

Elaine peered around the woman to see if his parents were anywhere in sight, but they weren't. It just was her. "What are you doing here? And, how do you know where I live?" She couldn't help but point her right index finger at her. The nurse being there made no sense to her.

Sure, she took care of Reginald during his coma, but why would the nurse be at their ... her apartment. There was also the fact that Gina was in something different than her usual scrubs. The nurse was in black herself.

"Well, his parents are running late, and they had asked me to come pick you up. They had given me your address, and I had accepted since you're right on my way to the funeral home." She chuckled nervously and stood in place awkwardly. Gina shifted uncomfortably in her black stilettos. "Sorry for the sudden change." Her eyes glanced to the side. "It had caught me off guard too." A bit of annoyance was evident in her voice.

"Would it be better if I drove myself?" Her tone was a bit snappish, and she hadn't meant to come out like that so obviously, but it was clear that Gina didn't want to be there. Elaine didn't desire her to be there. To Elaine, Gina simply was another nurse who had given her fake smiles and had acted like she had been more of a nuisance than anything else when she had visited Reginald.

"No, it's fine." Her friendliness was fading, and she stepped aside so that Elaine could exit her home. "I had promised that I would take you." Elaine gave her a questioning look before she locked the door and followed after the nurse.

Unlocking her black civic, Gina started the car soon after and before Elaine had even properly seated herself. One of Elaine's eyebrows twitched, and she now really wished that Edmund had been able to take her. They probably would be having a decent conversation at the moment if that were the case.

As they drove off to Petal Valley Funeral Home, a quiet air existed between them, and it was the uncomfortable kind. Elaine removed her phone from her purse and found herself scrolling over past text messages she had sent Edmund, though; there were few of them since she had preferred calling him.

What caught her attention, however, was when Gina placed a CD into the disc slot of the car. Her hands tightened around her phone, and her body seemed to freeze. Reginald's favorite song started to play. How would Gina know that information, or did she even know?

"Is this a song that you like?" Elaine questioned, her voice a near whisper.

"Yes, I used to listen to it a lot with ... well, a friend of mine." Gina tightened her hands around the steering wheel. "Well, I've always liked it too." Her nails tapped against the vinyl of the wheel, and she gulped quietly, but Elaine still noticed.

Something was wrong. A pit in her stomach formed. Gina was hiding something. Just what the h*ll had she been to Reginald? Elaine bit her bottom lip. "Had your friend been Reginald? Had you known him before the hospital?" Steadily, the nurse nodded her head, and Elaine's stomach knotted more.

## Chapter Seven: Rip

*Cherished music played in the background, but the notes began to decrease their pace. The music became warped, and ears listened to dreadful words as venom infected veins.*

"How had you known him from before?" Elaine's voice was only above a whisper. Each of her words felt like they were stealing all of the water from her body. Her mind swirled with negative possibilities, and her stomach only was feeling sicker.

Hesitation was clear across Gina's face. "... Well ..." Her pink lips parted, but nothing more exited them. They closed before they opened again. The action reminded the younger woman of a fish but only if that fish was the most awful being in the world.

"Just tell me." Elaine's tone was firm and demanding. A threat was laced behind it, but the younger woman appeared immensely sick regardless. Despite Gina being a nurse, she gave no motion to helping her younger passenger.

"..." The silence increased the impatience of Elaine. Her hands became fists around her skirt before she leaned over to the radio and turned off the song. She couldn't take it anymore. Both of her dark brown orbs remained fixed on the nurse. Almost, the younger could see sweat forming on the nurse's brow. When she still didn't answer, Elaine lost it and slammed her hands down on the dash. Gina jumped in her chair before she slammed on the breaks and took the car to the side of the road. Someone honked, but neither of them bothered with that individual. They only saw a car speed past, but even that soon faded from their minds.

"Tell me." Elaine faced Gina fully. Her hands tightened around her skirt again. "How had you known him before the hospital?" The younger stressed every word, every syllable. She appeared ready to pounce on the older woman if she was met with the quiet again.

Gina shut off the car and slid her hands onto her lap. She leaned back against the driver's seat and released a lengthy, worried sigh. Momentarily, she shut her brown eyes. "We had met at a small sandwich place." Her eyes opened, and her gaze stared to the road ahead. "We had bumped into each other and had started talking afterwards. A real cliché moment." A slight laugh parted from her lips, but Elaine didn't emit a sound. "We just had started meeting each other after that more and more. We had seemed to click so well. We ..."

"I don't care." Gina glanced over to her passenger, and she visibly scooted closer to the car door. A heavy frown was painted on the younger's lips. Her dark brown eyes were downcast, and she looked like a mannequin ready to come to life and strike. "Just answer this." The younger's next words parted from her in a cold, calculated manner. "Had he been cheating on me with you?"

It felt as though all of the air in her lungs evaporated. Gina choked on her words, and she couldn't meet Elaine's gaze. "How far?" The nurse carefully peered to her passenger in confusion. "How far had you two gone?" the younger repeated, her voice sounding like a volcano ready to erupt.

Rubbing her hands together, Gina felt a bead of sweat roll down the left side of her face. Her teeth bit the inside of her lower lip since she didn't wish to ruin her lipstick. "Tell me!" The nurse leaped up and groaned when she hit the back of her head on her headrest. Elaine's orbs now were pinned onto her. They burned with loathing and despair.

"W-we ..." Gina held her head down. Why had she been so stupid as to play that song in the car with Elaine right there? She hadn't been thinking since her mind had been too distracted by getting to the funeral. If only she could travel back in time. Then, there would only be the uncomfortable silence in the car. Breathing in deeply and exhaling, Gina sat up straighter and gripped the wheel as she was ready to start the car again.

"Several times ..." Gina placed her hand on the key and tried not to think about Elaine's next reaction. "... We had slept together." The atmosphere in the car grew to a dense pool of dread, hate and heartbreak.

Elaine slumped over on her chair. "Had his parents known?" she questioned quietly.

"Y-Yes."

"And, they had decided to let you pick me up." Elaine released a bitter chuckle. Her hands covered her face, and she laughed some more. "They favor you." Her lips twitched up into a broken smile. Gina's hands trembled. The nurse wanted to arrive at the funeral as soon as possible to get rid of the younger woman, who really was freaking her out.

Meeting Gina's eyes, Elaine sucked back her tears, but her eyes looked watery. "They like you more." She choked back a sob. "Right?" Elaine searched Gina's eyes while the nurse gulped. In Gina's brown orbs, Elaine spotted the truth, and it ate at her horrendously. "I'm correct." Sorrow dominated her voice.

Before Gina could get another word in, Elaine faced away from her and unlocked the passenger door. "I never want to see you again." Gina froze. The nurse feared that if she moved she would find herself dead. No words left the nurse either. She simply watched Elaine open the car door and leave. "Come tomorrow and pick his stuff up." The order was piercing, and Gina shook all the more from it. Her passenger door slammed shut. Hesitantly, the nurse peeked out the back window. Elaine was walking down the side of the street, keeping well off of the road.

Fearing that the younger woman would spin around and bolt right at her, Gina started the car and drove off. She would have some explaining to do once she reached Petal Valley Funeral Home, but she was thankful that she wouldn't have to deal with Elaine there. As she increased distance between Elaine and herself, she calmed down and was grateful that she would receive all of Reginald's things. And since the younger woman never wished to view her again, Gina doubted that she actually would have any direct contact with Elaine. A smile painted Gina's lips. The nurse turned on the radio again and sang along. With her passenger side empty, she easily could imagine Reginald sitting there and singing along with her.

Broken, Elaine desired to collapse on the side of the road and roll down the slight hill to her left. She'd be hidden from the other cars, and she'd be left to her own thoughts. Then again, she didn't know if she could even think straight. Everything seemed utterly ... pointless.

All of that time she had spent visiting Reginald was a giant slap to the face. Had he ever truly cared for her, or had she been simply a toy for him until he was bored with her? If he hadn't been in that accident, would he have ditched her for Gina all those months ago? Even all of her tears and mourning had gone to waste. That energy had been spent on ... nothing.

Now, she had new tears. They felt all the more painful. Her heart ached for her to run to the funeral and ask Reginald's parents. Part of her wanted to receive confirmation, but the other part of her knew that Gina hadn't been lying. Staring forward blankly, she wondered if she should even head home. She had shared that place with Reginald, and she now had to pack up his things. Those facts tortuously plagued her. In her own thoughts, though, she didn't note a certain car driving past. The woman didn't hear either that same car stopping and turning around. Elaine didn't spot that car making a u-turn and heading straight for her, and she only noticed it when it stopped right next to her.

Puzzled, she gazed over to it lifelessly. Her eyes squinted at the black 1965 mustang. They widened a bit in familiarity. The driver stepped out of the car, and her ears listened to the rushed footsteps of the individual. Before she could utter his name, she felt hands rest concernedly on her upper arms. "Elaine, are you alright?" Edmund glanced around before he looked back to her. "Why are you out here?"

His thumbs moved up to her cheeks and wiped tears from them. "Why are you out here?" She threw the question back at him, and it came out snappish even though that hadn't been her intent. He stood up a little straighter, but he didn't appear hurt. Instead, he continued to be worried.

"I had been on my way to a meeting." He removed his hands from her. "Now, your turn." She was about to mention how he should keep going then, but she held her tongue. Right now, she really did need the help. Elaine didn't know how long she had been walking for, but her feet hurt, and she was going to rip off her heels soon.

Not meeting his eyes, she bit on her lower lip and ruined her lipstick a little. She tried to think of some explanation to give him, but her mind seemed to shut down. Her legs felt wobbly, and she wished to cry more. "Elaine?" The woman didn't know what had come over her, but she closed the distance between them.

Without a word, she wrapped her arms around him and buried her head into his chest. Her tears and lipstick stained his shirt, but its black hue managed to hide the marks somewhat. A soft sigh hit her ears, but she didn't peer up at him. He probably was annoyed at her, but she didn't move. Elaine was grateful, though, when he secured his arms around her in a soft embrace. What she didn't sight, however, was that Edmund was smirking. Edmund hadn't expected such a hug from her that day so soon, but he loved it nonetheless. That didn't extinguish his growing anger, however.

# Chapter Eight: Drive

*Scenery passed by as the car's engine roared with life in the background. Hands trembled, but comfort was nearby in a handsome form.*

She didn't know for how long she was in his car or the exact location of their destination. All she knew was that they were heading towards his meeting. He had offered to drive her home, but she hadn't wanted him to be late on her account, so they had made the arrangement of him taking her home after his meeting. Apparently, his home wasn't too far from hers.

Presently, though, she was leaning her head against the car window. A frown remained on her lips. Sections of her lips bore a lighter shade of her lipstick due to it being ruined, but she didn't care. Her eye makeup too was probably in a horrendous state. Thankfully, Edmund hadn't mentioned it to her.

Silence existed between them, but it was comfortable. Edmund didn't bother her one bit, but she figured that he was waiting for her to say something. She didn't feel like talking, however. All she desired was to curl up into a ball and forget that the day was happening.

A soft tune started to play on the radio. It was pleasant, but it brought no smile to her lips. Rather, it caused her to bring her feet up onto the seat and fulfill her wish of curling up. Her shoes were long since kicked off, and she noted that the bottoms of her feet were red with soreness still. If she received a couple of blisters, she wouldn't be surprised.

Buildings passed by along with other cars and trees. Fields of grass sometimes greeted her eyes. A part of her wished to lie in the middle of them and fade into them. Maybe, that would be best. Something jolted her out of her dreary thoughts, though.

On her left calf rested Edmund's hand. Hesitant, she peered over to him. His eyes remained on the road, and it wasn't too long after that he removed his appendage from her but not before he gave her skin a comforting squeeze. "Do you need me to stay with you tonight?"

His voice was soft and smooth like honey. There was a sweetness to it that she couldn't resist, and it eased her troubled mind. Just above a whisper, she answered, "Thank you." She shifted her body and sat somewhat upright. Her legs remained on the seat, however. Elaine rubbed her fingers together, debating on whether she should say something else.

Her dark brown orbs stared over to him briefly. His gaze remained on the road, but there was a peaceful look upon his countenance. She wished that she could experience that feeling in the present moment. Oddly enough, though, her heart and mind calmed down. Gently, her hands traveled up to her chest and lied over her heart. A steady exhale left her before her eyes focused on the road ahead. More buildings filled their surroundings.

"I just don't ..." Another exhale escaped her. "I just don't want to go back."

"Do you want to stay with me?" His tone was casual, and the question seemed harmless enough. Elaine trusted him as well, and he always was so helpful to her. He never pushed himself on her even with that note. Edmund had been nothing but kind and considerate to her throughout their blooming friendship.

Regardless, she couldn't spend the night at his home. "I ... I can't." A large part of her did, but she had to pack up Reg ... his things for Gi ... that woman. "I need to get rid of his stuff." Barely, her voice was audible, but it appeared that Edmund heard her.

"You don't want to hold onto any of it?" He wore a mask of puzzlement. Internally, though, he was screaming with jubilance. Edmund wondered if she had found out that little secret of Reginald's. If she had, that would explain her sudden desire not to attend his funeral and her current behavior. Oh, that would be splendid. He supposed that he could've worn something else than all black, but he always loved to match her.

"No." A shaky breath parted from her. How he wished to catch it and then ensnare her lips with his. "He had ... he had ..."

"You don't have to tell me, Elaine."

Shaking her head, she intertwined her fingers and held her knees close to her chest. "I don't want to. I don't feel like saying anything to you, but ..." She trailed off and rested her forehead against her knees. "But, it's hard not to." A miniscule smile touched her lips. "You listen, and you're understanding. It makes it easy to confide in you."

Upon his lips, his own smile formed. Her eyes glanced upon it, and she felt a light dash of heat hit her cheeks. It wasn't the time to consider him attractive or anything of that nature. Right now, she needed those things gone from her apartment, and she required only his friendship. His lips parted as if to say something, but she beat him to it.

Uncurling herself, she stared down at her lap. Her fingers tightened around themselves. A bitter, pain-filled frown coated her lips. Tears threatened to fall again. "H-H-He ..." She took a deep breath in before she exhaled. Elaine's breath came out trembling.

Knives seemed to dig holes in her chest, and her stomach knotted. For a second, she thought that she might be sick. Her arms hugged her torso. Edmund shifted his foot towards the break. She shook her head. "No. Keep going."

Reluctantly, he did so. Elaine steeled herself and straightened her shoulders back against the seat. "It's just ... It's just ... Well ..." A sob escaped her. Her hands flew up to her face and covered her eyes. The feelings of hopelessness invaded her mind again. "I'm sorry. I can't."

No verbal response was given to her. Edmund opened the middle compartment and removed a thing of tissues. He closed the storage unit and set the tissues on top. "Don't apologize." If she hadn't been sniffling and sobbing, she wouldn't have missed the ticked-off tone of his.

As Elaine grabbed a tissue, Edmund tightened his hands around the steering wheel. If he could, he would bend the wheel completely. He was ecstatic that she finally knew the truth about Reginald and Gina, but he was beyond infuriated at her present state. The fact that Gina probably was smiling to herself due to Elaine not attending the funeral left him rage-filled. It didn't help that he comprehended that the wretched man's parents had been in on the secret too. Something had to be done, and he'd figure it out later.

When he finally stopped the car, he glanced over to her. Her nose was swollen as was the top of her upper lip. Both areas were rubbed dry too, and her lipstick was long since gone. Each of her eyes was red and puffed up, and her makeup was a waterfall on her cheeks.

It broke his heart to view her in such a state when she usually was so prim and proper. Not saying anything, he placed his keys in his left pants' pocket and left the car. He closed the car door, which didn't even catch her attention. Edmund opened hers and held out his hand to her. "I can't possibly leave you in there." An attentive and charming smile was directed her way.

Slowly, she diverted her eyes up to him. A look of shame crossed her countenance, and she quickly averted her eyes elsewhere. "It's fine. I'll stay in here." She didn't even glance to the building. "You have a meeting."

"Yes, I do. But, I'm not leaving you in my car." His hand motioned for her to grab it. She stared to him again and noted the kind look in his eyes, but there was a harsher note there too. It caught her off guard, but she pushed it aside as her mind playing tricks on her. Gently, she slipped on her pumps and let him lift her out of the car.

"I'm a mess. I really ..."

"You're beautiful." The compliment surprised her, and heat returned to her cheeks. She didn't dare meet his eyes then. He reached around her and retrieved a couple of tissues as well as a water bottle. Edmund wetted the tissues before he set the bottle down and placed his right fingers under her chin. "Close your eyes and hold still."

"But ..."

"Most of your makeup is gone anyway." He gave her an amused look, and she glanced to the side in embarrassment. "No need for the rest of it." Before she could get another word in, she felt the wet tissue against her skin. She really wished that she had brought makeup wipes with her. Elaine shut her eyes tightly and allowed him to finish taking it off.

"There." His fingers lingered under her chin for a bit longer. When she opened her eyes, she nearly took a step back. He was so ... so close. "Perfect." Her heart skipped a beat even if it was wrong for such a thing to happen on the day of that man's funeral despite him having cheated on her.

Just as she was about to take in his features all the better, he turned away from her and put the bottle back in the car. He closed the door and motioned for her to follow. "Let's head in."

## Chapter Nine: Shop

*Rows of glass beads sparkled under the bright lights, and fabric flowers bloomed to her right. Footsteps echoed down the nearby aisle before a form rounded the corner.*

Elaine didn't know what she had been expecting when she had entered the store. Her mind had been too sidetracked to read the building's sign. When she inspected her surroundings, though, the biography about Claude Monet and the interior design magazine with all of the paintings made sense. He worked in an art store or with one at least. Taking into consideration the cost of those magazine paintings, however, she wondered how high up he was in the business. Not to mention he had said that he had a meeting at the place, not a shift to cover.

A light, melodic chuckle hit her ears. "Have you ever been in an art store before?" She snapped out of her trance and glanced up to him. Some heat invaded her cheeks, and a small pout hit her lips.

Crossing her arms, she averted her eyes to the many aisles. "I just didn't know what part of the store you're working in." She looked back to him, and there was clear amusement in his eyes. "Are you a manager of this store?"

Edmund started to walk towards the cash registers, and he greeted the two cashiers kindly. They both exchanged a line of, "Good morning, Mr. Fex," as he walked by. Each of them returned to the customers they were currently helping. He exchanged a friendly smile to both of the customers but nothing more than that, trusting that his cashiers had asked them all of the proper customer service questions already.

"So, you are a manager?" She kept up right behind him, and she heard another chuckle from him. "Am I wrong?" Her tone held a little more frustration to it. "You can tell me if I am."

Reaching some stairs, he started to ascend them before he stopped midway. "You glossed over the sign?" he asked even though he had a knowing look within his eyes.

Hesitantly, she nodded. "But, I was ..."

Holding up his hands, he shook his head. "You don't have to explain yourself. I know that this day has been h*ll for you." He gave her an apologetic smile. "I really shouldn't be teasing you like this."

She sighed and she glanced down to her feet. "How about you tell me about your position once we get up these stairs?" She cracked a smile, trying to lighten the atmosphere once more. "My feet are killing me."

Agreeing to the proposal, he faced away from her and opened the door at the top. He held it open for her, and she headed into the small room. A light switch flicked on and revealed a carpeted room with a large table and several chairs in the middle of it. No doubt it was a space for meetings. Off to the right side, there was even a screen with a table and computer next to it. Up above was a projector. All around the room except for the back wall and part of the right wall were windows.

Closing the door, Edmund headed over to one of the front corners. He glanced out over the store as she walked up beside him. Her lips shifted in a manner that would indicate that she was about to whistle, but no sound left her. "This has a nice view."

"Yes, it does. And, the workers can look up here too. I didn't want it to seem like I was hiding anything from them, but the room had to have some barrier so that meetings could carry on without interruptions from the background sound of the store."

"If you're not the manager ..."

"The sign." She met his orbs. A proud gleam danced in them, and a small smile touched his lips. "We're in an art store. What do think it says?"

Furrowing her brow, she tried to think of all of the art stores in the city. Obviously, they were in one of the bigger ones, but there were two art store chains that had large buildings. If she guessed the wrong one, she might as well slap him. Her eyes searched for anything in the store that might clue her into the right one.

Staring to the front doors, she noted the words across it. She managed to make it out after squinting, but a laugh told her that Edmund was well aware of what she was doing. "Well?" His voice caused her to peer up at him, and she did somewhat desire to slap that smirk off of him.

"Ires's." Her eyes narrowed at him. "You're hinting that you're the owner." It certainly would explain how he would be able to afford that painting. "But, that's not what your employees addressed you as." She crossed her arms again. "I don't understand."

"That's my father's name." He fully faced her and walked over to the computer. Soon enough, the projector turned on, and light met the screen. "I changed my last name to my mother's after their deaths." There was a click of the mouse, and the computer home screen popped up on the fabric screen. "My father already has his name on the store." His eyes glanced to hers momentarily, and there was softness to them. "I figured that I would keep my mother's name alive too." A strangeness crossed over his orbs next. "Or, do you prefer my father's name?"

Not comprehending why her opinion would matter on that, she shook her. "I like both, but I like what you did for your mother more." She smiled gently. "That was sweet of you." Elaine wanted to know more about how they had died, but she didn't wish to pry. Not to mention that she couldn't be a good support at the moment. Her mind just was calming down from her previous shows of grief.

"Later." Confused, she tilted her head by a fraction and furrowed her brows. "You want to know about their deaths." A slight laugh left him, but there was pain in it. "I'll tell you another time."

"Sorry." She dipped her head in apology, ashamed that she had been so obvious. Footsteps greeted her ears, and his black dress shoes soon entered her field of vision. Fingers slipped under her chin and lifted her eyes to his. Warmth tickled her cheeks, and she was tempted to step back; however, her legs refused her that.

"Don't be. You're curious. I can't blame you." He removed his fingers and headed back to the computer. "Though," his eyes shifted to her momentarily, "I'm surprised that you're not more shocked."

At that, she couldn't help but chuckle. A teasing look crossed her eyes. "It's too late for that." She shrugged with her arms crossed. "I've met you too much." Elaine glanced over her right shoulder briefly towards the store's floor. "You owning the chain of Ires's fits along with what I know about you." Her right hand extended out a little, and she held up two fingers. "Your expensive taste and flexible schedule."

Laughing, he leaned on the table. "If that's all you know about me, I've done our meetings an injustice." She shook her head and smiled to him. "And, those two things could fit many jobs."

"Well yes, but I ..." Elaine shrugged her shoulders again. "I don't know. Maybe, I was thinking about the answer too much that it dulled the effect of the reveal." She pursed her lips as if trying to come up with another reason.

"It's fine." He stood back up straight and faced the computer again. "Your mind has a lot on it." His eyes averted to hers. "Go walk around and relax. I'll meet you when I'm done."

"Trying to get rid of me?" She raised a brow and pursed her lips all the more.

Not staring to her now, he smirked and continued to set up for his meeting. "Well unless you want to sit in on a business meeting and be introduced to several people."

Her eyebrow twitched. He already knew her answer, but she released a complying sigh. "Later, then." He nodded his head, and she left the office. As soon as the door closed behind her, his eyes shot towards the door before he smirked to himself. She was able to reason with so well. It truly was a lovely quality about her. There was also the fact that she was becoming more reliant on him, and that would increase tenfold now that she knew the truth about Reginald and Gina. It wouldn't be long before she agreed to be his.

Facing his work, he finished the setup before he heard the door open again. A professional, friendly smile greeted his lips as his employees walked through and into the space. Once the door closed, the meeting began, though; it was hard to keep his mind off of his perfect darling below, but he made sure that none of his workers noticed. No, he would keep those thoughts private.

After she stepped down the stairs, Elaine explored the store, but she stopped by the beads section, which was near to the fabric flowers. Her eyes trailed over the sparkling waterfalls of glass. She forced herself not to stare over to the flowers. Otherwise, she would be reminded of the funeral, so her body faced the beads at an angle.

Carefully, her hands slid across the rows of beads until they stopped on a row of light green ones. They glittered under the artificial lights, and tears threatened to fall again. Those beads were like his eyes, but now she could only picture them looking at Gina. Her fingers fell onto white beads, and she saw him lying through his pearly whites to her. Only footsteps drew her from her somber thoughts.

## Chapter Ten: Pick

*Dark green plastic twirled between fingertips as a separated silk petal drifted to the floor. Delicate fingers lifted it from the ground, but the petal was soon to be replaced by a full blossom.*

Leaning against the shelf to her right, Edmund stood. His arms were crossed over his chest, and she noted the worried look in his eyes. "The meeting's over?" she questioned quietly as her attention drifted back to the many beads. Footsteps hit her ears again, and he was soon beside her.

"Yes." His hand glided over a few of the beads before they stopped on a row of hot pink flowers.

She raised a brow, not expecting him to admire those. "You like those?" Skepticism ruled her voice, and she sounded somewhat rude, but a chuckle reaching her ears told her not to be concerned about that.

His hand slipped from them, and he shook his head. "No, I don't. Someone else might. There are a few gone from this row after all." He slipped his fingers back along the row, and he probably was counting them in his head. "Ah!" Despite his slightly raised voice, it maintained its low qualities and reminded her of soothing warm milk. "There are three missing."

They shared a glance. Before she knew what she was doing, she was covering her mouth with her right hand and laughing quietly. She comprehended that he had overreacted on purpose, but she was appreciating his efforts to cheer her up.

A pleased smile fell upon his lips before he faced her fully. "Good distraction?" he asked even though there was a prideful and knowing smile on his lips. She stared up at him, and her lips twitched up into a tiny smile. Instead of giving him a verbal answer, though, she closed the distance between them and wrapped her arms around him securely.

---

"Should I make another one?" His tone was teasing, but there was an undeniable softness to it also. Edmund's arms held onto her as he heard a light chuckle leave her. The distraction had worked better than he had anticipated, but he could feel the effects start to ebb away. Her shoulders sagged, and her hands slipped down his back a little as though she was melting against him and not in the pleasurable way.

"Elaine, what had happened?" His hands moved to her upper arms, and he held her at a slight distance. A frown was once again on her stunning, velvet lips, and it displeased him immensely. Her smiles complemented her so much more when directed at him. Both of her eyes were downturned as though she was ashamed of what she was about to admit. He already knew that no blame was to be put onto her.

No, the fault belonged to those two. He forced back a smirk and laugh. And, one of them was dead. The other ... Well, she wouldn't be let off of the hook, especially with how his lovely treasure was acting.

Her fingers intertwined in front of her, and no words left her. If anything, she looked to be a perfect statue of silence. Gently, he removed his hands from her before his right fingers lifted up her chin. "Elaine?" He observed her lower lip quiver, and he noticed the tears threatening to spill again.

Glancing around, he made sure that there was no one else in the area. There were the video cameras, but he could care less about that. The cameras didn't have audio. He focused back on her, and her eyes were directly on his. His heart felt a painful tug at her glassy eyes and ripped apart expression.

Sucking back a shaky breath, she tried to compose herself, but that ended in failure. His grip on her chin tightened, but she didn't flinch. Rather, it seemed to calm her. He would've smirked if the present atmosphere wasn't so grave. Her lips parted, and she released that trembling breath.

"Reg ... H-h-he ..." She swallowed a sob. "And, G-G-Gina ..." Her legs grew wobbly. Before she could stop herself, she collapsed against him. His hands supported her up, and he kept a firm hold on her. Elaine was pressed to his chest once more. He could feel her fingers tighten around the fabric of his black suit coat.

"What about them?" Even though he knew the answer, he wanted to hear it from her lips. He desired for her to admit it to him. It was selfish, and it hurt her, but he needed her to state out-loud how terrible a person Reginald was. Once she verbally voiced that to him, he had a feeling that she would grow all the nearer to him.

Burying her head further into his chest, she muttered something against him, but he couldn't hear a word. He leaned his head down a little. "It's fine, Elaine. You can tell me later." On cue, she raised her head and shook it slightly.

"N-no." Perfect. He had trouble keeping the grin off of his lips. She had fallen right into the palms of his hands. Such a delightful woman. "I need to ..." Elaine took a deep breath in before she exhaled. "I need to talk to someone." Her eyes locked onto his as if he was her last support in the world. It touched his heart in all the right ways. "To you."

Edmund sent her a simple nod. Gently, she rested the left side of her head against his chest. Her arms swirled around him before her hands gripped the back of his jacket. Elaine's fingers rubbed parts of the fabric between them, and he wished that she was performing that action on his hair.

As quiet as a soft breeze, she mumbled, "He had cheated on me ... with her." Her fingers stopped their motions and tugged on the fabric as if she was holding onto a ledge for dear life. His hands slackened against her, and the rest of him tensed. Edmund stared down at her in shock, but he made sure that its falsity was hidden from her even if her gaze was lifelessly on the shelf to their left.

"All of it ..." Her voice was barely audible, and he felt her body tremble against him. "It had been for nothing." She shut her eyes tight, and tears trickled down her cheeks. Instantly, he turned her face to him and wiped them away. Once again, her eyes shifted their focus to the floor. "What had I ..."

"It's not your fault." Her mouth shut, and he could tell that she was beginning to grow distant in the sense that her mind was turning off. He had to act fast. "You had done everything for him it sounds like. You had told me how dedicated you had been about visiting him while he had been in the hospital. You had told me about some of your dates with him in the past, and you had been perfect to him on those."

Sliding his hands up to the sides of her face, he softened his gaze and searched for sparks of life and not dullness. "Do you hear me?" There was a slight demanding tone in his voice, but he didn't shy away from it. She needed to understand that no blame resided on her.

Worried, he was about to repeat himself before she released a sigh. Her eyes met his, and a small smile touched her lips. Relieved, his thumbs wiped away any remaining tears. "Thank you." Briefly, her hands rested over his before she pulled away from him. She walked around him and towards the fake flowers. They made her heart ache, but their colorful petals also distracted her from her thoughts.

Pinks, oranges, blues and many more greeted her eyes. If she stared closely, she only saw the individual petals and not the whole flower. That made them easier to bear. Lightly, her fingers glided over a purple rose. They brushed against the silk petals, and one broke off from the rest of the flower. Her eyes observed it float down to the ground before she bent over and picked it up. Footsteps reminded her who owned the flower. She stood up and started, "I'm ..."

"Don't apologize." His left hand squeezed her right shoulder. She glanced up to him, and he gave her a reassuring smile. "If you only break one thing in my store after what you've told me, I'm going to be relieved." A light chuckle left him to cheer her up. "After that news, I'd want to demolish something." And, he most certainly would ... but later. Elaine's entire reaction and all of her pained words, though, caused him to speed up his plan for that disgusting woman.

"Thank you." A light laugh escaped her, but it was short-lived. Her eyes fell back on the flowers, and she watched a non-ruined rose be plucked from the shelf. Facing him, she saw him hold it out to her.

When she didn't accept it immediately, he moved it closer and removed the small tag. "Take it. It's yours." Hesitantly, she reached out and wrapped her fingers around it. A slight, appreciative nod indicated her gratitude. He smiled to her before he removed the ruined flower from the shelf too. "I'll go pay for these, and we can leave."

Holding out his right arm for her, she stepped up beside him and accepted it. The rose twirled in her right hand as their steps carried them to the front. Despite the depression that desired to control her mind, she managed to push it aside momentarily and enjoy Edmund's company. Thankfully, he had found her walking on the side of the road. Otherwise, she most likely would still be out there with large blisters forming on her feet.

To distract herself further, she asked, "Why are you paying? Haven't you already paid for them?"

"I have, but my employees have to pay for items here. I'm an employee too." His eyes didn't avert to hers. Rather, he continued to stare somewhat ahead, but he was aware of the fact that she smiled at his response.

## Chapter Eleven: Confront

*Subtly, the door opened, and the visitor walked in. Before him, there were various people underneath a warm glow of lights, but there was only one that held his interest.*

Sitting upon her bed, Elaine leaned further back against the headboard. She could see out into the small hallway and towards the front door. There, several boxes were stacked. All of them contained R ... his items. A blank stare covered her expression as her fingers twirled the purple rose between them.

She was forcing herself not to shed another tear over what had happened, though; she had a feeling that she would break that policy sooner or later. Thankfully, Edmund had helped her pack things away after they had arrived at her apartment. There were moments, however, where he had to step away from aiding her and take meeting calls since he had switched such meetings from face-to-face to phone conference calls. That gesture alone had been sweet, and she had thanked him for it several times.

Now, though, he was gone, and a dreary quiet hung over her apartment. Steadily, she forced her eyes from the boxes to the door. Where had he gone? He had seemed to be in a rush. Maybe, he had another meeting that he hadn't been able to change in time.

Her eyes landed on the alarm clock in her room. *5:00 pm.* She brought her knees up to her chest. The reception just started. Had Regi ... Elaine couldn't even think about his name let alone speak it fully. Bringing her right index finger and thumb to the bridge of her nose, she rubbed it. A slow exhale left her.

Had his parents even wondered why she had been absent from the funeral, or had they not cared? They probably hadn't and still didn't. After all, they had known about their son cheating on her, and they hadn't said a word to her. Probably, they thought that her lack of presence made things less complicated.

Relaxing her legs, she slid them down the sheets. She rolled over onto her right side. In front of her, the flower stared back. Its lavender-purple petals brought a slight smile to her lips. Her very first call to Edmund had been truly lucky. If she hadn't called him, she knew that she would be in worse shape.

Rolling onto her left side, her eyes drifted back to the clock. *5:05 pm.* She blinked as her mind seemed to click something together. Edmund had left about thirty minutes ago, which was the distance from her apartment to the post-funeral dinner. His state of urgency had been ... odd.

Instantly, she sat straight up. She winced and looked down. The plastic stem had bit into her skin by a little bit. Elaine removed her hand from the flower. No blood had been drawn, but there was a red mark there. It most likely would fade away soon.

Was he going to the reception dinner? If so, was he already there? She had told him the location earlier before what had happened ... in the car, and she had noted the sparks of anger in his eyes at various points while he had been at her apartment. Those sparks had formed whenever she had started to break down again and when she had choked out either that nurse or her ex's name.

If that was his plan, what was he going to do? He didn't seem like the type to create a dramatic scene, but his anger could turn him into that. She didn't wish for him to get hurt in the process because of that cursed nurse and her ex's parents. Worried, she reached over to her left nightstand to retrieve her phone. Her hand stopped midway, however, and she lowered it back to the bed.

Perhaps, she shouldn't stop him. She had left Gina and his parents off of the hook easily. Elaine knew that she should be the one to confront them, but her present state of mind wouldn't last long before any of them. If anything, she might have another mental breakdown, and Edmund could handle himself. He ran a popular chain of art stores after all, so he probably had dealt with all sorts of people already.

Still, a part of her didn't feel right just letting him go into that chaotic storm without some form of warning. Besides, she didn't even know if the reception dinner was his true destination, though; it was likely. Once again, she reached for her phone. That time, she grabbed it. Dialing his personal number, she waited.

"Elaine, is ..."

For once, she cut him off. "Are you heading to the dinner?" Her tone was rushed and firm, but she didn't want to delay. If he was there already, he probably wouldn't spend too much time on the phone.

Silence greeted her at first before a slight chuckle hit her ears. It could've easily been replaced with a sigh as though he was saying *you found me out.* "Yes. Is that why you called?" There was a tinge of annoyance in his tone, and it gave her pause, which allowed him to speak before she could. "Are you worried that I'm going to do something?"

"You're already doing something." Her air quotes could practically be seen by her tone, but she sighed in the end. "I originally had been, but I trust you." He remained silent as if to ask the purpose of her call, then. "I just ..." Suddenly, she felt somewhat embarrassed and childish. Edmund knew what he was doing, and it sounded like he was irritated at her call. She could practically hear him tapping a finger against the phone. "Well, I just wanted to tell you to be careful."

"..." For a moment, she thought that she heard a chuckle on the other end, but his following soft tone pushed that thought out of her mind. "Thank you. I'll be fine." She could hear the sound of a car door closing. "Do you want me to come back when I'm done?"

"No." She heard a pause in his steps. "Well, I want you to. And, I had told you earlier to stay the night, but ..." His steps continued again. "But, I don't think that it'd be wise since that nurse will be picking up R ... his things tomorrow." Silence met her, so she explained further. "If you're going to confront her, it might be better if you're not at my apartment in the morning."

"I should've brought the boxes with me, then." He chuckled a little. "But, that would've blown my cover, though; that happened regardless." She laughed lightly, and she could easily picture him smiling on the other end. "Call me when she's gone." Elaine hummed in response, and he hung up. His tone had been somewhat commanding, but she figured that his mind was elsewhere currently, so she hung up and brushed it aside.

Edmund placed his phone into his inner jacket pocket, and a small smile formed on his lips. He had expected her to get after him, yet he pleasantly had been surprised. Maybe, he would purchase her a bouquet of real purple roses the next time they met up or a few more fabric ones. Those didn't die.

His smile morphed into a neutral expression, however, as he approached the restaurant. He buttoned up his jacket and adjusted his black tie. The gel in his hair had worn off some, and more than the usual few strands hung over his forehead. Edmund pushed them back and hoped that they would stay in place for a little bit. Even if he disliked the person he was about to converse with, he wished to keep up his appearance.

Barely, he glanced up at the restaurant sign as he headed into the establishment. A waitress stood at the front, and he could hear a large group of people talking in the room to his left. She glanced to him as if determining whether to smile or not since there was a funeral reception in one part of the building, so he smiled to her. It wasn't a genuine one, but she wouldn't be able to tell. "I'm here for Reginald Daxni's reception."

By a little bit, her eyes widened before her shoulders sagged. Clearly, she was emotionally exhausted from all of the guests. "To your left." She pointed tiredly. "You can sit anywhere except the long table at the back."

"Thank you." She nodded to him, and he moved around her and into the room. His eyes scanned over the crowd. Not everyone appeared to be there yet since not all of the chairs were full. Then again, some could remain empty.

Peering to the back table, he saw who he assumed to be the disgusting man's parents. While he had been at Elaine's apartment, she had described them a little bit to him along with Gina and their son. They seemed to fit her description, but they weren't his target. The nurse was.

Scanning over the crowd again, he felt someone bump into the back of him. He caught himself before he stared down a little to find the woman of interest. "Sorry." Her voice was scratchy like she had been crying for some time. Almost, he glowered. She had no right to cry. When she met his eyes, she furrowed her brow. "I don't believe that we've met before."

"No, we haven't." He kept his tone even and controlled, though; he would like to strangle her ugly little neck. "I'm George." Edmund held out his hand for her to shake.

Lightly, she grasped and shook it. "Gina. Umm ..." She retracted her hand awkwardly.

"Why don't we get a drink and sit down? I'm sure that we both need it after today." A warm smile decorated his lips, and he indicated to a table far from the back one. "And then, we can talk." Hesitation filled her orbs, but she didn't deny him, and they headed over to the indicated table after getting drinks.

## <u>Chapter Twelve: Unnerve</u>

*Bubbles rose to the top of the champagne, and if one listened closely, they could hear the bubbles pop at the top. By each glass, an individual sat: one puzzled and the other infuriated.*

A bright light shone on the table next to them, casting their table in shadows. Edmund's face was partially covered by those shadows. Some of the bangs that he pushed back earlier fell forward again, but he acted as though he wasn't bothered by them. His long fingers wrapped around the stem of the hand-blown champagne glass, and he steadily lifted the rim to his lips.

Easily, he could've snapped the glass in half from his fury towards the woman across from him, but he forced himself to be satisfied with making her highly uncomfortable. Her eyes stared down at her glass nervously, and her long nails tapped the base of it. When she glanced up to him, he was lowering it down on the table. "How had you known Reginald?" The question was casual enough, but he heard the hesitation she was holding back. There was a fraction of determination in her tone too, however, as though she suspected his actual claim for being at the reception.

Edmund crossed his legs and sat up a little straighter on the dark oak chair. "I had met him at a bakery in town." Her brow furrowed, and she sipped at her drink. His right fingers moved onto the oak table and tapped against them. Each strike carried anger, but she wouldn't notice that. She wasn't that observant, or she would've seen him around the hospital when Elaine had been there. If she had viewed him there, she would comprehend that he wasn't at the reception dinner for Reginald at all.

"Bakery?" She set down her glass confused. He had trouble restraining a dark, knowing chuckle. "He never had gone to bakeries unless ..." Gina paused, and she bit her bottom lip. Almost, she had let her secret slip, but it wasn't a secret to him.

"At the time, he had been there with a woman." Edmund had trouble not complimenting Elaine, but he couldn't give himself away yet. No, the nurse had to squirm first.

"What had happened?" Her right index finger ran along the base of the glass, and her nail occasionally hit the glass. The woman's brown orbs were dominated by fear, but she was trying to hide it behind an expression bearing curiosity.

"The bakery only had accepted cash, and he only had a credit card." For a moment, he recalled the outfit upon Elaine's gorgeous form and how it had complemented her so well. When he had first seen Elaine with that man, he knew that they weren't meant to be a pair. That man hadn't appreciated her beauty and charm at all.

Lifting his glass to his lips, he took a sip before he set it back down. "I had loaned him the money to pay for his order since it already had been made. There was a brief conversation after that. An exchange of thanks and such. After that, I got to know him better."

"And, the woman?"

A pretend appearance of curiosity covered his countenance. "Why are you interested in her?" His eyes scanned over the restaurant and the guests. "In fact, I don't see her here now." Edmund had difficulty keeping the venom out of his tone. "Was or is there a problem with her?" Gina attempted to hide a gulp, but it didn't go unnoticed by him. Her eyes shifted to her left and down towards a cloth napkin on the table. Moving her fingers over to it, she began to rub the fabric between her fingers like the action would transport her somewhere else.

"Aren't you his girlfriend?" Her head perked up at that in shock. "He had talked about you." Edmund sent her a false kind smile, but the illusion wasn't revealed to her. "All good things." She breathed a sigh of relief. "I had assumed that other woman to be simply a friend of his." A chuckle left him, and its tone was anything but welcoming. "Though, he had kissed her on the lips a few times. So, maybe, very close friends."

By a fraction, his eyes narrowed as he lifted his glass up to his lips for a third time. Gina froze in her seat, and her fingers fell onto her lap. The napkin descended onto the floor. Champagne traveled down his throat in a smooth motion before he placed it down with immense grace. A neutral expression took over his face. "You act shocked, yet you also seem to have known about that."

Visibly, she gulped. "L-Lo-Look, I ..."

"Are you about to say the typical 'I don't know who you are' line?" Her mouth shut tight, and a gleam of amusement entered his eyes. "I thought so, but the thing is that you do know. I had told you previously."

"H-Had y-you ..." She coughed and composed herself to a degree. "Had you been lying?" He raised a brow. "About the bakery?" Edmund leaned back on his chair and watched some individuals in the crowd as if her words were but a nuisance to his ears. And, they basically were.

"How silly."

"What?" she asked completely perplexed.

"You know the answer." His eyes landed back on her, and they were piercing in a chilling way. Her body appeared to be paralyzed. "Everything I had told you is true, though; I had left out some details." He stared out over the crowd again since he didn't wish to look at her. "After my show of kindness, I had ordered something for myself and had taken a seat. The only available table had been the one behind your dear Reginald." His tone was soaked with poison at the end. Gina appeared ready to bolt of her chair, but a harsh stare put her back on her seat.

Focusing on his glass, he brought it to his lips once more. After the sip, he held it in his hand and twirled the champagne inside a bit. "And while he had been telling that woman sweet nothings, he had sent a peculiar text message to someone." Over the rim of the glass, he met her terrified orbs with a raptor-like gaze. "Can you tell me what that message had said?"

"I-I-I ..."

Chuckling bitterly, he shook his head. "Wrong. Would you like another try?" Only stuttering greeted him. "I thought so." Edmund rested his glass on the table with a sense of finality to it, and the infuriation in his orbs finally became visible to the nurse. "Let me tell you what that message had said. *Afternoon. Your place. 3:30 pm. Wear that sheer nightgown I like, Gina. Love you.*" Sweat formed on her brow. "You may have been his girlfriend, but you most certainly hadn't been his first one. The failed secrecy had given that away in a heartbeat."

"What do you want?" Her voice was strong but fearful.

"I want you to move by the end of week. Arrangements will be made so that you don't have to worry about finding a new job or apartment on such short notice." Baffled wouldn't begin to describe the expression on her face. "You harmed her, and I want you far away from her. Really, I should throw you out on the street, but I'm giving you a kind alternative."

Not being able to control herself, her hands gripped the table. "Who the h*ll do you think you are?"

"I'm a man with the right information and connections. I'm George."

Anger built up in her face, and she looked ready to explode. He wasn't amused, however. She had no right to be furious after what she had done to Elaine. "Why do you care?" His eyes held hers, and that gave her the answer. "Elaine?" Gina leaned across the table some like a snake ready to strike, but he wasn't intimidated in the slightest. "You're close with her."

"I'm a friend, yes." Her teeth grinded, but his expression didn't change. "But, she didn't send me if that's what you're getting at. I came of my own accord after I saw her condition today."

"If you're her friend, why hadn't you mentioned the cheating to her? Does she even know that you had known before her?" A malicious grin tugged at her lips, but it only made her more hideous, not frightening. "She doesn't know, does she?"

"No, she doesn't." A chuckle left him. "Do you intend to tell her?"

"I do. Tomorrow." She stood up from the table like she had won. "You probably know that I'll be stopping by her place to pick up Reginald's things. Originally, I doubted that I would see her again, but it'll be hard not to if I'm right outside of her house."

"Yes, that would be difficult." Edmund stood up from his seat after he finished his champagne. His eyes stared down to her with ill amusement. "Remember, my offer, though. Mess with me too much, and that might change, but it's your decision. I'll deal with whatever actions you take. Unlike you, I can face the consequences of my actions."

"Then, you wouldn't mind if I told the whole crowd your reason for being here." A grin stayed plastered on her lips, but he only shook his head like she was a fool. And, she was.

"Yes, tell everyone why Elaine's absent and how you had slept with him. They might understand why you would move, then." She stood still, and her grin fell. He smirked to her before he walked off.

59

## Chapter Thirteen: Ring

*Boxes practically were kicked through the open doorway. Eyes wouldn't even meet while from a short distance away the entire scene was observed.*

Sheets were haphazardly strewn across the bed, and the form beneath them was spread out across the plush mattress. Her face was half-hanging off of her pillow. There used to be a second pillow on the bed, but that had been removed the day prior. The woman's right arm was underneath her pillow, and her other hand's fingers were placed on the edge. Needless to say, her current position indicated that of a rough night.

An empty mug rested on the left nightstand. Hibiscus raspberry tea had filled it in the evening. Beside it was a half-eaten bar of dark chocolate. Elaine hadn't cried herself to sleep. She had refused that method. Rather, she had read a mystery book at the time or had tried to. If someone asked her what had happened for the first hundred pages, she'd most likely stare at them blankly. The chocolate bar and tea had captivated her attention a bit more.

When her alarm ringed, she groaned and rolled over before her hand basically slammed down on the button. Groggily, she opened her eyes and forced herself to sit up. She blinked a couple of times as she took in her bed's condition and reassured herself that it could've been worse.

Her hands rubbed at her eyes, and she felt something wet there. A sigh escaped her. It seemed that she had cried in her sleep. Then again, it didn't surprise her since her sleep had been filled with that nurse's words on repeat. It made her wish that she had asked Edmund to stay the night, though; she probably would've joined him on the couch midway through.

A slight dose of heat touched her cheeks at the thought, but that didn't stop her from considering having him over that night. Her lips formed something between a pout and frown. Maybe, she was becoming too dependent on him, but he didn't seem to mind. Still, his company eased her mind from all of its present troubles, so was it bad to be so reliant on him? Not to mention that she actually had laughed around him despite the current troubles in her life.

He even had confronted the nurse last night. She hadn't received a call from him after she had called him, but she figured that he had kept his promise. Elaine only hoped that the nurse wouldn't come barging through her door like a rampaging bull. If the nurse did show up to her apartment like that, she suspected that Edmund might not be far behind. He wouldn't leave her to handle that woman in such a state even though she had told him not to come. That was just how generous and kind he was.

Unfortunately, those thoughts reminded her of her oncoming headache: G ... the nurse. She ran her hands down her face before she looked over her appearance. A thulian pink cotton nightgown covered her form, and the sleeves hung loosely on her shoulders. Elaine patted her short, curly dark brown locks to test their state, and she found her hair to be an utter mess. Her emotions may be in every which way, but she wasn't going to allow that nurse to see that. That woman had witnessed enough yesterday.

Sliding her legs off of her bed, she headed over to her closet and slipped off her nightgown before she changed into her white blouse with chiffon sleeves, black chiffon skirt and plum purple strappy wedges. Since she was staying in her apartment for the day, the heels were unnecessary, but she wanted to appear her usual self as though her heart hadn't been shredded and stomped on. Elaine made her way into the bathroom next and brushed her locks several times to give them an ideal shine.

Some makeup even decorated her face at the end of her morning routine. A matte red-purple lipstick adorned her lips, and light smoky eye-shadow complemented her look. She leaned forward on the bathroom counter, wondering if she should just throw the boxes outside. Yesterday, she had told the nurse that she had never wished to see her again. Part of her claimed that to be a childish and unrealistic statement, but the other part announced that it was appropriate.

Resonating throughout the apartment, a ring alerted her. She groaned inwardly before she pushed herself off of the counter and made her way to the window by the door. Elaine peeked out it and saw the cursed woman. Maybe, she could make her wait outside for an hour, but she did want the nurse gone sooner than later.

Reluctantly, she unlocked the door and opened it. A slow creaking noise hit the air. An uncomfortable silence followed. Elaine briefly glanced to her before she focused on the boxes. "They're right there. Take them and go."

Gina stepped some into the apartment, ready to grab one, but she paused. Her brown orbs looked over the younger woman. "You're dolled up." She directed a slight glare to the younger. "Are you meeting him?"

"Him?" Elaine was disinterested in the conversation already. She knew who the nurse was referring to, but that was none of her business.

Standing up straighter, Gina scowled. "You know who I'm talking about. You might've not sent him to the reception, but he claimed to be your friend." Her eyes performed another scan of Elaine. "Maybe, he's actually more. And, you walk off yesterday like you're actually hurt. I bet that ..."

Skin impacted skin. Gina's head turned to the right as a handprint started to form on her left cheek. "I never had cheated on Reginald." Harshly, Elaine pointed to the boxes. "Take them and leave. Your welcome here is over." If her eyes could've burned holes into the older woman, they would have. That fury kept tears from falling, but she would probably cry later again.

Instead of anger falling on Gina's countenance, a smirk tugged at her lips. She stood up tall. Elaine held onto the door firmly as if meaning that she would slam the door on the nurse whether she was out of the way or not. Gina ignored the warning. "He still hasn't told you?" An ill chuckle left her, and the younger did her best not to appear puzzled. Annoyingly, the nurse noticed.

"So, he hasn't. Well ..." Suddenly, though, she stopped. She glanced back outside and surveyed her surroundings. No one was there, yet it felt like someone was staring at her intently. Was he nearby? Her confidence began to fade. Hesitantly, she grabbed one of the boxes.

"Well what?" Gina's pause had given Elaine enough time to compose herself. Her tone was demanding and impatient, and her right nails tapped against the wood to emphasize that further.

Up the nurse's spine, a chill traveled. Her next words got caught in her throat, and stuttering became her answer. Elaine rolled her eyes and leaned against the door as if to say that she was tired and bored of Gina's presence. The nurse hardly paid attention to that before she quickly answered, "Nothing."

"Then, get going." Without another word, Gina left with the first box. She came back for the following ones. Thankfully, it didn't take her long to load up all of his things, and she didn't come back after the last one.

Elaine watched the black civic drive out of the complex's parking lot. If things went well, she would never lay eyes on that woman again. A sigh left her, and she closed the door. Her mind did wonder what the nurse had been about to tell her about Edmund, but it probably had been nothing more than a lie. She trusted Edmund, not that nurse.

Retrieving her phone, she dialed his number to let him know that the nurse was gone. He picked up on the first ring, and a slight smile graced her lips. She leaned back against her kitchen counter a little.

"She's come and gone?" Edmund asked, though; he already knew the answer. He had observed it too. Binoculars were a wonderful device. The male heard a relieved sigh on the other end, and he could picture her nodding.

Edmund would've viewed the action if she was standing in front of her kitchen or living room window. "Yes, thankfully ... Are you going to come over later?" He held in a delighted chuckle and crossed his legs as he leaned back on his chair.

"If you want me to." A pause greeted him, and he smiled. "Do you?" Another pause was his reply, but he comprehended her answer. She just was being polite and not wanting to seem needy. It was cute how she thought that she could hide that.

"... I do." She paused again, though; her voice sped up next. "But, later on. You're probably busy."

"Any time will work, Elaine. I don't have to go anywhere today. If you need me now, I'll come now." A smirk pulled on his lips when she came into his view again. Her right arm was under her chest and supporting her left elbow as that hand held her phone. She was doing her best not to bite on her lower lip, but that caused him to bite his lower lip in turn.

"Whenever then ..." A smile gradually formed on her lips. "Surprise me." His lips stretched into a smirk. Oh, he could most definitely do that.

## Chapter Fourteen: Rearrange

*Clear glass sparkled with the light passing through it. Delicate, soft petals were opened wide to the rays, though; they didn't depend on such illumination to live.*

Not sure of when Edmund would be stopping by, Elaine picked up the apartment a little as soon as she hung up the phone. Most of it was already tidy, and she knew that he would understand if her apartment became a mess, but she wished it to look new. She would've held onto its old appearance had yesterday not occurred. Probably, she would be on her bed and curled up under the sheets.

Presently, though, her mind was continuing to cope with all of the dreadful information that had passed. That was why she wanted things to be clean. She would probably even rearrange several pieces of furniture so that her apartment would appear like R ... he never had resided there. His memory was painful and now tainted because of that nurse.

Resting her hands on her hips, she scanned over the contents of her apartment to see where to start first. Her eyes landed on the bedroom. She had changed the sheets last night and had thrown out the old ones. Elaine had even opened a new package of sheets. Her ex had never once touched them. Excellent, though, she needed to make her bed. The sheets remained in disarray.

Entering the space, she fixed the sheets and fluffed her pillow, which used to be only on the right-hand side of the bed. Maybe down the road, she would purchase a new mattress and headboard. In the long run, hopefully, all of her furniture would be replaced so that his presence in the apartment would be nonexistent.

Or, she could move and sell off the furniture to afford new items. As lovely as that option sounded, she would wait at least until the lease was up on the place. Besides, she now had to pay for the monthly bills on her own, which would eat up a good portion of her budget, but she could still afford the payments.

Her eyes trailed over to the silk rose, which she had placed on the right nightstand. Steadily, she walked over to it and lifted it up. She twirled the plastic between her fingers, and a light smile touched her lips before a peculiar thought crossed her mind. He could move in with her ... Elaine snapped her eyes open and shook her head. They only had started meeting each other for about a week. That was too short in her head to warrant them living together.

Placing the flower down, she rubbed the bridge of her nose. What was she thinking? Had she grown to like him that much? He was only a friend, right? A groan left her, and she forced herself to turn from the rose. She had other things to clean and rearrange; she could think on it later.

Heading into the bathroom, she grabbed a rag and some dust cleaner before she went to work on dusting down the whole bedroom. She left the window open as she worked and hummed along. Most of the room was dusted until she came upon the left nightstand. That had been his beforehand, but he had put her alarm clock on it since he typically had woken up before her. Now, she wondered if he really had started work so early in the morning.

A knot formed in her stomach, and she scowled. That was no longer important. She placed the rag and cleaner aside before she removed the clock. Elaine bent down and pulled out the lamp plug before she wrapped it around the stem of the item. Once done, she removed the lamp from her room and set it by the door. Following it was the nightstand. Those would be the first items for her to sell.

After she stood up straight from the moving, she jumped a little. She was caught off guard by the doorbell ringing. Elaine stepped over to the window and peeked out of it. A smile fell upon her lips before puzzlement set in. Edmund was there, but he was holding something also. From her angle, she couldn't make it out.

Going back to the door, she unlocked and turned the knob. When it opened, Edmund smiled to her before his eyes fell onto the furniture by the door. "I thought that you had given everything to that nurse already?" His eyes glanced back to her, and one of his eyebrows was arched.

"I did ... Well ..." She peered over her right shoulder to everything in the apartment. "Not the furniture. It wasn't only his, but I ..."

"I understand." She met his eyes again and gave him a thankful look that she wouldn't have to explain herself further before she moved aside and indicated for him to come in. He dipped his head in thanks before he walked right past with the item in his hands. Elaine thought that she saw lavender-purple, but she noted something else about him.

His outfit's colors matched hers like they had in the past. Edmund's suit jacket and pants were black as were his dress shoes; however, he was wearing his plum and black striped button-up. To top that off, he had a white tie on.

"Do you have a vase?"

The question brought her back from her staring, and she realized that she still had the door open. "Wh-wh ..." She shook her head, and he shifted his orbs back to her. An amused smile tugged at his lips, and they parted as if to ask her again. Hurriedly, she chuckled her behavior off and answered, "Yes. The cupboard on the right side of the window." He nodded and faced away from her. "Why?"

Movements pausing, he set the item in his hands on the counter. His back currently blocked it from her view. "You'll see, but you should close the door unless you like the cool breeze coming through." He started to move again, and he opened the proper cupboard.

Heat dusted her cheeks in embarrassment, and she quickly shut the door and locked it. Elaine didn't even know if there was actually a breeze. Her mind just had trusted him, and she almost face-palmed from that. She scolded herself for worrying too much about his clothing options. Maybe, it was odd, but it could be a reoccurring coincidence. That sounded ridiculous, but if she didn't focus soon, he might call her out on her seemingly zoned-out state.

Pinching her wrist a bit, she woke herself up and joined him in the kitchen. Curious, she moved to his left side to spot what was on the counter. Just as she did so, however, he picked the item back up and walked past her with the vase too. "Would you mind getting that rose I had given you yesterday, Elaine?"

Edmund continued to face away from her as he headed towards her bedroom. She followed behind him. "Well, it's in my bedroom." He paused, and she couldn't view the smirk on his lips. "That's where you're going, right?"

"I am." He advanced towards the room again. "Why'd you put it in there?" His steps were slow and calculated, and they created a somewhat intimidating vibe around him as though he already knew the reason; however, that didn't draw her away from him. If anything, it made her move closer so that she could try and steal a peek at his facial expression. Unfortunately, he remained one step ahead of her, and not once could she view his face as they traveled down the hallway. "Elaine?"

Noting that she actually hadn't responded, she coughed awkwardly before she noticed that heat tickled her cheeks again. "I ... I ... I'm not sure." His silence signaled her to continue. "Well after you had left, I just had ... Well, I just had brought it in with me."

Entering her bedroom, he stopped and averted his eyes to her nightstand. A smile, almost a grin, took over his lips. As Elaine stepped up beside him, it morphed into simply a soft smile before amusement painted his eyes. "And, what happened to the petals?"

Momentarily perplexed, she diverted her gaze to them. More heat decorated her cheeks. Each petal was slightly crushed. She must've slept on it at times during the night. Not knowing what to say, she replied meekly, "Sorry."

Laughing gently, he shook his head and stepped over to the area. "It's fine." Towards the back of the nightstand, he placed down the vase and moved aside. Now, she could see that there were a dozen of the lavender-purple roses in the glass container. She suspected that he had been holding flowers, but she hadn't wanted to assume anything until she was sure. Her eyes brightened a bit, and she moved over to him while he delicately held onto the flower from yesterday.

"Thank you!" She couldn't resist giving him a hug to which he almost lost his balance from surprise. An entertained chuckle escaped him, and he wrapped his right arm around her while he stood up straight again. His left hand deposited the single rose into the vase, and he had put two and two together. Elaine had slept with the flower, and that had made his heart tighten with jubilation.

In the future, it would be him instead of that flower. He held back a smirk and forced the grin away from his eyes. Instead, he maintained a calm countenance. "You're welcome. I thought that just one rose wouldn't suit you."

Staring up at him with her arms still around him, she smiled again. Her words were clear across her lips, but she spoke them anyway. "Well, they do brighten up the space."

"Should I decorate the rest of your apartment?" At his words, she chuckled and winked playfully.

## Chapter Fifteen: Drift

*Folded paper flew through the air as its wings danced upon the light breeze. Down below, something of similar origin glided along effortlessly.*

Streams of pale sunlight broke through the thin, grey clouds above. Their heat wasn't too hot. Rather, it was calming and created the perfect weather for a stroll outside. Some seized such an opportunity, and their forms could be viewed upon the cement sidewalks that bordered the streets.

A pair of dark blue one-inch wedges protected the feet of one of these individuals. Light pink flowers decorated the design of the shoe's fabric. Accompanying these was a short, dark blue dress, and there was a black belt around the waist. Within the individual's ears was a pair of light pink flower earrings. The woman carried a black leather purse, which held a piece of green paper and other items inside.

Elaine had her hair tied up in the back with a black and dark blue ribbon. Her locks were brushed to perfection, and when the streams of sunlight hit them, they seemed to glow. Upon her lips was a striking dark red lipstick, and her eyes were piercing with the right amount of mascara and eye shadow.

As if those features didn't grab enough attention, her walk was powerful. Every step held a purpose, and her eyes were determined to find her desired location, yet her mind wasn't so fixed on a singular goal. She had her plan for the day set into motion, but she couldn't help the smiles that formed in her mind.

It had been a week since Edmund had given her that bouquet of flowers, and they still sat marvelously on her nightstand. Since then, he had aided her in cleaning up her apartment and rearranging the furniture. At first, she had thought that he only had been joking about his offer to help her, but that had been far from the case. He even had posted a few items online for her to sell and had shown her how to continue to do that for other items.

Tomorrow, they were even going to pick out paint for her place, which she had received permission to do from the landowner as long as she repainted the walls an off-white before she left. Not only was he helping her to remove signs of R ... him from her apartment but also he was making her laugh and smile, which eased her mind immensely from the beatings it had taken previously.

Eventually, she couldn't keep the smiles to herself, and one stretched across her lips in a small, delicate manner. She downturned her head, trying to keep it private, but she figured that some saw it. Still, she had to perform something today. It would be another way of removing her ex from her mind and heart.

When she lifted her head back up, she saw the park coming up. She took a right and headed down the smaller sidewalk, which led to the batch of birch trees. They grew by the stream that traveled through the park and gave the visitor a peaceful, quiet retreat.

Once the sidewalk ended, she stepped onto the grass and gained her bearings before continuing forward. She maneuvered around the many trunks and stepped up beside the water. Her reflection looked back at her as the water carried on at a gentle pace. No smile greeted her lips now.

The present spot had once been a special location for that man and her. He would lay out a large, fleece blanket even though it would pick up the dirt and leaves if there were any on the ground. That man had wanted her to be comfortable, though; she wasn't so sure now that he ever actually had cared about that. She scowled at the memory and kicked some of the dried debris and dirt away.

One by one, she tried to remove the memories of their conversations by the water away. They didn't serve a purpose anymore but to torment her; however, some of the memories remained powerful in her mind, and they all had one connection. She reached into her purse and pulled out the green paper. It was like the color of his eyes.

Nearly, she crumpled it up. She wished to slam it to the ground and stomp endlessly on it. It was a curse, a poison. A slight growl left her at the rush of negative emotions. Elaine took a deep breath in before she exhaled. Practically, she could feel the anger, sadness and depression leave through that breath, but that relief wouldn't last long. All of those emotions would come flying right back at her unless she carried on with what she originally intended.

Her fingers, though shaky from fury, began to fold the paper. She had trouble standing still, but she planted her feet firmly on the ground and refused to move her legs yet. Steadily, the paper took shape. When she was finished, a paper airplane rested on the palms of her hands.

Every conversation they had out by the current spot had ended with them throwing a paper airplane across the water. It never made it to the other riverbank. Rather, it sailed through the air before it met the water and floated along its surface. Written within each of those planes had been a line or two of their wishes. Such a tradition had been their version of wishing upon a star.

Presently, the green plane had a message written within it. It wasn't so much as a wish as it was a demand, a requirement for her to move on. She placed the plane between her right index finger and thumb, but she didn't throw it immediately. No, she waited to make sure that her heartache was deposited into the piece of paper.

Positive that she was ready, she tilted her hand back before she rushed it forward as she released the plane. It soared through the air and even managed a spin, but she was waiting for it to make contact with the water. Almost, it looked like it would make it to the other shore, but it plummeted and crashed into the water before then.

Water soaked the paper as it drifted downstream and out of her field of vision; however, something peculiar traveled towards her on the water. All of her focus shifted to it as the plane became forgotten by her. She took a few steps forward and crouched down to the water.

On two sturdy, wooden sticks, there was a paper boat. Water was held off by the wood, and the boat maintained its crisp and elegant shape. She stared up and around her to see if she could find the owner, but there seemed to be no one else in the vicinity ... How odd.

Hesitantly, she reached towards it and removed it from the water. Water dripped from the sticks, and she noted that the bottom of the boat had been hole-punched. Strings were laced through the holes and secured the item to the sticks. It certainly was a neat art project. At that thought, she smiled a little. Edmund probably would appreciate the craft.

What sparked her interest further, however, was that there was something written along the deck of the boat. *A new life awaits.* Her brows furrowed at the message, and she couldn't help but glance over her shoulder. The plane was gone, and she was glad for it. That part of her life was over, and she had a new section ahead of her. She froze. The message on the boat was strangely and worryingly close to that.

Immediately, she stood up. Just who was in the area with her? She hadn't seen the boat until recently, but she hadn't heard footsteps around her either. Elaine performed another check of her surroundings, but that didn't produce any results either. Maybe, she was over-thinking things.

Perhaps, the person simply was referring to the fact that the boat would have a new life. It was sailing down the river with no given purpose but that. Many things could happen to it along the way, and those would all be contained in its new life upon the water. Or, there was the possibility that someone just liked inspirational phrases.

Yet, a troubling question remained. Who had set the boat on the water? She gave the area one last inspection before she decided it time to leave. Elaine wouldn't come to the area again, especially after the mysterious boat.

Setting the boat back on the water, she turned away and started her way back to her apartment. From the other shore, however, a form hid among the trees. His tall body leaned against one gently as though he were but a tilted tree in the small forest area. Edmund's orbs followed Elaine the entire time until she moved out of his sight.

Like usual, he matched her outfit choices. A black jacket, tie, pants and shoes adorned his form while a dark blue button-up accompanied them. His suit jacket had light pink flower cufflinks.

In his hands, however, there was a soggy piece of green paper. He had unfolded the plane, and his eyes glanced down at the ruined message again. *I d-n't l-ve R ... him a-ym-re. Let h-s m-mory d-own a-d f-de.* Letters were illegible, but he figured out the message well enough. Besides, that pathetic excuse for a human being's memory already was disappearing, and he was replacing it.

Just like the boat, he would provide her a sturdier, more supportive life. Something as gentle as a stream wouldn't be able to tarnish their bond. Edmund watched the boat sail further down the water until it made a turn and vanished from his view, but he smirked. Despite it being out of view, he trusted that it would hold just like he trusted that Elaine would be even closer to him now.

## <u>Chapter Sixteen: Examine</u>

*Careful steps ascended upwards, and quietness reigned around the individual. Hands grabbed the door handle and opened the doorway, which unveiled something worth pausing for.*

Waking up early, Elaine glanced to her alarm clock. *7:00 am.* She hadn't been up that early voluntarily for awhile, but when she tried to fall back asleep, she found that she couldn't. Elaine even tried switching her position on the bed multiple times, but that didn't work. Her mind was still focused on what had occurred yesterday. That boat's message bothered her too much.

Sitting up, she combed her right fingers through her dark brown locks and huffed. Today, she would be meeting Edmund at his art store for paint, which would keep her mind off of the boat. At least, she hoped that to be the case. His company did always ease her mind. Maybe if she was lucky, she would even forget about the boat. Besides, she would make sure to upkeep her promise of never visiting that spot again. She wouldn't even visit that park. A safe distance from that area would serve her well.

Draping her legs over the bed, she stood to her feet and proceeded with her morning routine. When she finished, she checked her clock again. *7:30 am.* She was supposed to meet Edmund at eleven in the morning, so she would need to leave at about ten-thirty, but she would be ready to depart long before that. Elaine slipped out of her olive green nightgown and tossed it into the hamper.

The soft pads of her heels touched the apartment flooring lightly as she moved to her closet. She opened the closet door and shifted her weight on her feet a few times before a smile tickled her lips. There was a simple and easy solution: meet him early. That did have an issue, though. He would've picked her up on his way to work since he had said that her apartment was on the way, but he was going to be in a meeting from eight-thirty to ten-thirty. So, she had told him not to worry and that she would drive herself there.

If she arrived early, she wouldn't be able to talk with him, but she supposed that she could begin to look at the paints. Or, she could surprise him in the meeting room once it was over. Would that bother him? She chewed on her lower lip a little and leaned against the side of the closet doorway. In all fairness, he had surprised her on a few occasions, so she didn't see an issue with returning the favor.

There was the option of working before she had to leave, but she had finished all of her tasks on her agenda last night like she had planned. She could always read over the blog pages again, but she felt that would waste both her employers' time as well as hers, not to mention her employers' money. Having convinced herself that it would be fine, she pushed herself off of the closet frame and selected her outfit.

She changed into her black button-up dress, with its plum-colored ribbon around the collar, and her black pumps. Heading back into the bathroom, she brushed her hair, leaving it down, and applied a red-purple lipstick along with a little bit of mascara and eye shadow.

Her next task on her agenda was breakfast, and she would leave at eight. She wanted Edmund to be in his meeting when she arrived so that he wouldn't notice her coming in. Spending two hours in an art store was easily possible, and she had no idea what color or colors to paint her apartment so that would take time on its own. Edmund was supposed to help her, but he could towards the end.

With that in mind, she followed her plan and was in her car at eight. The drive to the art store was pleasant despite the fact that she had to use the same road that she had been walking down the prior week, but she wasn't about to take a long detour because of that. She wouldn't let that deceased man and that nurse control her driving patterns. No, she had dealt with that nurse and had thrown that paper airplane.

Instead, she switched on her radio and sang along lightly to whatever song was playing. At the moment, she didn't care about who the singer was or what genre the music was in. She simply liked the tune, and it kept her mind off of annoying thoughts. Elaine would've opened her window and relished in the wind racing by, but she didn't wish for her hair to be a mess. It was for herself that she maintained her appearance, but she would be lying if she said that she didn't like retaining her groomed looks for Edmund.

At such a thought, her cheeks heated a bit. Again, there was the dilemma that she hadn't known him for long, but she now had known him for a little over two weeks. She almost rested her forehead against the steering wheel. It felt like she had met him ages ago. More time ... maybe. At least, she would try and wait another week before she definitely admitted anything to herself.

Then again, she might be over-thinking the whole thing, but her mind had been on a rollercoaster. Extreme emotions had invaded her in the past weeks, and she just was beginning to get them fully out of her system. Those facts had to be affecting her opinion on Edmund, so another week would be wise.

All of her thoughts distracted her from the remaining distance to Ires's and the clock in her car. Soon enough, she found herself turning into the parking lot. Easily, she spotted his black 1965 mustang. It was the only one in the parking lot, and there weren't too many cars there to begin with. Checking the clock too, she read *8:30 am.* Right on time.

Grabbing her purse, she shifted it onto her right shoulder and locked her vehicle. Her heels clicked against the asphalt before they tapped on the tiles of the store. She nodded her head at the one cashier at the front of the store, who had greeted her, and smiled. The cashier had been different from the previous two, which she was thankful for. Then again, those two probably hadn't remembered her, though; it probably wasn't every day that their boss bought a customer fabric flowers.

Facing away from the cashier, she somewhat hurried to the cover of the shelves. From the meeting room, Edmund would probably still be able to see her, but she liked to think that she would be hidden in the back where the paint was. The paint might give her away, but if he was in a meeting, he hopefully wouldn't be examining the store floor.

For the next two hours, she inspected some of the paint color options and grabbed a few pamphlets on how the colors looked in various rooms. There were several that she liked, but she decided to wait on what to choose. She did desire to hear Edmund's opinion, so she started to explore the store's other contents.

Browsing the aisles didn't keep her, though, from checking the time on her phone every now and then. The paint had held her thoughts for some time, but walking around wasn't producing the same effect. There were items of interest to her in the store, and she thought of various craft projects while examining them, but she was a little too excited to surprise Edmund.

It was somewhat childish, but she rarely ever surprised anyone. Beforehand, she really only had spent time with her ex, and her ex always had kept to schedule. He hadn't liked to break it. Now, she knew why. It wouldn't have benefited him if she had discovered him cheating on her. She frowned, and she would've spat the thoughts out if she could have, but she reminded herself to pay attention to the present and the future.

So when her phone depicted that it was ten-thirty, she grinned a little bit. She maneuvered around the shelves as quietly as she could with heels and towards the stairs. Elaine heard voices, and Edmund's was among them. Steps followed down, and not too long after they exited through the front doors.

A door clicked shut at the top. She hoped that it didn't lock. Peeking around the shelf, she saw that the cashier was wiping down the register. Quickly and softly, she headed for the stairs. When she reached them, she checked on the cashier again, who wasn't looking her way. Step by step, she advanced up the stairs. Once by the door, she practically cheered, but she reminded herself where she was and of her goal. Steadily, she placed her hands on the door handle and pressed down. To her relief, the door opened, and she sneaked in.

Edmund was sitting on the chair at the head of the table. A folder was in his hands, which were near his lap, and he was reading through papers. To her reassurance and amusement, he didn't notice her. Silently, she managed to close the door without it clicking into place. When she stared back to him, his eyes remained on the documents. A smile cracked on her lips, and she had to hold back a laugh; however, her lips soon fell, and her gaze pinned itself on him.

Presently, there were some atypical things about him. He didn't have a tie on or his jacket. His jacket rested on the back of his chair, and his tie was flat against the table. Her eyes scanned over the top of his shirt. Only the top button was undone, but it still brought warmth to her cheeks. Elaine's orbs trailed up his neck of perfect length to his face. It was the first time that she truly examined his facial features, and she couldn't avert her eyes. Edmund was exceedingly handsome.

His jaw line was strong and angled while his lips were in a straight line, portraying that he was both focused and serious. Due to his head being tilted down, his nose was angled down too, but it was of a medium pointed shape. Green-hazel eyes held a calculating and comprehending gaze while pitch black eyebrows were furrowed in concentration but not enough to cause a wrinkle to appear on his skin. Atop his head was pitch black hair, which was gelled back; however, a few strands were loose and curled at the front. On each side of his head was an ear fitted to his head ideally.

Simply, she couldn't divert her eyes, and she began to feel awkward standing there. A light cough left her, which immediately caught his attention. Instantly, his eyes met hers.

## Chapter Seventeen: Worry

*There was a lack of purple in the room, and someone paused as concern began to eat at her mind. That worry, however, vanished when embarrassment took its place.*

It was the first time that she could remember him looking completely shocked. "Elaine ... you're early." She couldn't tell if he was angry or not, but he certainly seemed out of sorts. He placed the folder on the table and went to stand, but she held her hands out and shook her head.

"It's fine. You can stay sitting." She smiled and lowered her hands. "I'm early. No need to rush or anything." Her smile fell a little when he didn't return it. Hesitantly, she shifted her weight between her feet and became nervous. "You're not mad ... are you?" Elaine was tempted to bite her lower lip, but she instead released a sigh when he shook his head.

"No, just ... You startled me." He sat up straight on his chair and indicated to another in the room. "Please, have a seat." Edmund pushed back his loose strands of hair, which fell in front of his face again. A slight groan left him, but a chuckle left her. His eyes met hers again, and she was laughing lightly behind her right hand. She always knew how to look stunning, yet his present appearance was a mess, or so he thought anyway.

"You should leave them." She stepped over to the table and close to the chair to his left. "Your hair looks nice like that."

Slowly, his hand drifted down from his forehead. "I am done with my meeting, but I still ..."

"Your workers won't mind. Besides, there's only the cashier on the store floor right now, and I doubt that customers will recognize you unless they've met you before." He remained silent, waiting to be convinced more, and he was inwardly entertained that she had cut him off. She was taking after him, but he didn't desire for her to do that too often. "And, I think that they'll like the look too." Edmund continued not to let a word slip past his lips, and she was about to seat herself out of nervousness until her eyes landed on his black tie.

"But," she reached over and grabbed it while his eyes followed her every movement, "you may want to put this back on." Her eyes focused on his, and she could finally note amusement in them. That eased her heart and mind.

"You do have a point." He held out his hand to take the tie from her, but, admittedly, she surprised him again. Instead of handing it to him, she closed the distance between them and rested the tie around his neck. Not a syllable was able to leave him. Rather, he focused on how her hands glided over the fabric of his shirt, but he could feel her fingertips through the cloth. They were like delicate kisses teasing him.

It didn't help that if he stared straight ahead, his eyes would be aligned with her chest. Was she really not aware of that? She couldn't have been; she must've not noticed. Refusing to keep his eyes there, he peered down to his lap. "Why did you come early?" Her fingers paused momentarily before they continued their delicate touches around his neck and upper chest.

"I wanted to surprise you." A smile tugged at his lips. She tied the knot at the top, and her fingers' movement seemed like that of a gentle, receding wave as they drifted away. He'd love to pull them back and have them pressed firmly on his chest.

Taking her seat next to him, she crossed one leg behind the other and placed her hands on her lap. A slight shrug followed before she laughed. The sound reminded him of rich honey being poured into warm tea. "I think that it worked."

"Yes, it did." He stood up from his chair and grabbed his jacket before he slipped his arms through and buttoned it up. "I wasn't expecting you to view me in such casual dress."

At that, she couldn't help but laugh loudly. Her right hand covered her mouth, and her eyes closed before they reopened. When they met his gaze, she felt her heart skip a beat. His eyes held warmth and mirth even though she noted that there was a tiny bit of annoyance there.

"Had I looked that awful without my jacket and tie?" He retrieved his folder, his arm extending out across the table and coming near to her. She almost scooted back in her seat, though; she wasn't aware why, nor did she want to dwell on that action since a little bit of heat touched her cheeks.

Making eye contact with him, she smiled and shook her head once more. "No ..." She stopped since she didn't wish to tell him that his looks had frozen her for a bit. Her mind thought back to that one unbuttoned button, and her cheeks grew warmer. Elaine had to shift her eyes elsewhere. For a moment, she had to remind herself of why she had laughed. Besides, her quietness probably was raising suspicion in him.

"No?" His arm was holding the folder to his side now. "You don't sound convinced." Despite his curious gaze, he was smirking on the inside. She hadn't even registered that her eyes for a brief second had drifted to where his tie now was.

An adorable pout formed on her lips. "That wasn't the reason why I had paused." Her voice was firm, but her countenance took away from that. She huffed and crossed her arms before she smiled again at the memory of his words. Elaine averted her dark brown orbs to him. "Most wouldn't consider dress pants, a ..."

All of sudden, she noted something very different about him. She looked over his black dress shoes, pants and jacket. Elaine stared to his shirt and tie next. Was it because she had surprised him? But, what would that mean? Hesitantly, she stood up and took a step back.

"Is something wrong?" She could hear the concern in his voice. Maybe, she was over-thinking things, but why did such a horrid feeling enter the pit of her stomach, then? Fingers rested under her chin and forced her to stare into his orbs. Something felt off. "Elaine?" His hand moved from her chin to her forehead. "No fever, but you look sick all of a sudden."

"You're not matching." Her voice was barely above a whisper. Gradually, his hand left her. "You don't have any purple on." Edmund about stood still, but he composed himself before she noticed. Instead, he acted perplexed and made sure that his inner worry wasn't shown to her.

Since she had entered the office unexpectedly, he had forgotten to grab one of his other ties from behind the podium. If he had seen her coming, he would've retrieved the plum purple one. "I don't understand. Are we usually matching?" He stood up straight and asked in a tone that was between confused and accusing so that she would feel guilty for bringing it up.

That snapped her out of her trance. "Had you really not noticed?" Her eyes searched his for any shred of a lie as he shook his head. He had to maintain his composure, or he could lose her and over such a simple thing too. Her shoulders relaxed.

"Would you like us to?" Now, he smiled and looked plainly entertained by such an idea as if he had mulled it over and found it to be something enjoyable. A desired reaction greeted him. She became embarrassed, and her eyes diverted themselves to another spot in the space.

Her fingers rubbed against each other, and she bit her lower lip before she responded, "It's just that ... Well before today, we always seemed to be wearing the same colors." She stared to him again as if to check that he wasn't going to be offended by such a claim. He would've shown his relief that the situation had turned in his favor if she weren't in the room with him. "Now that I surprised you ..."

"I'm not wearing any purple." Slowly, she nodded. He walked past her and to the door before he opened it and signaled her to go on ahead. Steadily, she left the room, and she was glad to see that he was following her down the stairs. "That can be fixed."

Once at the bottom, she peered back to him. "What ..."

As typical, he cut her off. "We're in an art store. We can always add some purple." Her eyes widened in realization. "So, you really do want us to match?" She seemed to become paralyzed, but he was pleased to know that she did appreciate his usual attention to detail. A light laugh left him, and he moved past her. "Well, are we going to look at paint like we planned?" His hazel-green orbs averted back to her, and she met them eventually. "We can adjust my tie after."

"... Right." She moved her feet before she caught up to him so that she could walk at his side. As if to move past what just transpired, she mentioned, "I looked at the paint earlier, though; I'm surprised that you have paint like that in here. Usually, that's in places like hardware or home improvement stores."

Keeping his eyes fixed forward, he nodded. "Yes, but I wanted to expand a little into that. Besides, your apartment is far from either of those places. Thirty minutes isn't a short drive either, but it's better than an hour. This is more convenient for you, right?"

Smiling a little, she nodded. "Yes, it is." She walked towards the back with him and entered the paint section. He stopped about midway through the color selections, and she stepped right up beside him. "So, any recommendations, Edmund?"

## Chapter Eighteen: Choose

*Colors from bright pinks to soft yellows to fiery oranges lined the shelves on small pieces of paper. Fingers reached forward and plucked a color from the many options as a smile touched painted lips.*

"I think that a soft, pale or a rich, dark hue will suit your walls best." Edmund pointed to several colors along the wall, and she nodded in agreement. "Remind me." He glanced to her slightly. "Are you wanting to paint each room a different color? And, do you want them to fit together if so?" His right fingers hovered over a certain color: light lavender.

"I think that a different color for each would be fun." She chuckled a little. "I think that you've already picked one out, though." Elaine reached and slipped her fingers under his to the color choice. Her fingers plucked it out from the holder, and she held it up. "For my room, right?" Another light chuckle escaped her. "You want it to match the roses."

He stood up straight and seemingly analyzed her before he smiled a bit. "Yes. I think that lavender suits you. It's soft and gentle."

A light bit of heat touched her cheeks before she puffed them out. "I'm not always like that." She stood up tall and tried to look intimidating. "You should've seen how I had slapped Gina the other day." Elaine huffed and abruptly turned her orbs back to the color options.

Laughter hit her ears, and she found that she couldn't maintain a frown on her lips for long. She relaxed again and shifted her eyes over to him somewhat. "Then, I'll keep that in mind." Amusement continued to fill his orbs. It was like he knew what she was capable of, but it still didn't intimidate him in the slightest. His fingers lifted to more hues. "Why, though?" The mirth in his tone faded and was replaced by curiosity.

Her fingers paused over a very pale blue, which could work well in the bathroom, but her mind distanced itself from painting for a moment. As her lips became downturned, her fingers fell from the color option. She stood straight up. Part of her didn't want to say anything because she didn't know how Edmund would take it.

Larger, yet graceful fingers picked out the blue color she had been examining. "This would go well with the purple. You're wanting to keep it to paler tones, then?" A slight smile cracked on her lips, and she looked up to him appreciatively.

"Thanks." She nodded to the paint hue. "I'll use it in the bathroom." He smiled to her and slipped it into one of his free jacket pockets. "But ..." Before she could stop herself, her right hand reached out and tugged on his left jacket sleeve. Edmund halted immediately and peered back and down at her.

Brow furrowed, she didn't speak instantly, but her lips steadily parted as she straightened herself out. "But, you don't have to change topics." He faced her fully. Edmund probably was going to inform her that he didn't mind, but she did. Another part of her didn't wish to remain silent, and that part was winning over.

"She had accused me of something." Her hand slid from his sleeve, and she found her eyes on his tie again. Hesitation remained in her, but his silence pointed to him waiting for her to continue. Idly, her hands reached up and traced over his tie as though she was about to adjust it for him. He made no motion to stop her. If anything, she thought that she saw a slight shiver travel through him, but she brushed it off as her imagining things.

"After your talk with her, she ... Well, she brought you up." A warm smile tugged at her lips a tiny bit. "You had called us friends." Her fingers trailed up his tie before they stopped at the knot. "But she ..." Elaine met his piercing orbs that displayed complete comprehension.

"Had she accused you of cheating on him with me?" It was hard to keep his eyes from narrowing, but he managed to maintain a neutral, knowing expression. How dare that garbage of a woman mention such a thing. If she understood ... Almost, he chuckled. That fool couldn't understand anyone but herself. It was no wonder why she would try to bring his treasure down to her disgusting level.

"Yes."

Barely, he caught her answer, but her quiet reply caused him to wrap his hands around hers. A slight frown coated his lips. "I'm sorry." Her hands moved slightly in his as if he had tugged on her heart a little. Maybe, he did.

"It's not your fault." She removed her hands from his only to wrap hers back around his. Her hands tugged on his a little and drew him closer to her. He doubted that she even fully realized what she was doing. That made it hard to contain a smirk. "You stood up for me. Defended me. What she did next was entirely on her own. She made that choice, not you."

"Are you certain, Elaine?"

Resolutely, she nodded her head. "Positive." A small grin tugged at her lips as she stared up to him. His shoulders visibly relaxed before he appeared somewhat confused by her look. "And, I know what color to paint the kitchen."

Slipping her hands from his, her fingers dived into the pool of colors, and she lifted out a mint green paper. She tapped her right index finger against it. "It's not the exact color of a rose stem, but it's still green and fits the light tone theme." That actually did give him pause, and he understood that she noticed. A grin tugged at her lips. "You based my room off of the petals. I'll carry on the theme of the rose.

"The bathroom can be the water even though water technically is clear, but we can adjust that." She winked to him a bit as a joke to his tie, and a light chuckle left him. "The kitchen is the stem, and the living room is the ... Is the vase!" Elaine snapped her fingers before they fell a little with her countenance. "But, what..."

"Color? Leaving one room white isn't a bad thing, Elaine. We just can paint it with a new coat to give it a fresher feel." He pulled the brightest white from the selection and handed it to her. She inspected it and envisioned her living room with the look before she nodded in agreement.

"Excellent." Edmund took the remaining colors from her and placed them in his pocket too. "I'll bring what you need to your apartment tomorrow." He started to turn from her, noting her lips parting as he did, but he didn't stop. He continued before he started to walk away. "Now, we can work on the issue of my tie."

"Wait!" She grabbed his left arm. His feet halted, and he managed to withhold a smirk. "You can't pay for all of that." Her hands dropped from his arm, and she moved to the front of him. "You may own a chain of successful art stores, but I'm not going to be eating out of your wallet." Elaine lifted her right index finger and poked him in the center of his chest.

"I'm not asking you too. I told you that I was going to help you pick out paint colors. My paying for them was an implied part of that."

"B*llsh*t." She stood up straight and appeared slightly shocked that the word left her lips so easily. Elaine coughed lightly but maintained a firm gaze. Edmund couldn't help but chuckle, which made her frown all the more. Crossing her arms, she stood like she could easily block him even though she knew that she was losing. He simply found her behavior amusing, not threatening, and she didn't know how much longer she could hold off a smile.

"I'm not going to change my mind, Elaine." He moved to step around her, but she blocked him. Edmund quirked a brow, and he couldn't hold back his smirk anymore. It tickled his lips, and he spun on his heel to head in the other direction.

"... Hey!" Once more, she latched onto his left arm. "I'm not finished." He stopped again, but she supposed that he wouldn't stay still for long. "If you're buying the paint, then we're not adjusting your tie." A light laugh left him as though that wasn't much of a sacrifice for him to make. "I'm going to buy you a really nice plum purple one." At that, his eyes met hers.

Now, she smirked, and she dropped her arms from him. "In fact, I'm going to do that right now." Before he could react, she spun on her heel only for her to lose her balance in the process. Her form ungracefully descended to the ground, but two arms wrapped around her waist. Her form spun again, and she found herself staring up into Edmund's eyes. A slight touch of heat filled her cheeks out of embarrassment and ... the unexpected closeness to him.

"I'll allow that." He moved her from her dipped position to standing upright. His hands now rested on her waist and slid down to her hips before they left her. A chill flowed through her body while she felt warm also. She shifted on her feet uncomfortably. "I'll see you at your apartment tomorrow." Before she could get in a word, he moved around her and headed off.

From her lips, a long sigh left her before she felt her heart pounding somewhat in her chest. She could feel the heat in her cheeks, and her hands touched them lightly. That had been ... nice.

## Chapter Nineteen: Hurry

*A small, black box seated itself upon the kitchen countertop. Atop it was a satin plum-purple ribbon, which flowed along the sides of the box like a graceful waterfall.*

Hangers were pushed aside, shoes were scattered outside of the closet and organizers were removed from the closet. In the center of the chaos, Elaine sat cross-legged. Frustration was evident on her face, and she couldn't help but groan every now and then. Admittedly, she never had worked repainting the apartment into her plans for the future, so she now had quite an annoying problem. Her fashion sense didn't exactly equate to home painter.

Climbing ladders in heels and a skirt or a dress didn't seem like the best of options to her. None of her clothes were incredibly short, but there remained the possibility of Edmund viewing her underwear. She didn't think that he would be that sort of person; however, an accident could occur, and that would be embarrassing.

That didn't even delve into the domain of her heels. Elaine could envision herself slipping all too easily on a ladder while she painted. If she didn't catch herself or if Edmund wasn't nearby, she could incur a serious injury. She ran her hands over her face and groaned into them. There wasn't time to go out and buy a new outfit, and she cursed herself for not thinking of it yesterday.

When her eyes landed on her clock, her heart about leaped out of her chest. She had lost track of time. It was nine thirty. Edmund would be at her home in fifteen minutes! A string of curse words filed out of her mouth as adrenaline kicked through her. Elaine scrambled to her feet to rush into the bathroom before a dreadful sound reached her ears: the doorbell's ring.

Entirely, she froze. Why was he early?! She was still in her satin, navy blue nightgown. Her fingers combed through her locks in a panic. Was he getting back at her for yesterday? The doorbell rang again. For a moment, she was tempted to jump up and down in a panic.

Thinking fast, she ripped a cotton, black bathrobe off of a hanger and threw it on. As she tied the knot, she hurried across the flooring and peeked out the window. Edmund was indeed standing there. She had been hoping that maybe the mail had arrived really early, though; she knew that was ridiculous since the mailman never came to her door.

There remained the possibility of keeping him out there, but she noticed the cans of paint by him. He was even holding a few, and he probably had more of the supplies in his car. Again, he rang the doorbell, and she wished momentarily to disappear.

Smoothing out her locks a little, she hesitantly opened and unlocked the door. Her head peeked out from around it, and she couldn't keep the nervous smile off of her lips. "Come in ..." As he stepped into her apartment, he gave her a puzzled look as to why she kept hiding behind the door. "Umm, you're e-e-early."

Facing her fully, he understood why she was acting so unusual. Her dark brown hair was in tangles, her bathrobe was haphazardly thrown on, her nightgown sleeves were beginning to slip off of her shoulders and she had no shoes or makeup on.

"I was expecting to surprise you for yesterday, but this ..." He couldn't help but chuckle. Edmund set down the paint cans by the door. "Did you sleep in?" His green-hazel eyes gleamed with amusement even though he knew the answer.

Earlier that morning, he had seen her in the kitchen filling up a glass of water, and he had been waiting to see what she would wear so that he could match her. For some reason, though, she never had changed, so he wore all black. It would be rather strange for him to match her nightgown's color from her perspective until they were a couple and living together. Then again, he had matched her nightgown's color when that weak excuse of a man had died, though; she had left her apartment that day, so it had been more reasonable for him to match her.

Huffing, she broke her gaze with him and stood up fully. She adjusted her bathrobe a bit. "No. I didn't." Her voice was resolute, but her overall look was too adorable for her to be taken seriously. "I ... I ..." Elaine pursed her lips, and only silence followed.

Raising an eyebrow, he scanned over her apartment before he noted something out of the ordinary. He leaned forward a bit more before he headed in that direction. Before she could register what he was noticing, he was already halfway down the hallway. Instantly, Elaine felt her cheeks burn as she realized what he had caught sight of.

Hurriedly, she raced after him and tried to cut him off, but she was too late. He stepped into her room. "Are you changing your wardrobe too?" There was humor in his tone, but a miniscule amount of disappointment too. That gave her a slight pause before she raced into the room.

His eyes landed on what she was worried about, and she swore that he took a step back. Immediately, he stared in another direction and coughed awkwardly. "Your entire wardrobe?" Heat remained on her cheeks, and she swiftly kicked the organizers of her lace undergarments back into the closet. She slammed the door shut. "I'll retrieve the rest of the paint."

"And, wait out there in the living room until I'm ready!" she called after him, completely embarrassed. She received no verbal response from him, only a simple nod. Quickly, she closed her room door and sank down against it. The heat seemed to pound in her cheeks, and her heart raced. Her morning was really spiraling out of control.

Certainly, that had been a ... discovery. His right hand covered his lips by a little bit, and his steps paused momentarily. He wasn't aware that she appreciated lace so much. If that's what she wore under ... Before his mind could dive into that realm too much, he put two and two together. She had been looking for an outfit suitable for painting. Painting walls in a skirt or dress with heels only asked for trouble, especially if she was wearing ...

"D*mn it, Elaine," he muttered quietly to himself. He only could keep himself composed so much. Edmund slid his hand down his face and tried to brush off the warmth in his body. Forcing himself out of her apartment, he brought in the rest of the paint and supplies.

Once done, he closed the front door, but he didn't lock it. He saw that her room door remained shut. She probably comprehended that he understood the situation and didn't want to face him any time soon. His eyes landed on a magnet with post-it notes attached to it on the fridge. Just what he needed. Walking over, he uncapped the pen beside the notes and wrote a quick message to her in case she left her room. *I'll be right back with some clothes for you.* He put the pen back and ripped the note off before he gently stuck it to her room door.

Leaving the apartment, he debated on stopping by his home to pick up some of his clothes that could potentially fit her with a few adjustments, or he could make the ten minute drive to the closest clothing store. There remained the issue of him not knowing her size. He could ask her, but given what had occurred previously, he doubted that she would respond favorably. Edmund decided to utilize guess work, and he headed for the clothing store. His own clothes could wait for later.

The shopping experience wasn't horrendous. His main objective was to grab things swiftly that would work well for painting walls. In the end, he selected a pair of black boot-cut jeans and a black t-shirt so that they would be matching. He did receive a few odd stares from other people in the store, but his priority was Elaine, not bothering himself with them.

At the cashier, he gained another couple of looks from the male employee, but Edmund was pleased that he was asked no questions. Still, he was about to rub the bridge of his nose in irritation. Once he had the bag in his hands and paid, he left the store immediately and drove off to her apartment. Entering it, he closed and locked the door behind him. The note on her bedroom door was untouched, but he heard movement on the other side of it. He stepped up towards it and knocked softly. "Elaine?" No answer. "I have clothes for you." Still, no answer. "May I slide them under the door?" That time, the door opened a crack, and one of her hands reached out.

Depositing the bag into her grip, she took it back into her room and closed the door after her. Entertained, he smirked before he removed his jacket and placed it on the back of the couch carefully. Now only on his chest was a black t-shirt. An old pair of dress pants was on his legs, and if one examined them closely, they would spot the worn-out state of them. His shoes weren't even dress shoes but tennis shoes. Rarely, did he wear such things, but he didn't desire to ruin one of his typical outfits. Besides, Elaine was so distracted by her own state of dress that she didn't notice his. He didn't know how long that would last, but he was grateful for its present effectiveness. About to set up the paint items, he paused. His eyes caught sight of a small, black box on the kitchen counter. A plum-purple satin ribbon secured it shut. He didn't even have to open it to understand what was inside. Edmund smiled and wondered how long she had spent searching for the item inside. All of his attention, though, soon snapped to her bedroom door.

It opened, and she stepped out. To his relief, the clothes fit her well. Her eyes didn't meet his, but she mumbled, "Thank you."

## Chapter Twenty: Snap

*As if being touched by flower petals, fingers glided across skin as though they would break the skin upon contact. Such fingers moved from skin to fabric as if the action was of the greatest skill to possess.*

Entering the living room, she finally met his eyes. "The size ..."

"I guessed." She gave him a doubtful look, and he held up his hands in mock surrender. "I swear, Elaine. It was all guesswork." He did leave out the fact that he had stared at her enough in the past to make reasonable guesses as to what her sizes were.

"The clothes are just right." She stepped a little closer to him, but he didn't back up. If anything, he was tempted to move nearer to her, but he held his ground. "That's some guesswork." Elaine crossed her arms. "When did you look?"

Maybe, it was out of character for Edmund to snag a glance at her clothing sizes, but she didn't understand how else he could've done it. Guessing right on point with her pant size was a little preposterous. At least in her opinion, it was.

"I didn't look. That would've been wrong of me unless you wanted me to look." His brow furrowed a bit. Did Edmund seriously consider that a possibility ... Wait, did she think it to be one too? Heat crept up to her cheeks. Elaine found that she couldn't deny it.

Awkwardly, she broke her stare with his. She rubbed the bridge of her nose. "Fine, you didn't." If she argued more, she would only get more embarrassed at that point. There was something else to note anyway. Elaine spun on her heel. "But, you did match us on purpose!"

At her behavior, he couldn't help but emit a chuckle. "Yes, I did. It's not every day that I get to pick out your clothes for you."

She pursed her lips a bit before she broke out into a smile. "Well, you did also get me some suitable clothes for painting." Elaine scanned over him again before she chuckled behind her right hand. Her eyes met his, and they were like glowing, beautiful gems. "But, you do look funny in such casual clothes."

Elaine closed the distance between them and crouched in front of him. Her right hand moved to his left shoe and poked at it. "It's definitely a tennis shoe." Laughter hit her ears, and she felt her heart skip a beat. The low, relaxing tones in it really were refreshing. "Is there a dress shoe under it?"

"No." He shook his head amused and felt her poke at his foot again. "Like you, I wasn't about to paint in my regular clothes. Paint splattered on one of my favorite suits would ... Well, I wouldn't prefer it."

Standing back up, she quirked a brow. "All of your suits are the same, though." He seemed taken aback by that, but she only chuckled. "Hurting one wouldn't really do that much." A rough cough hit her ears, and her heart nearly jumped into her throat.

It was then that she realized how close they were to each other, and she had been the one responsible for that. Mentally, she cursed herself. His lips weren't even inches apart from hers. Despite the irked expression on his countenance, she couldn't prevent heat from touching her cheeks.

"They are different from each other. Each of them is a different brand." He blew the loose bangs to the side, and her nose picked up on ginger and peppermint. The combination was revitalizing and made her realize their heart-pounding proximity even more.

Edmund was well aware of their present positioning, and he loved every moment of it. He was stressing his suits, though, so that she wouldn't focus on the fact that he was taking advantage of the situation. To her, he was very much livid about her observations about his suits. Almost, though, he could feel the heat radiating off of her cheeks. If he didn't have restraint, he would've kissed her already both on her lips and on her neck.

Unfortunately, she stepped back from him. "Okay, okay." She tried to brush aside the fact that she completely was embarrassed. "I get it." Her eyes peered over to him as she crossed her arms firmly. A small pout formed on her lips. "But, I do like this look on you." Elaine didn't state how his shirt hugged his torso in all the right places and displayed a little the toned muscle underneath.

"Your face would say otherwise." He moved over to the kitchen and leaned against the counter to relax his left elbow on it. Her pout dropped. Delight dominated his tone. "Are you perhaps mad about that?" Edmund laughed a little. "Did you expect me to only wear suits and only look decent in suits alone?"

Now, she smiled and shook her head. She held up her right fingers like she was pinching a grain of salt. "Maybe a little. Though, you did look nice yesterday ..." Elaine hadn't meant to say that. Yesterday, she had complimented him on his loose bangs but not his entire look. A growing desire to hide for a couple of minutes tugged at her.

"I ..." Her lips parted to speak and interrupt him, but he held his left index finger against his lips. The action didn't make him appear cute in any way or form. Rather, it gave him an almost threatening atmosphere. When he was certain that she wouldn't speak, he continued, "I was wondering if it had anything to do with my lack of tie. So, did it?" As if to tease her, his fingers created an unbuttoning action.

Instantly, she froze. Had he caught her staring yesterday but had pretended not to notice? Rapidly, she was sinking further and further into a hole of distress. Her eyes landed on the box on the counter. Hurriedly, she rushed over to it. "Since you mentioned a tie ..." She chuckled nervously and quietly as she slid the box across the counter to him.

An entertained smirk coated his lips. "You're dodging the question." His eyes shifted from her to the box, however, indicating that he wouldn't press her about it. She comprehended, though, that he had connected the pieces together, but she was glad that she didn't have to explain herself. Edmund placed his fingers on the two ends of the bow. "May I?"

After she nodded, she leaned on the counter herself, though; both of her elbows were on it. She watched the ribbon pool around the base of the box before his right hand snapped the box open. Inside, a plum-purple, silk tie rested. Elaine bit her lip, wondering if it was to his tastes or not. There wasn't a pattern on the tie since she hadn't seen any pattern on his other ties. "... So ..."

"It's excellent." He removed it from the box. "Thank you. Maybe, I should wear this at least while we paint," he joked only to find the tie taken from his hands. Edmund averted his orbs back to her.

"Maybe." She winked playfully to him, which caused him to chuckle. He didn't even have to ask her to tie it around his neck. Already, she was on it. Like yesterday, her fingers on his neck sent him into rapture. Nearly, he leaned into her so that he could feel them press harder into his skin and not tease him so with their delicate touches. How could she possess such fingers that caused such temptation?

Internally, a sickness plagued his mind. How she could ever give a similar treatment to that dead waste of a man pained him. On some mornings, he had seen her tie that man's tie before he had gone off to work. How he had been so jealous back then. Almost, a cruel smirk decorated his lips. Things had worked in his favor in the end, and he refused to be taken out by a car accident or any method for that matter. No, he would remain by his treasure's side throughout their entire lives.

With the knot formed, she retracted her hands. He snapped his thoughts back to her before he looked down and smiled. His eyes diverted back to her. "Does this fit me better?"

Chuckling, she shook her head. "No. One or the either." He reached up his hands. "No, let me." Once again, her lovely hands were back on him. A light laugh escaped her. "I tied it after all." She had no clue what she was doing to him, and the more she stayed in her present position, the more he wished to make them a couple then and there.

The knot came undone, and the two ends of the tie hung around his shoulders loosely. Her hands didn't leave him immediately. Rather, they remained placed on the ends gently. It was as if she was debating on something, and he swore that he saw her gulp. He wished to chuckle loudly. She was having the same problem as him it would seem. No, he knew that she was.

Gradually, her hands left him. It was as though a long breath passed between them when her hands rested by her sides again. She seemingly jolted back to her usual self. "We should start painting!" Elaine moved around him and to the supplies. Her hands placed themselves on her hips. "Where do we start?"

Going back to a less intense atmosphere wasn't easy. He breathed in deeply before he exhaled near soundlessly. Edmund stepped up beside her and pointed to the cans of primer. "Before we even paint the actual colors on, we need to put on the primer so that the paint sticks better to the walls. There are steps before that, however."

"Like moving the furniture and putting tape up so that we don't spillover onto the ceiling and floor?"

"Exactly. We'll start with the living room and work our way from there." She nodded in agreement, and they both started on the long project ahead of them.

## Chapter Twenty One: Repaint

*Hands gripped onto fabric in a surprised and panicked effort. They tugged further as other hands reached out to hold onto the individual.*

Furniture was moved out from the walls, and it clustered in the middle of the rooms. Blue tape was along the ceiling and floor. There was even more in the kitchen so that the paint wouldn't get on the cupboards. A ladder was in the middle of the bedroom in case either painter required it for the next painting section in their area.

Elaine was in the bathroom, and Edmund was in the bedroom. Both of them were still putting the primer up on the walls. They had taken a lunch break after the kitchen and living room had been completed, but she was still tired. Presently, she was cursing the small wall space between the toilet and the sink. To reach it, she had to kneel on the porcelain top of the toilet, and it wasn't comfortable in the slightest. Why had she allowed Edmund to prime the bedroom?

Once they were on the color paint, they were going to switch. She wasn't going to submit herself to toilet kneeling again. When she completed the spot, her shoulders sagged, and she smiled to herself. Done. Finally done.

Getting off of the toilet, she set down the roller on the paint tray and glanced down to her knees. Bruises were already forming on them. She reached down and rubbed them only to wince in the process. No more kneeling for the day, that was for certain. Her eyes examined the bathroom, and she only had the sections up by the ceiling left. Then, she could relax for the day as the paint dried. In fact, she wouldn't have to paint again until the next week since Edmund would have the weekend off.

Standing up completely, she glanced over to the ladder. Edmund wasn't on it. She examined the room further but couldn't sight him. Her eyes moved towards the back of her bed before they found evidence of him. His shoes were sticking out, and more of his legs were showing themselves slowly. If he had been wearing one of his typical suits, she would've laughed at how silly he would've looked.

Entering the room, she inspected Edmund's progress. He was about halfway done. Despite the hard-to-reach places in the bathroom, it was significantly smaller than her bedroom. Maybe, she would reconsider and buy a kneeling pad.

She grabbed the ladder and began to carry it back into the bathroom, but she stopped when she found Edmund staring at her. Her heart jumped a little, and she could see specks of amusement in his eyes. "Are you almost done?" he asked, sitting up on his knees. He had placed the roller on the tray.

Calming down and figuring that he hadn't been staring for long, she nodded. "Just the areas around the ceiling." She chuckled a bit. "You, though, have quite a bit left to do." Elaine shifted the ladder in her hands, and a small grin tickled her lips. "Also, your gel is really starting to wear off."

Instantly, his hands reached up to his hair. An annoyed groan left him as he tried to smooth some of the locks back. "Maybe, I should switch brands."

Shaking her head in humor, she mentioned, "You're on your knees painting. And, you've been painting the whole day. That gel didn't stand a chance unless you put half the container on your head." A joking smile touched her lips as she now leaned against the ladder. He didn't seem satisfied by that answer. "If you're that worried, we can put some water through it and restyle it to how it was."

"Is it that bad?" It was like her words completely flew over his head except for the part about him needing to restyle it. She rolled her eyes and moved away from the ladder and into the bathroom. "Is it?" he repeated, now a little bit of concern in his tone. Elaine had a hard time not laughing.

Grabbing a glass from the medicine cupboard, she filled it with water. She had no idea how he would react, but she was going to try it regardless. After she turned off the faucet, she grabbed one of her combs and walked back into her bedroom. Edmund was vigorously pushing loose strands of hair back only for them to fall back out. Ultimately, he only was causing more strands to fall out of their slicked-back positions.

He didn't even view her coming. Before he could react, she seated herself in front of him and dumped the glass of water on his head. A sputtered sound came from him. It was probably between a shout and a gasp. She could tell that he was about to yell at her, so she reached her hands forward and started to comb back his hair, trying to get it to look as it did before.

Wiping the water from his eyes, he blinked a few times as he found himself willingly lowering his head so that she could get at it better. He was soaked, however, but he supposed that the water did feel nice after working for so long. "I could've followed you into the bathroom," he pointed out as a sigh left him.

An airy, cute chuckle parted from her. A gentle, knowing smile graced her lips. "I don't think so." He rolled his eyes, but he couldn't keep a smile away, especially when she was running her hands through his hair. It felt intoxicating, and it was addicting. The typical curls fell onto his forehead still, but he didn't complain. She did like them after all. "Besides, I think that I'm doing a good job."

"I'll have to check in the mirror." A slight glare was sent his way, but he could tell that it was playful. Soon after, a smile formed on her lips, and she leaned forward slightly more to get some of the strands in the back. His head was dipped down quite a bit so that she could reach them, and her chest probably was closer than she realized. Edmund shifted his orbs to his right, glad that he had bought her a crew neck and not a v-neck. It didn't help that she practically was sitting on his lap.

It was hard not to grab her waist and bring her closer so that he could kiss her. His head was already loosing itself in the thoughts. "Done." Gradually, he came back. He had to blink a few times, and when he finished, she was already back on her feet. An approving smile coated her lips. "You look good as new. Probably need more water later, but I think that'll do for now." She pointed to the bathroom with the comb. "Want to check?"

Shaking his head, he picked up the paint roller. "No, I'll trust your work." She appeared a little caught off guard by that, but he could tell that she appreciated his words too. An inward smirk formed, but he did also reject her offer because he didn't wish to stand so close to her for awhile. If he did, he probably would kiss her.

"I won't question that." Her smile morphed into a grin before she picked up the ladder and traveled back into the bathroom. Edmund forced himself to turn away from her direction. She would be finished before him with painting, so he had to remain focused so that he didn't keep her waiting for too long. With the roller in hand, he returned to painting the lower sections of the walls.

As time passed, he heard the ladder move again before footsteps followed. He now was on the middle sections of the walls, which were his last parts. His back was turned to her, and he figured that she was taking the ladder back into the living room. After he heard metal being shifted, running water hit his ears. A glass of water did sound refreshing.

No, he needed to finish. Nearly, he rested his forehead on the wall until he remembered the wet paint there. That would've definitely ruined his hair. His mind kept returning to her, though, and to her fingers gracing his locks. Frustrated, he ran his free hand down his face. A small break wouldn't hurt.

Turning around, he placed the roller on the tray and headed for the kitchen. His steps weren't hurried, but his mind was racing. He closed his eyes momentarily and rubbed the bridge of his nose. Edmund rounded the corner and entered the hallway only to feel a swift impact to his chest.

Immediately, he opened his eyes only to feel his shirt being tugged on. His eyes widened, and he reached out his hands to attempt to stop the fall, but he was too late. No groan of pain left him. He was more worried about Elaine since he had landed on top of her. Quickly, he picked himself up and stared down at her. "Are you alright?"

A discomforted moan escaped her, and her eyes opened up steadily. "Ow," she mumbled as she gazed up to him. Her eyes instantly widened, however. Then, he realized the position that they both were in. His hands were pinned by the sides of her head, and his legs straddled her hips as his body hung over hers, yet he couldn't move. His lips didn't part either to confirm her wellbeing again.

Heat burned her cheeks, but she couldn't break her eyes from his. Her head hurt, but her heart thumping loudly in her chest blocked that out. She supposed that Edmund had been leaving the bedroom to check on her or to get a drink himself. In fact, she had been on her way to ask him if he wanted anything. With their present position, she wondered if he was wishing for the same thing as her.

They may have only really known each other for about two weeks, but she couldn't stop the rush of emotions that were invading her mind and heart. Edmund's silence too wasn't helping. He seemed to be debating something similar, or, at least, she hoped that to be the case. Gradually, her hands reached up and wrapped around the back of his head and neck.

Her action motivated him to lower himself and close the distance. Before she could rethink her action, his lips were on hers in a smooth, delicate embrace. His lips molded ideally against hers, and their touch spread a warmth through her. She felt like she was being wrapped in a blanket of soothing flames, and she didn't want it to end.

## Chapter Twenty Two: Recount

*Knees were touching her chest, and her arms were wrapped around her legs. Fabrics of the bed didn't cover her; they only were wrinkled beneath her form.*

On constant replay, his words continued on and on in her head. She couldn't remove them, nor did she desire to. They were music to her ears; they were like a soft lullaby, yet they kept her from sleep. Her lips were curled up in a small, embarrassed smile. *After my work next Wednesday, join me for dinner. I'll be at The Fox's Garden at six in the evening. I'll see you then.*

He hadn't asked if she could make it or not; he simply had told her where he would be and that he expected her to be there. Normally, she would've turned down such an invitation. With him, though, she overlooked his command-like delivery. All she could do was smile and recall that kiss.

Edmund had stayed after to finish the primer on her bedroom, but they hadn't talked until he had invited her to dinner next week. She hadn't minded the silence. If anything, she had been appreciative of it. It had allowed her to get her thoughts in order, but now her only thoughts were about next week.

She brought her knees close to her chest and hugged them tightly. By that point, her sheets were kicked to the end of the bed. Underneath her, they were all wrinkled. Her thulian pink, cotton nightgown barely was covering her lower half since it had climbed up her form from all of her movement. The sleeves were messed up too and were falling down her shoulders.

Thankfully, Edmund wasn't there to witness her in such a state. Her cheeks warmed up at the thought, and she rolled onto her back. She stretched her legs out and curled her toes in the sheets. All of her hair fanned out around her head. Elaine glanced around the room bathed in the night's pale light.

A happy huff parted from her lips. She couldn't sleep. Elaine threw her legs over the side of the bed and stood up before she checked the clock. *2:00 am.* A late night snack wouldn't hurt her, and she could watch television and even fall asleep on the couch. That sounded relaxing for her mind, which was going through various scenarios of how the dinner could transpire.

Her hands came up to her cheeks and rubbed them a bit. All of those situations ended in another fiery, yet soothing kiss. The touch of his lips simply was too much. She still could feel the presence of them on hers. Back then, she had loved her ex, but they never had shared a kiss like that. It was such a cliché thing to think, but she couldn't help it.

That kiss made her lips desperately ache for another. Her lips felt like pudding waiting to be solidified and enjoyed by another. Touching her lips with her fingertips, she paused before she flicked on the kitchen light. Slowly, she dragged her fingers down before her hands fell to her sides. She hung her head and sighed. If she didn't distract herself soon, she probably would find herself calling him, and he most likely didn't want to be contacted at such a time.

Switching the light on, she adjusted her nightgown a bit before she opened the fridge. Nothing of interest caught her eye. She turned to her cupboards that held boxed snacks, canned goods and peanut butter. Elaine didn't grab anything immediately since her attention shifted to her kitchen window. Across the street, there was another apartment complex. The apartment directly across from hers had lights on inside.

At least, she wasn't the only one in the vicinity still up. She wondered if Edmund was up ... "No, stop," she mumbled to herself and rubbed the bridge of her nose. Elaine forced herself to stare at her food selection. Chocolate gram crackers and peanut butter. Never had she tried that combination, but it was chocolate and peanut butter. It had to be good unless the crackers were old and stale.

Checking the box's expiration date, she grinned. Another two months before it expired. Great. She retrieved the peanut butter and a butter knife from one of her drawers. Elaine scooped a decent amount into a small bowl before she put the peanut butter back. With the bowl and box in hand, she maneuvered her way around the new furniture placements and seated herself on her couch.

After she flipped the television on, she dipped one of the crackers into the peanut butter before she tossed it into her mouth. To her delight, it was satisfyingly delicious. When she tuned into the program on the screen, however, she frowned. A romance movie. That definitely wasn't what she needed at the moment. Oh, the convenience of the world.

Setting down her treats, she switched from channel to channel. Every single one had something to do with romance. She was certain that it wasn't Valentine's Day. A sigh left her lips, and she considered purchasing cable for the future. For the moment, it was time for a movie. Her eyes switched to the two small stacks of films.

Among the stack, there was a dvd on rain forests. She couldn't remember why she had bought it since she normally didn't watch documentaries on nature, but it was there, so she slid it into the television and nestled back down on the couch.

While she relaxed on her sofa, Edmund exited his bathroom. He pushed back his wet bangs and headed down the hall to his bedroom but stopped midway. His eyes stared out his hallway window and across the street to Elaine's apartment. Her kitchen light was on. It hadn't been on when he had gone to take his shower. A smirk tugged at his lips.

He stepped forward a bit more and leaned against the window seal. Luckily, she wasn't standing in front of either of her windows. Otherwise, she would be able to note him standing there. She wouldn't know that it was him, but she would be able to make out that someone was there.

Crossing his arms, he continued to smirk. He wondered if the thought of their date next week was keeping her up. Then again, he really didn't have to ponder on the topic. Most certainly, that was the reason why she was up still. It was causing his mind to be more energetic than it usually was at such a late hour.

Even after his shower, he could remember every detail of their intimate exchange. Her fingers snaking their way through his locks and pulling him down towards her was alive in his mind's eyes, and her lips were of a silky smooth texture. It had been like kissing real rose petals: velvety and rich.

Reluctantly, he pushed himself off of the seal. His towel was beginning to slip, and even if no one was looking at him, he didn't wish to be on full display to the outside world. He entered his bedroom, and his toes curled into the plush beige carpet as he walked across it.

Since his bedroom window was across from the wall of another apartment building, he didn't have to worry about anyone catching sight of his exposed form. He permitted the towel to slide down from his hips and to the floor in a pool of fabric. Edmund stepped over it while droplets of water dripped down his figure.

Retrieving a pair of green pajama pants, which matched his eyes, he slipped them on and tied the drawstring at the top. He would put on boxers in the morning before he headed out. At night, alone and asleep, he could care less about such an item of clothing.

Ringing caught his attention. He shifted his orbs over to the phone on the bed. Was she calling? Chuckling, he moved over to the device and checked the caller. A frown painted his lips. Edmund didn't recognize the number, and he slid his thumb across the red mark on his phone. Even if he did receive worthless calls in the middle of the night, it was worth it since there always was the possibility that Elaine would contact him. She could have an emergency and need him, so he refused to turn his phone off.

Tossing his phone back onto the bed, he snatched up his binoculars from his nightstand top and headed back into the hallway. He brushed back his bangs again, but a few curls refused to be restrained. At least, Elaine liked them like that.

Again, he was back at the window seal. That time, though, the hallway light was off. He moved his improved gaze to her living room window. She must've been watching television since he couldn't spot her in the room, nor was she in the kitchen when he double-checked. Either that or she had gone to her room or bathroom for a short bit.

How he wished to be over there or for her to be with him, but he had to be patient. It wouldn't be too long before their date. Soon enough, they would be at The Fox's Garden enjoying a pleasant dinner, and she would be no doubt dolled up for him. He wondered if she would purchase a new dress or wear one that she had hidden away in her closet for a special occasion that hadn't happened yet.

There was the option that he could buy her one, but he preferred the surprise. Of course, he would learn of her attire before dinner. He did finish work at four, so he could return home and discover what she was wearing to dinner so that he could match her. A strange coincidence for her but it was a necessity for him.

Instantly, he broke from his thoughts. Elaine stood up and was headed for her kitchen. He diverted his eyes to her kitchen window. She was grabbing a napkin from the napkin holder, but he could care less about that. No, he was focusing on how her nightgown fit her. Goodness, she was beautiful.

## Chapter Twenty Three: Dine

*Folds of fabric waved back and forth as steps struck the tile floors. Each step echoed down the hall, and some heads turned, but only one held her interest.*

Parking her car, she turned the key in the ignition and removed it before she left and locked her vehicle. Street lamps along the nearby sidewalk illuminated the parking lot and her. Their light bathed her dark brown, curly and short locks in a soft, gentle glow. A shadow was cast over her face as she walked across the asphalt until she neared the door of the establishment.

Briefly, her dark brown eyes glanced up to the sign on the wrought iron archway. *The Fox's Garden.* Tiny spheres of light gave the sign life and highlighted the various vines wrapping their way up the structure. Beyond it, there was a set of stone steps, which led to a dark-stained oak door. In the center of the door was a paned window, giving the guest a view inside before they entered.

She viewed a waitress taking a family away to a side room for seating while a waiter remained at the front. A small, stone fox statue rested atop the waiter's podium. There were patrons sitting upon long wooden benches too. No doubt, they were waiting to be seated themselves. Elaine opened the door and allowed herself in. It shut near soundlessly behind her.

Before she had turned off her car, she had checked the clock. It had been five minutes to six. Most likely, it only was a couple minutes more to the hour. She adjusted her purse on her right shoulder and advanced towards the waiter on the plush red carpet. A few of those waiting glanced up at her, but she ignored them.

"Hello, I'm here to meet with an Edmund Fex."

The waiter glanced down upon his list of reservations before he nodded once he found Edmund's name. "Ah, yes." He looked back up to her. "Your name is Elaine Margarit, correct?" She nodded in response. Signaling a free waitress over, he mentioned, "The back table outside." His eyes met hers once more. "Enjoy your dinner, Ms. Margarit."

"Thank you." Elaine faced away from him and followed the waitress through the restaurant. Calming lights hung from the ceiling, and plants grew around pillars in the restaurant. Little candles twinkled amid bouquets of fresh flowers, and a wonderful, floral smell complemented the aroma of fine food.

Occasionally, her eyes would glance upon a dish that looked too scrumptious to pass up. It was obvious that she would have a hard time choosing a meal to settle on. The waitress took a left and headed for a pair of double doors. Paned glass was in the middle of each door, and the waitress grabbed both before she headed out.

Leaving the inner dining area, Elaine was directed by the waitress to stare to her left and towards the back. "He's back there, and both of your menus are on the table. The wine will be brought out shortly." The waitress dipped her head a bit and smiled before she left to the inside and closed the doors behind her.

Dark brown orbs landed on him. He hadn't noticed her yet. His chin was resting on the palm of his right hand as he looked out over the row of candles and past the trees surrounding the present part of the restaurant. The street had to be nearby given the sound of an occasional car driving past. She didn't check, however, since she remained focused on him.

Like usual, his hair was gelled back, but he left the few curls at the front down. A smile touched her lips before she felt a knot in her stomach. He was matching her again, yet she hadn't seen him before the restaurant. He wore his typical black jacket, pants and shoes, but he had on a maroon button-up and a black tie. Decorating the tie was a gold tie clip.

Maybe, they both thought that the colors would suit their first date together. Elaine permitted that thought to fill her mind so that she wouldn't worry. Besides, the knot didn't last long as butterflies took over, and her lips tingled at the memory of his upon hers. She breathed in a little before she let out a quiet exhale and headed towards him.

Maroon heels with golden clasps clicked against the tiles while a maroon fit-and-flare dress adorned her figure. It traveled down to just past her knees. A maroon belt was around her waist with a golden clasp while the sleeves of the dress were off-shoulder and crisscrossed. Thin, straight gold earrings dangled from her ears as her loose, well-brushed locks framed her face gorgeously. Matte maroon lipstick painted her lips while a soft eye shadow complemented her eyes.

Attention from some of the other customers outside fell upon her, but she held her gaze on him. He finally looked over to her, and a smile steadily tugged at his lips. A dose of heat touched her cheeks as his eyes stared and analyzed her with pure rapture. "Right at six." His left hand indicated to the pulled-out chair for her. "Make yourself comfortable."

Taking her seat, she smoothed out her dress. She didn't quite know how to act around him after that kiss. Part of her wanted to move to his seat and kiss him then and there while the other wanted to fiddle with her silverware and cloth napkin. Ultimately, she started to play with the napkin tips. "How ..."

"Elaine, are you about to ask me how I've been?" Her eyes stared at the napkin more, and she wished to hide under the table. When she did peer up at him, amusement danced in his eyes, and she had to break her gaze with him once more. "We don't need those questions right now." His tone wasn't criticizing but knowing and teasing.

Hesitantly, she averted her eyes to his, waiting for him to continue. "You want my opinion on our kiss. Or, you want another one. Maybe, both." Her cheeks warmed up considerably. The waitress returned with a bottle of wine, and Edmund signaled that he would open it himself. It was a bottle of expensive Pinot Noir. She hadn't tried the wine before, but she had read good reviews about it; however, there was a more pressing matter than the wine, and the heat wouldn't leave her cheeks.

Edmund popped the cork and set it aside before he poured her a glass first and then one for himself. He placed the bottle in the center of the table but also off to the side. His right hand lifted up his glass and swirled the drink lightly inside as the aroma of sweet black cherry, raspberry and rose petals wafted to his nose. After a brief sip, he placed the glass back down, but his fingers remained on the handle. Out of nerves, she wished to down her glass, but she moved her fingers to her lap and intertwined them there. "Which is it?"

Not expecting a question to be directed at her, she sat up straighter and tightened her hold on her fingers. "Edmund, that's ..."

"Unfair of me to ask? Embarrassing to answer?" He chuckled, and a gleam hit his green-hazel eyes. "I know, but I'm curious about your opinion on the kiss too." Her lips parted slightly before her right fingers slipped themselves around the stem of her glass. No words left her. She couldn't describe it so openly to him, but her heart rate was beginning to pick up. "But, I would like another one."

Instantly, she diverted her attention to him and not the glass. A pleased, humored laugh escaped him. "Is it that much of a surprise?" He gestured to the restaurant with his left hand. "I wouldn't have asked you here otherwise if I didn't want to advance our relationship more."

Gradually, a smile touched her lips again. Her eyes fell on her wine, and she shook her head lightly. "You know that this wasn't necessary. I would've been happy eating at a fast food restaurant like the first time we had met up." She raised her glass to her lips and partook of a sip before she set the glass back on the table and relaxed her fingers around the stem. A pleasant taste settled on her tongue, and she would enjoy another sip soon.

"Can you still tell me, though?" she asked meekly. Her eyes rested upon his as they tried not to drift down to his lips. "About what you thought?" A miniscule smirk graced his lips before he took another taste of his drink. He rested the glass back on the table and removed his fingers from it.

"I wish that I had met you sooner. Then, we would've had more than one by now." A light chuckle past her lips while her cheeks stayed warm. An appreciative smile soon overtook her. "And, I do hope that you don't become too distracted when we work on painting your apartment again." At that, her cheeks burst into flame.

Out of embarrassment, she crossed her arms and averted her dark brown orbs back to the door as if she was hoping the waitress would return. She didn't want that at all, but he had caught her head on. There was a fair chance that she would become distracted a decent amount of times on the weekend. "You'll be distracted too," she muttered, still keeping her eyes off of him.

"I never said that I wouldn't be. I'm distracted right now." Her heart skipped a beat at that, and she found that she had to look back at him. There probably was a charming smile upon his lips, and she didn't desire to miss it. At least, that's what she thought until her eyes caught sight of two figures.

Immediately, her spirits vanished. Her eyes made contact with two pairs of other eyes. To her utter dismay, the people started to walk her way. Edmund caught onto her mood change swiftly, and he spotted the figures too. A frown controlled his lips as he made sure that he was sitting upright on his seat. The two should've walked away.

## Chapter Twenty Four: Threaten

*Anger bubbled but remained hidden in front of the two who were standing. Wine was sipped at, yet it begged to be brought to another location and enjoyed elsewhere; where was that, though?*

Their steps ended, and fake, horrid smiles graced their lips. Why couldn't they just have left? Elaine shifted herself on her seat, aching to move to the far end of it, but she didn't wish to cower in their presence. Edmund, however, was the braver one. He met their orbs: light brown and light green.

"I do hope that you know we weren't expecting guests." Edmund's tone was calm and collected. His eyes were on them, but his gaze looked bored and unimpressed. "I hope that you don't expect us to move." He looked away and partook of a little of his drink. The sip was steady as if every drop of crimson mocked the older couple's existence.

Elaine had trouble enough staying on her seat, so she was very thankful for Edmund's display. Her fingers wrapped around the stem of her wine glass, and a few of her nails tapped against it lightly. "We won't take ... much of your time," Mr. Daxni remarked as his attention shifted onto Elaine. She wanted to shrink on her chair, but she forced herself to maintain her posture. Edmund, however, lowered his glass slowly while his eyes watched her ex's father like a hawk. The hesitation in the older man's voice was anything but reassuring.

"We just wanted to check on Elaine. We haven't heard from her since the funeral." Mrs. Daxni contained sympathy in her eyes towards Elaine, but Elaine refused to meet the woman's light brown eyes. "But, it would seem that she's doing quite fine." Her tone was accusing as if she was doing something wrong. That struck both the wrong cords in Elaine and Edmund.

"Yes, I am." Now, her eyes fell upon the two. Mrs. Daxni had her sandy brown locks pulled back into a tight, tidy bun. An off-white, blouse and skirt covered her form while her feet were in matching linen heels. Pearl accessories decorated her. "And, you look fine as ever." Whether that remark was an insult, compliment or both, Elaine didn't care, but her tone was harsh and unforgiving.

"We're glad to hear that." Mr. Daxni stepped in front of his wife a little. He wore a grey suit, blue and white striped shirt and red tie. His sandy brown locks were combed to the side, but the look didn't do anything for him. "Though, don't you think it's too soon?"

She could tell that the man was attempting to hold back a small smirk, and that fueled the fire within her more. Almost, she felt like she might break her glass in two. "No. Now, you've checked on me." Her eyes glanced between the two of them. "You should leave."

Mrs. Daxni shifted on her feet awkwardly as her lips were pulled into a tight line. Her cheeks heated a little at the disrespect offered to her. "You ..."

"I don't want to hear it." Her dark brown eyes pierced into the older woman's. "I'm doing nothing wrong. If anything, both of you should apologize to me. You had known about him cheating on me, yet you hadn't said a word. Instead, that nurse had informed me. And, now you're reprimanding me about moving on?" She released a sharp laugh. "You have no right."

"Apologize?" Mr. Daxni laughed in bitter amusement. His eyes turned over to Edmund, who wore an unreadable expression. "You sent this uninvited man to our son's funeral and had him threaten Gina."

"Threaten?" Elaine resisted the urge to glance over to Edmund. That had to be wrong. "He hadn't threatened her. He had gone over there to defend me after what the three of you had kept from me. Unlike all of you, including your son, he actually cares about my wellbeing."

"And, she hadn't sent me. I had gone on my own." Edmund brought his glass to his lips, but he paused midway. His left hand reached out and stopped Mr. Daxni from spilling his wine. When Mr. Daxni went to retract his wrist, Edmund held firmly onto him. "And, I hadn't threatened her. I had given her options. She had chosen wisely."

As the two men stared the other down, Elaine furrowed her brow. Edmund never had told her what he had said to that nurse even after the nurse had come to her apartment the following day. "If you're wondering what George had done, he had Gina pack her bags and move to another city," Mrs. Daxni explained to Elaine. Edmund stared over to the woman while her husband ripped his wrist from Edmund's grasp. A displeased huff left the older man, and he nodded to his wife's words.

"George?" Elaine muttered in confusion, trying to keep a laugh from leaving her. She did her best to hide the amusement in her eyes, and she couldn't help but avert her eyes over to Edmund. Her look said her words clearly. *Really?* A small smile, only noticeable to her, touched his lips before he took a sip of his wine.

Bringing her gaze back to her ex's parents, she managed to control her laughter at the older male's words. "He hadn't made Gina do anything. It had been her choice. Besides, she's probably fine. Or maybe, you two could go check on her." She lifted her wine to her lips and sipped some. Out of the corners of her eyes, she stared to them as she parted the glass from her lips. "Or, do you not prefer her anymore? Had her move raised too many questions from others that had attended the funeral?"

Immediately, Mrs. Daxni grew furious. The older woman stepped forward, but she hadn't been paying attention to Edmund. He already was up and moving. Mr. Daxni hadn't noted him either since the flames in his eyes were directed at Elaine. Before her hand could reach Elaine, a loud impact sounded throughout the outside seating area. Heads turned, and Elaine instantly placed down her glass.

Taking a step back hesitantly, the woman peered up at Edmund. Surprise was written all across her countenance. Edmund didn't touch his cheek, and his head never had turned. The entire time, his gaze was pinned on the woman. "I suggest that you two leave."

"Or, you'll threaten us?" Mr. Daxni asked, a roll of his eyes following. Edmund didn't relax his stare. Elaine couldn't view it, but a suffocating atmosphere was around him and directed at the couple. Mrs. Daxni moved closer to her husband.

"I don't threaten. I give choices." A pleased smile fell upon Edmund's lips. "Besides, I think that everyone else out here would like you to leave too." He didn't avert his eyes to the other patrons and the waitress outside, but Mr. and Mrs. Daxni did. "Your wife's slap really put the both of you in a poor light. And if you don't leave, I think that you'll find the restaurant threatening you to do so." His voice had grown quiet, but its bite hadn't lessened.

The waitress stood her ground, and her gaze indicated for the two to leave as they were causing quite a disturbance. Fury shot through Mr. Daxni. "You shouldn't have made fools out of us." He abruptly turned away from Edmund and Elaine with his wife.

"I didn't. You did that on your own." Mr. Daxni appeared ready to punch him, but the waitress's cough signaled the older couple to be on their way. The couple soon left, and the waitress came over to their table.

Dipping her head in apology, she remarked, "I'm sorry for that. I'll speak to the manager. You both ..."

"It's not yours or the restaurant's fault. I'll still pay for the wine I purchased, but I do hope that you understand that we'll have food elsewhere." Edmund glanced back to Elaine momentarily, and she indicated that she was fine with that decision. He faced the waitress again. "I'll make sure that the restaurant receives a good review regardless." A wave of relief washed over the waitress before she thanked him and went on her way.

Movement was heard behind him, but he held out his hand. Edmund diverted his focus to Elaine. "You don't need to get up. I'm fine." Due to the size of the chairs, which were more like miniature benches, Edmund seated himself beside her. His fingers glided under her chin. "Are you alright, though?"

Lightly, a bit of heat touched her cheeks, but she raised her one hand and moved his to her cheek. She leaned against his touch and smiled softly. Her hands felt like the velvet touch of rose petals to him. "I'm fine. I just wish that they hadn't come over." Elaine locked her orbs with his. "About the nurse ..."

"She's working at another hospital in another city. She's making the same amount that she was earning here, and the rent of her living is the same too. I had it arranged so that you would never see her again." Despite the confidence in his words, he was worried that she would think that he had taken it too far regardless of how she had defended him earlier.

Silence existed between them, but he grew relieved when he sighted her smile. "You had given her an option. I knew it, and you got her to move farther away from me." She lowered his hand from her face before she leaned forward. He met her halfway as he intertwined his fingers with hers and kissed her.

Like before, that comforting fire grew within her, and her free hand rested on the back of his head to pull him closer. She didn't care that there were others behind them. Elaine simply was thankful that she had him in her arms at that moment. When she pulled back, her breath was uneven, but she couldn't keep a grin from forming on her lips. "So, we still have a place to go?" Edmund smiled to her and answered her with another tender kiss.

## Chapter Twenty Five: Drip

*Mint green coated black fabric, but the accident was hidden and disposed of. Such an occurrence couldn't be forgotten because of the end result.*

Sitting on her living room couch, she leaned back into the cushiony surface and wrapped her arms around her legs. Her eyes shifted to her right and towards the kitchen trash can. The lid was closed. Within it, the mint green mess lived. It had been an accident even though it was somewhat reminiscent of what had happened last week.

At the time, she had been leaving the kitchen with the paint tray. There had been a considerable amount left, so she had been going to pour it back into the can. Edmund had been turning the corner unexpectedly, and the paint tray had met his chest. In the process, it had splattered all across his face and had dripped down his pants and onto his shoes.

Despite his reassurance, she had rushed out of her apartment after she had asked him his sizes. Meanwhile, he had gone to use her shower. When she had returned, he still had been in her bathroom. Then again, she had been away for about twenty-five minutes, and he had to wash paint out of his hair.

Elaine sat upright when she heard the water turn off. She looked to her right again even though she couldn't see down the hallway and into her room, but she had left his replacement clothes there. Swiftly, she removed her gaze from that direction and rested her chin on her knees. Her teeth chewed on her lower lip lightly as she tried to get various images out of her mind.

Her attempt to distract herself ended up failing too since her mind traveled to the memory of her date with him a few days back. After they had finished the bottle of wine, Edmund had paid the check and tip and had given the restaurant a favorable review. That awful man and woman had drifted from their minds as they had switched dining locations to her apartment and had watched old movies based on Roman mythology. On the way there, they had stopped at a drive-through at the nearest fast food place per her request.

To her, those vanilla and strawberry milkshakes had tasted better than they ever had in the past. Probably, that had been due to Edmund and her switching shakes throughout the movie. The food hadn't been exempted from that policy either.

Warmth touched her cheeks all the more at the memory of him feeding her a French fry. She leaned her forehead against her knees and groaned lightly into them. Elaine supposed that it was better than the alternative, which included too many drops of water and ... a towel slipping. Instantly, she cursed herself for reminding herself of the image.

A pout rested on her lips. She needed to move. Elaine stood to her feet and walked towards the kitchen. All of her paused, however, when her bathroom door creaked open. Before she even processed what she was doing, her head turned in that direction.

By a little bit, he stepped out of the bathroom. His pitch black hair was slicked back by beads of water while a few strands hovered around his forehead and framed his face. Edmund glanced down and noticed the pile of clothing before he bent down and picked the items up.

Finding herself unable to avert her eyes, she steadily shifted her orbs from the droplets of water on his face and perfect lips to his torso. His chest and abs were sculpted to his form in an exceptional and natural way. Her jaw couldn't help but open a little as her cheeks felt like volcanoes erupting to dramatic classical music.

Heartbeat increasing, she took a hesitant step to her left, but her eyes wouldn't leave him. They didn't want to miss a moment of him. Unfortunately, her unnoticed staring soon became the opposite. When he stood up fully again, he caught sight of her out of the corners of his eyes. A smirk tugged at his lips, and he made direct eye contact with her.

Practically, she jumped before she scurried off into the kitchen. An amused chuckle hit her ears, and she rubbed her cheeks furiously. She shook her head a little and opened the fridge door. The cool air hit her, and she felt like sticking her head in to clear it, but she resisted that urge.

Without much thought, she snagged a jar of grape jelly and slid it across the kitchen counter. She shut the door and figured that a peanut butter and jelly sandwich would be as good as any other sandwich at the moment. The sweetness might distract her from the model-like man in her home. Retrieving two butter knives, some whole wheat bread and peanut butter, she went to work on crafting the easy meal.

"Did you go to the same store that I had gone to?" A tone filled with quiet laughter reached her ears, and she stilled. Hesitantly, she peered up to him. Her cheeks, which had been starting to cool down, flared up again. "Well?" Edmund soon leaned against the fridge as his fingertips tugged at the hem of his shirt some.

All her mind could think about was what was under his shirt, and she had to set the knife down so that she wouldn't accidentally stab the middle of the bread. "Umm ..." Her lips parted, but nothing came from them. "... Sorry." She broke her eyes from him and rubbed the bridge of her nose. "I'm just ..."

"Distracted?" If she could've looked him in the eyes, she would've glared at him due to the teasing nature of his tone. She heard his steps and tensed when she felt him stop behind her. His arms maneuvered around hers before he lifted up the knife and continued her work. Her shoulders relaxed while a tiny pout remained on her lips. Elaine crossed her arms but didn't object to being within his. "I had asked because we're still matching."

Raising an eyebrow, she asked, "What do ..." She faced him before her eyes widened by a fraction. A black crew-neck and black pants were on him. Her mouth opened again in surprise. Stuttering occurred next, and she lifted a finger to point out of shock. "I-I-I ..."

Setting down the knife, he moved half of the sandwich to in front of her while he shifted his orbs to hers. Gradually, she reached forward a little and took the food. "I don't mind, Elaine. We're almost always matching after all." She couldn't deny that even though it was still odd.

Biting into the sandwich, she managed to avoid saying anything else. He picked up the other half and moved away from her a little. His gaze diverted to the living room and around the kitchen too. "Two rooms done. Two to go." She hummed softly in agreement. "We should work on the same room together."

Swallowing a bite, she managed to compose herself and look to him. "Why? It might take longer."

Laughing, he replied, "So, we don't bump into each other again." A slight wave of heat hit her cheeks out of embarrassment. "Though, both times have been enjoyable." Carefully, she met his orbs. They were knowing and alluring. "Maybe, we should try it a third time."

"No, we'll paint together!" The answer slipped out of her lips so quickly that she only comprehended her words afterwards. Instantly, he started to chuckle loudly. He leaned forward on the counter and set the sandwich down so that he wouldn't squish it out of mirth.

Feeling all the more embarrassed, she lowered her sandwich. "It's just that ... It's just that ... Well ..." Her eyes shifted to her right a little. "What if ..." Before she could finish her thought, she felt fingers slip under her chin. His simple touch brought flames to her skin, and she nearly dropped the sandwich in her hands.

With ease, he removed it from her hands and placed it upon the plate with the other one. Soon enough, he was back in front of her. "What if what? We share another kiss?" Her eyes couldn't help but snag a glance at his lips, which were so close. "I wouldn't mind that." He lowered his head more, and his breath blew back a few loose strands of her dark brown hair as a light chuckle left him. "Besides, I'm not leaving until I have a few more." She felt her heart skip a beat.

Not being able to control herself, she raised her hands before she wrapped her arms around his neck and stood up more on her feet to close the distance between them. She could taste remnants of jam and peanut butter on his lips, and he tasted the same on her. Edmund backed her into the fridge, and its cool metal seemed to awaken her senses to him all the more. Elaine wished to capture the warmth from his lips like it was her last breath.

Every kiss with him was so utterly intoxicating, and she had to hold onto him tighter so that her legs wouldn't give way. His hands settled on her hips and pulled her closer while his fingers pressed and rubbed into her skin. When a drawn-out moan escaped her, her other senses returned to her, and she moved away for air. Edmund's fingers remained on her, but their touch grew lighter. "Better, Elaine?"

Even if she wished to glower playfully at him, she threw away that idea and instead pecked his lips one more time. When she pulled back, she smirked. "I don't know. Are you?" She giggled and spun out of his hold before she made her way over to the light lavender paint. Lifting up a can of it, she asked further, "Ready?"

## Chapter Twenty Six: Complete

*Four sides were smoothed and spread out while bowls with food inside were on top. The single lamp in the room illuminated the dining space and allowed the two to see the other.*

The bedroom was finished, and the bathroom was near to being done; however, Elaine was no longer painting. Edmund had insisted upon completing the space by himself since there only had been a little bit left. She had argued that it would be quicker if she helped, but he had shooed her away. Elaine had figured that if he was that desperate to clean her bathroom, so be it.

In thanks, though, she was making dinner for both of them. It was nine at night, and she only had ice water since that sandwich earlier. Needless to say, she was hungry, and her stomach constantly reminded her of that while she cooked. Thankfully, Edmund was in the other room.

She stirred the soup a bit more before she carefully tasted the concoction. To her delight, she had seasoned the soup perfectly. It wasn't anything extravagant; it was chicken noodle soup with rice instead of noodles. Still, the food was warm and comforting, which her muscles needed after all of the painting.

When it was finished, she switched off the stove and moved the pot to another burner before she retrieved bowls, plates, spoons and napkins. She set all of the kitchenware on the counter before a further idea popped into her head. Elaine quietly stepped into her room and sneaked into her closet.

Removing one of her older blankets from it, which her ex never had used, she crept back into her room and smoothed it out on the floor. A light breeze came in through her window, which they had opened earlier to vent out the paint smell, but the wind wasn't strong, so she didn't have to hold down the blanket with anything. Satisfied with her work, she reentered her kitchen and prepared everything.

Once everything was ready, she set it all onto a food tray, though; she noted that she forgot drinks. Based off of their first date, she supposed that Edmund appreciated wine, and he did seem to enjoy that brand that they had shared. She had nothing like that, though, in her apartment, but she might have some alcohol.

There was a cabinet designated for liquor, but she didn't restock it often. Usually, there would only be three to five bottles in there anyway. Reaching up, she opened the small wooden door and peered inside. To her surprise, there were no bottles in it. She furrowed her brows before she recalled why. All of the remaining bottles had been drinks that her ex and she had shared. They had been added to the boxes of things given to that nurse.

Closing the cabinet, she checked the fridge. There was blackberry iced tea, grape juice, almond milk and regular milk. She supposed that the tea would work. After she poured the two of them each a glass, she put it back and added the two glasses to the tray.

Lifting it up, she noted that it was somewhat heavy and could easily tip over if she wasn't careful. She had balanced both sides out, but that didn't stop the dishes from wanting to slide across the tray every now and then. When she reached her room and placed it down, her shoulders immediately relaxed.

A soft sigh escaped her, and she arranged everything onto the blanket before she stood back up and took the tray back to the kitchen. Edmund, however, heard movement of various things in the bedroom. They had finished painting the space, and the furniture wouldn't be moved back until it was dry. Curious, he finished the last section of the walls swiftly and in a quality manner before he placed the roller onto the tray.

Heading into the bedroom, he paused at the sight before him. She had set up an indoor picnic for them. A smirk touched his lips. How cute and thoughtful. He supposed that he did deserve the treat since her apartment would be painted over again within a month or so. At least, he planned for her to move in with him by then, and he couldn't see why not. Elaine already was in his hands, and he had no intention of letting her out of them.

"What do you think?" a hesitant and soft voice asked. He was brought out of his thoughts by her enchanting voice and stared over to the doorway. Her fingers were fiddling with each other in front of her as she glanced between the food and him. "You like soup and tea, right?" Her dark brown eyes landed on the tea, and she looked disappointed. "I didn't have any wine or liquor, so I ..."

"It's wonderful." Instantly, she averted her eyes back to him, and a smile tugged at her lips. Already, he knew what she was going to say. "And yes, really." She diverted her orbs and smiled to herself. Edmund took that opportunity to step forward and intertwine his fingers with hers. Elaine put up no resistance and permitted him to guide her down towards the blanket.

Seated, she stared up at him. "Aren't you going to sit?" There was a tinge of concern in her voice, and it made his heart swell with bliss. He removed his hands gently from hers, and he noted that she was resisting the urge to reach out to him again. Goodness, her dependence was rapture.

"I will. I need to wash the paint off of my hands." Glancing towards her hands, she checked them for paint. "It's dry, but I'd still like to wash it off." Her eyes met his again, and a miniscule smirk crept onto her lips.

"Or, is it an excuse to fix your hair?" she teased, a laugh dying to escape past her lips. "It's a little untidy." She quirked a brow as a small smirk touched his lips in return.

He held his hands up in mock surrender. "My hair may need some fixing, though; you might just mess it up again." At that, her humor fell, and embarrassment took its place. "Another distraction might happen." She crossed her arms and refused to make eye contact with him. Elaine mumbled something. Edmund couldn't catch it, but he laughed regardless.

Turning on his heel, he headed into the bathroom. "Just don't take too long." He paused. "The food will get cold. I won't wait forever." Edmund smiled before he continued into the bathroom and washed his hands. As he did so, he looked into the mirror. Admittedly, his hair was hanging loosely in multiple sections. Not that he minded her hands running through his locks and her fingers getting tangled in them.

With the paint all gone, he turned off the water, switched off the light and reentered the room. She was playing with one of the corners of the blanket idly and rubbing the fabric between her fingertips. Her eyes seemed to notice the difference in light, and she glanced over. It was like she woke up from a trance when he arrived. Elaine really knew how to have an effect on him. Gaze shifting to his hair, her cheeks heated a little. "So, you decided not to fix it." He walked over and seated himself on the blanket. Before he could answer, she leaned over and ruffled his locks all the more. A victorious smirk painted her lips. "There, now it's even worse."

"It may be worse, but does it look bad?" He picked up his bowl and spoon as he glanced towards her out of the corners of his eyes. She paused as if her deepest secret had been unveiled. Silence was her answer before she copied him in picking up the bowl and spoon before her. "Ah, you prefer it."

Gripping her spoon a bit tighter, she muttered, "I like both." He chuckled and took a careful bite, and a smile formed on his lips. She followed suit, though; her smile was because he liked her cooking.

Lowering the bowl, he couldn't help but remark, "Though when my hair is like this, it reminds you of our intimacy, right?" She nearly spit out her bite of food but managed to swallow it in the end. Elaine shakily set her bowl and spoon down before she cast a scowl at him. In the process, he rapidly grabbed another bite of food and shoved it into her mouth. Her eyes widened before she swallowed as he pulled the spoon away. "One to zero."

Grabbing her napkin, she wiped any broth away from the sides of her lips. For a moment, confusion crossed her face before she caught on. "I'll catch ..." Another spoon past her lips, and he quirked a brow. She took the bite begrudgingly.

"Two to zero." Elaine parted her lips from the spoon. He didn't immediately go for another one, but she had a feeling he was planning the perfect timing. Well, she wouldn't let him. A minor stare off occurred between the two of them. When she saw his hand move, she sprung into action.

Her hands reached out and grabbed his wrists, though; their combined weight sent them to the floor. An entertained laugh left him, and she felt heat dance upon her cheeks. "Reversing the tables, Elaine?" She pushed the heat away and pressed his wrists to the floor more, trying to forget that she was straddling him. His eyes watched her every move, and she noted a gleam of lust in his eyes.

"Now, who's distracted?"

"I was distracted back then too, or would you like me to go to another level?"

Narrowing her eyes a bit, she shoved the thoughts that entered her mind aside. "Well, I'd like you to ..."

Once again, he cut her off. He pushed up against her and shifted their weight, and he was on top of her. A smirk touched his lips, and he lowered his lips to her right ear and whispered, "I never lose."

## Chapter Twenty Seven: Win

*Hands held tightly while fingers left soft trails of touches. A kiss upon the neck and several upon the head left the pair. They were lovingly administered. Though, was one ... obsessive?*

Heart pounding in her chest, she observed his every move as she found it harder and harder to breathe normally. He pulled his lips farther from her ear, but they were centimeters away from her jaw. She could feel his breath tickle her skin, but she didn't dare turn her head. His movement was too precise and perfectly timed, and she couldn't avert her attention from it.

She didn't even register him switching her wrists to one hand while his other retrieved his soup bowl. Her eyes trained themselves onto his. An irresistible gleam shone in his green-hazel eyes. Before she could utter a word, he sat up and tugged her up with him. A slight surprised cry left her until it was silenced by a spoonful of soup in her mouth.

"Three to zero." A grin decorated his lips while her cheeks burned with embarrassment and frustration. She swallowed the soup and pulled away. Elaine crossed her arms and rolled her eyes. "Are you going to surrender?" While he chuckled, she acted fast.

In a heartbeat, she retrieved her bowl and forced the spoon past his lips. His eyes widened while she removed the spoon. "Three ..." Another spoon found itself in her mouth. A determined fire lit up in her eyes. She would prove him wrong!

The next several minutes were a blur. All she knew was that the blanket would need to be washed due to broth spilling onto the fabric. Their clothes were stained in various places, but most of the soup did go into their mouths. Despite the minor mess, she was laughing and enjoying her evening to the fullest. Based on Edmund's smiles and chuckles, she presumed that he held similar feelings.

When his last spoonful traveled past her lips and into her mouth, a smirk stretched upon his lips, and she roughly took the spoon out with a huff after she swallowed. "I never lose, but," she gave him a hesitant look as he continued, "I'll continue to let you feed me. You do owe me."

"I have a better idea." She positioned herself to sit on her knees and motioned him to come closer. Edmund quirked a brow and didn't budge. A slight groan escaped her much to his amusement. Scooting across the blanket, she soon sat right in front of him and picked up her bowl.

"I thought that you had a better idea." He was permitted no opportunity to analyze her behavior closer. All he saw was her hand dive into her soup bowl before it met his hair. It combed through his locks and pushed the untidy strands back. Meanwhile, Elaine wore a smile of complete payback for his arrogant remarks.

His lips parted in surprise; however, a frown soon met them. Instantly, her hand froze. Had she caused him to become angry? Slowly, she retracted her hand, but he grabbed her wrist. "Finish it." Edmund's hold disappeared. Hesitantly, she combed her fingers back through his locks, but an arm soon wrapped around her waist and pushed her onto his lap.

"E ..."

"Shh, just finish it." He leaned forward and rested his forehead on her left shoulder. A slight dose of heat touched her cheeks as she lifted up her hands and smoothed back his locks, which would need to be washed again. She wished to ask him a few questions, but she figured that he would ask her to be quiet once more.

Even if she had upset him, she wouldn't take back her action. His presence was comforting, and she was relishing the quiet peace between the two of them. Before she could stop herself, her hands slid back down his head and halted. She leaned over and pressed light kisses to the top of his head. He tensed a bit, but his arms soon wrapped around her, and his fingers rested near her shoulder blades.

While kisses continued to be applied to his hair, he shifted his head to be more comfortable against her. Upon his lips, an unseen smirk painted them. She played so easily to his every action, and he didn't even have her upon strings. Her lips parted from him and didn't meet his head again. His smirk fell a little, but he didn't move from his spot. "Edmund?"

That time, he would let her speak. "Hmm?" he hummed in response, his fingers delicately rubbing at her shoulders. He felt a shiver run up her spine, and it truly was delightful.

"You're not actually mad at me, are you?" Almost, he chuckled. He loved how she couldn't read him. To her, he was a closed book, yet she trusted the words that danced off of his tongue. Such devotion was a rare treat, and it was all his. She belonged to him. "Are you?" she repeated, worry evident in her melodic voice.

"No." He turned his head in more and pressed a light kiss to her neck as he felt her visibly relax in his arms. What a darling woman. "But," she tensed again, "I would like another shower." An audible sigh escaped her.

Combing her fingers through his hair again, she chuckled out, "That I'm fine with." Her laugh was short-lived when she realized what that meant. "Are you ... Are you going to be okay wearing those clothes?"

Edmund gripped her back with a slightly harder hold while he leaned forward more. Confused, Elaine was about to ask him what was wrong until her ears caught hold of laughter. Her fingers stopped their movement, and she stared down at him. His face was out of her field of vision, but he continued to laugh. She didn't know what to say, so she waited for him to calm down and explain himself.

Loosening his hold on her, he composed himself. "I can shower at my home, Elaine." Heat engulfed her cheeks at that obvious option. She hadn't even considered it, and she felt the urge to hide somewhere. Gradually, he lifted his head up. His eyes stared into hers, and she couldn't remove her eyes from him again. They were too attention-grabbing. "Or, I can shower here and change back into my clothes with paint on them."

At that, she managed to break out of her slight trance. "What?!" She shook her head. "I'm not going to have you change into dirty clothes. You helped me paint my home. That's not a good way to repay you."

"I think that you've repaid me enough." He smiled to her and raised her chin with his right fingers. "Your company brings me immense pleasure, Elaine." Heat dusted across her cheeks, but she moved his fingers away from her face, ready to argue. "And, you've already bought me another outfit. I won't have you go looking for another. It's night, and I'll be at my home tomorrow. Or, I can leave after I've helped you clean this up."

Without any thought, she mumbled, "I don't want you to leave." She caught herself too late, but she didn't retract her statement, nor could she. Elaine stared up at him shyly, hoping that he wouldn't tease her again. Luckily, he understood her message quite clearly.

"Then, tomorrow." Gently, he moved her off of his lap. He stood up and held out his right hand to her. She took it, and he lifted her up. "Let's pick this up first."

"No, it's fine. You get a shower. I'll figure something out for you concerning your attire." He looked reluctant to leave her to the mess, but she smiled reassuringly to him. "It's fine." Her smile vanished a little and was replaced by a fraction of embarrassment. "Though, don't leave the bathroom again. I'll just hand them to you when you're ready." He gave her a curious and entertained glance. "Just extend out your hand, though! Don't open the door the whole way!" she exclaimed swiftly so that he wouldn't say something that would make the heat in her cheeks rise. Elaine faced away from him to pick up the indoor picnic.

"Should I prepare the couch when I'm done?" he asked, stepping away from her and towards the bathroom. When he reached the doorway, he leaned against it and waited for her reply. She stood fully back up and had all of the dishware and such in a nice, neat stack.

Her back faced him, but she shook her head. "No, you can sleep beside me." He raised his eyebrows a little, but his heart gave a harsh pound out of joy. Slightly, she looked over her right shoulder to him. "But, I'll find you something to wear so that you're not just in ... your boxers." Edmund had to refrain from chuckling. It was obvious that she was doing her best not to avert her eyes to his lower half.

Roughly spinning on her heel, she left her bedroom, and he watched her make the turn into the kitchen. Slowly, he stepped into the bathroom and shut the door. He locked it and leaned his head against the door. She would be in one of her nightgowns, and if she failed in her task, he would only be in his boxers. That much skin-to-skin contact caused him to drag his fingers down the door. Almost, his nails dug into the surface, but he forced himself away from the wooden object.

If he didn't turn on the water soon enough, she might become suspicious. He doubted it; however, he wished to remain cautious. Slipping out of his clothes, he entered her shower and couldn't wait for the day when she joined him in it. The water left the shower head and coated him in its embrace, but its touch couldn't even compare to that of his treasure's.

## Chapter Twenty Eight: Discover

*A folded piece of paper seated itself upon wood while rays of sun peeked under the door and through the window. Lavender roses bloomed brightly like always even though someone was missing.*

Reaching out, her left hand subconsciously grabbed at the space next to her. Her fingers curled into the sheets, and she rolled onto her stomach. No warmth was felt next to her, and her brows furrowed in confusion. Warmth had been there before. Gradually, her eyes blinked open. She closed them again when morning light broke into the room. Both of her eyes squinted open towards her alarm clock. *9:00 am.* Elaine didn't pay attention to the alarm for very long, however. Rather, her eyes shifted to the empty space beside her. A slight frown covered her lips, but she supposed that his absence saved her the embarrassment of waking up next to him ... or on him for that matter.

She rested her head back on her pillow, which originally had been on ... Edmund's chest. Her cheeks heated a bit, and she reminded herself that she had allowed him her pillow since she only had one. Elaine pressed her face into the pillow more, but that didn't remove the memories at all. If anything, it caused them to become stronger. A faint scent of him was there, and her lips twitched up into a tiny smile.

Last night, she had discovered something for him to wear: her black bathrobe. It had been a little short on him, but it had covered him more than just his boxers would. Yesterday night, however, had made her regret a little not purchasing any nightclothes but just nightgowns. She had decided to wear her thulian pink cotton one since the cotton had seemed more casual than satin or the chiffon-like fabric of her olive green one.

Biting her lower lip, she recalled the goodnight kiss they had shared, well more like several, and her cheeks grew all the hotter. A quiet little squeak parted from her lips. Her fingers gripped her pillow, and she shoved her face into the pillow roughly. Even the memory of his kisses sparked roaring, soothing flames within her.

Despite her mind being relieved that she wouldn't have to handle embarrassment so early in the morning, her lips desperately wanted his back on them. A pout formed onto her lips while she mentally sighed in frustration. It was far too easy to imagine her hands accidentally running past the bathrobe and across his well-toned chest. Eventually, they would find their way to his perfectly sculpted face, and her lips would land upon his again. Roughly, she switched to lay on her right side. She frowned heavily while her cheeks burned. It was even possible that he had woken up with the bathrobe in complete disarray. That would've been quite the sight to wake up to.

Blowing a couple of strands out of her face, she finally noted something new on her nightstand. She scooted across her bed and pushed herself up onto her hands before she supported her weight on her right hand. Her left hand retrieved the folded piece of paper before she sat up, leaned against the headboard and unfolded the paper.

*I was called in to a shipment gone wrong at one of my stores. Apparently, the glass in several boxes of picture frames arrived completely shattered. I'll call you later in the day or evening depending on how long it takes to sort out this mess. I didn't want to wake you; you're far too adorable for that.* She paused in reading and permitted a smile to creep upon her lips while a light bit of heat tickled her cheeks. Elaine turned back to reading. *There's breakfast for you in the fridge. Enjoy.*

Carefully, she placed the paper back on her nightstand and slipped her legs over the edge of the bed. Standing up, she stretched her limbs. For the moment, she skipped her morning routine as her feet led her to her kitchen. Her pace abnormally was fast, but she didn't mind at all. She was curious to find out what he had made her.

Opening the door, she scanned over the items inside before she saw a note beside a yogurt parfait. Layers of vanilla yogurt, which was what the note mentioned, blueberries, strawberries and peanut butter granola were packed into the glass. A spoon was beside it too.

Not being able to wait, she retrieved the item from her fridge and closed the door behind her. She seated herself on the couch and flipped on the television. A lazy hour in the morning wouldn't hurt her. Admittedly, though, she was looking forward to his call later on. Part of her was tempted to text him her thanks for the note and breakfast, but she didn't want to draw his attention away from the problem that had occurred. Besides if she called him, her lazy hour might morph into several hours. Elaine needed to focus her mind on other things than him, which wasn't easy; however, she could manage it.

~ ~ ~ ~ ~ ~ ~ ~ ~ ~ ~

Warm water filled the sink as bubbles covered dishes. Some floated, and others didn't. Black fuzzy slippers covered her feet, which she probably could've worn during painting. That might've gotten them covered in paint, however, and she was happy that they were still paint free. Her red pleated skirt flowed down to her knees effortlessly while her red blouse with ruffles around the collar and sleeves decorated her torso. A red hair bow held back some of her locks, and her face held no makeup. She hadn't left the house, and it was late in the evening. Edmund hadn't called yet, and she doubted that she would see him before the next day.

Shutting off the water, she grabbed a clean dish rag before she heard her phone ring. She draped the rag over the sink counter and recognized Edmund's number. A smile touched her lips, and she leaned against the counter as she answered. "How'd it go?"

His immediate answer was a drawn-out sigh. "Not well. I had to call the seller, and the exchange hadn't been pleasant with him." She could envision him rubbing the bridge of his nose, but she heard a car door open and shut shortly later. He probably just arrived home.

"Have you bought things from him before?" She crossed her left arm under her chest as cleaning the dishes steadily faded from her mind.

"No, but he carried a particular frame that I thought would be a good addition to the stores. He seemed reliable when I had met him, but he was the complete opposite today. I managed to receive a refund back, but business with him is forever off."

"Did he blame you for it?"

"Not me directly but he called my workers incompetent." Most definitely, he just rolled his eyes. His tone was bitter and insulted. "I have cameras at my stores, and I saw that they hadn't dropped any of the boxes in the delivery room. They had arrived like that."

"Then ..."

"No, the frames are gone. He wanted them back. It's been a headache." She pushed herself off of the counter and leaned against the one by the window. Elaine rested her chin on the palm of her left hand. Before she could try and make him feel better, he continued, "I'll use my money that I received back to design a new frame that I like even more and have some custom built for me with a reliable contact." Another heavy sigh met her ears.

"Are you going to be alright?"

Gently, a soft laugh met her ears, and she glanced out the window as if she expected him to be there; however, something did catch her eyes. She stood up straight, and she leaned towards the window more. A man was walking on the sidewalk across from her apartment complex. It looked like he was on the phone since his right hand was up to his ear. Elaine couldn't make out his exact features due to the shadows cast over him by the streetlights.

"... I'll see you sometime next week. I want to settle all of this first." Elaine missed most of what he had said except for his last two lines. Her eyes remained focused on the man walking, though. "Elaine?"

Hearing her name, she rapidly made up an excuse. "Ah, sorry. I'm in the middle of washing dishes." It really wasn't an excuse. There were ready-to-be-washed dishes in the sink. The man entered the apartment complex across the street. Something just didn't sit well in the pit of her stomach. Had that been Edmund? Had he been living across the street from her all this time, and she simply never had noticed?

"Would you like me to call back later?"

"No, you're fine." She forced herself to move away from the window. "Will you call me again while you're settling this, though?" Now, she wanted to ask him where he lived but not make it obvious.

He chuckled. "Yes, I'll still call you. Your voice is welcome after today."

Despite the compliment, she didn't smile. Her mind was too concentrated on what she just had viewed. Maybe, she was over thinking things, but she desired to double check. "I enjoy listening to your voice too." She heard a light chuckle in response, but she barely registered it against the sound of her thoughts.

## Chapter Twenty Nine: Investigate

*Lying on the table, the phone was plugged in and charging. A call just had ended, but no smile greeted lips; however, eyes stared out ahead, curious and troubled.*

A week had gone by since it had taken Edmund longer to handle the issue of the frames than he had expected. He also had his other plans for his work on top of that, so they simply had called the other during the week. Even though she hadn't seen him in person, she hadn't been down about that. Rather, her mind had kept returning to that man from the other night.

The likely answer was that he had been nothing more than stranger, who just had happened to be on the phone at the same time as Edmund and her. She had tried to ease her worry by attempting to get Edmund to mention something about his home, but the conversations conveniently had changed topics. Or, he had to hang up since work had been calling. Those factors only had caused her to become more suspicious. Something about his place of residence had to be odd.

Elaine crossed her legs on the sofa while her arms were crossed under her chest. Her back leaned against the couch, and her eyes trained themselves on her phone. She just had ended a conversation with Edmund. He had been apologizing for not being able to meet up for the week or to help move her furniture back, but he had promised to come tomorrow.

All of her wasn't excited about his visit. She had moved her furniture back into place and had taken down all of the sheets of plastic and tape from painting since it had taken her mind off of that man for a bit earlier in the week. Now, though, she had barely anything to distract her. Elaine had finished her work for the weekend, and television wouldn't help her with how strong the nagging of her curiosity was.

Edmund was still at work, or he had told her that at least. If he hadn't been lying and if he did live across the street, she quickly could check. The idea sinking in, she sprung to her feet and looked out her living room window. No one was walking on the sidewalk on either side of the street.

Time not being on her side, she grabbed her phone and keys before she hurried out of her door and locked it behind her. She forgot that she had her black fuzzy slippers on, but she didn't bother to head back inside and change into heels. Heels would create too much noise. Her black chiffon skirt rippled along with her fast-paced steps. Elaine slightly regretted wearing her white blouse with chiffon sleeves since the color made her stand out in the night, but that made her increase her speed all the more.

Before hopefully anyone saw her, she entered into the apartment complex across the street. It was certainly nicer than her own, and she had heard that each room had two floors. Given the income Edmund probably collected, the added bonus fit with his paycheck. Even the entrance hall to the apartments depicted that residents had to have a decent pay wage.

Polished, dark-stained wood tables lined the hallway to the elevator and to the stairwell. Crystal vases sat atop them, and bright pink lilies bloomed within them. There were a couple of maroon leather chairs within the space, and they were seated upon the sparkling tile floor. In the center of the hall, a crystal chandelier hung and illuminated the space.

"Are you here to see someone?" Elaine about leaped into the air. She rapidly glanced to her left and spotted a desk, matching the tables in the space. A man stood behind it, and his blue eyes were focused purely on her. "I don't recognize you." He broke his gaze with her and scanned over the desk as if he was searching for a specific note. "And, none of the residents told me that they were expecting someone today."

"I'm surprising him!" Her voice was a little too loud, and she winced after it. The man raised a dark brown brow, clearly skeptical of her excuse. His eyes moved from her face down to her feet, and she suddenly wished that she had spent the extra time to change her shoes. "I live just across the street." She even pointed with her left index finger. "I didn't feel like switching my shoes." Elaine felt compelled to move closer to the desk as if that would convince him more of her uncreative excuse.

"Who are you surprising?" He crossed his arms and leaned against the wall. Probably, he had heard the same excuse before. Her plan was falling apart, and she most likely even wouldn't reach the elevator let alone the stairs.

Hesitantly, she took a few more steps towards the desk. "...
Edmund Fex?" She didn't mean to sound so much like she was
asking a question, but she couldn't help herself. Ultimately, she
hoped that he didn't reside in the complex. Otherwise, her
questions would increase tenfold, and she definitely wouldn't leave
until she saw him that night.

Surprise crossed the man's face like he actually hadn't
expected her to give him a valid name. Did he really live across the
street from her? Her heart pounded, and she placed her hands on
the desk shakily. "... Well? Can I see him?"

Steadily, the man pushed himself off of the wall. Instead of
answering her, he picked up the phone on the desk and dialed a
number. She watched him press the digits. Her heart dropped, and
her stomach twisted into dreadful knots. Edmund's personal phone
number. Elaine didn't need another answer.

Legs feeling weak, they wobbled before she collapsed to her
knees. Immediately, the man behind the desk set down the phone.
"Miss, are you alright?" She waved her hand feebly. Hesitantly, he
picked up the phone again.

"Ah, sorry about that Mr. Fex." Elaine's lips parted. That had
been him last week. "Yes, I did have a question for you. There's a
woman here saying that she came over to surprise you. It's not
much of a surprise now, but you know protocol, so ... Ah, okay. I'll
tell her." He hung up the phone and peered over the desk down to
her. "He would like you to wait here for him, and he'll take you up
once he arrives ... Do you need anything? You don't look well."

"I'm fine." Gradually, she picked herself up to her feet and
used the desk as a support. She did feel lightheaded. "Maybe, some
water." He nodded and opened a small refrigerator behind the desk
before he handed her a cold water bottle. "Thank you ..." Elaine
squinted her eyes since she couldn't focus on her surroundings too
much. "Gerald."

Making her way over to one of the leather chairs, she plopped
herself down. She noted slightly that Gerald was staring at her as if
he wished to ask her more questions, but he eventually looked away
and seated himself on the chair he had. He pulled out his personal
phone and focused on it, but he probably was watching everything
else too in the area.

Removing the cap from the water, she took a sip before she capped it again. She slid off her slippers and brought her feet up onto the chair. Part of her desired to head straight back to her apartment and avoid Edmund for awhile, but that part didn't win over the side that wished to face him. Despite the oddity of him living right across the street from her and never mentioning it, she wanted to continue to date him. Elaine didn't wish to give him up; she simply desired an explanation or two so that she could trust him completely again.

Idly, her fingers picked at the label around the bottle. Her fingernails tore into it a little, and the simple action allowed her to maintain her composure, but her thoughts were chaotic. She was so wrapped up in her own mind about what she had discovered and what it meant that she didn't register the passing of time and the entrance door opening.

"Good evening, Mr. Fex."

That caused her to sit up straight. Her eyes switched over to the door's direction. Edmund closed the door behind him and gave Gerald a small smile. "Thank you, Gerald. Have a good evening." He changed his gaze to her, and she froze. His steps sounded like earthquakes, and his expression completely was unreadable.

"Elaine, are you ready to head up?" She stared up to him as he extended out his right hand for her to take. Her heart pounded in fright, but her hand reached out to him regardless. He intertwined his fingers with hers and lifted her from the chair as she slipped her feet back into her slippers.

Meekly and worriedly, she started, "Edmund ..."

"I'll explain when we're upstairs. I should've told you when you indirectly had been asking this week, but I wanted to tell you in person." So, he had known. She felt even smaller next to him.

He gave a grateful nod to Gerald before he took her over to the elevator. Edmund pressed the call button, and the doors immediately opened before they stepped inside. His right index finger pressed for the third floor, and the doors shut. Elaine only hoped that his calm demeanor wouldn't drastically change into one of fury when they arrived at his room.

## Chapter Thirty: Disclose

*Grey metal pendant lights brightened up the place from the darkness of night. Two metal stools were pulled out from the counter, but only one was occupied.*

Walking down the polished tiles, she somewhat slid across on her feet, and she stood a little behind Edmund. He remained quiet and didn't try to retrieve her hand back. Edmund was too calm for her liking, but he might also be worried and attempting not to display it. Perhaps, she should tell him that he had nothing to be concerned about with regards to her leaving him. That wasn't her intent in the slightest, but if she revealed that, he might not explain the whole situation to her. She desired the complete truth from him.

They stopped in front of the last door in the hall. He removed his keys from his right pocket and slipped the house key inside the lock. With a click, the door opened, and he indicated for her to head in first. Her feet remained where they were. A sigh parted from his lips before he entered his home. Hesitantly, she followed him in before he closed and locked the door behind them.

Noting her gaze pinned to the lock, Edmund held out his keys to her. She gave him a puzzled stare. "Take them if you're worried." Despite the simple gesture, it was much more than that. It was a test of trust, but she wished to hold onto the keys. Her right hand reached out before it hovered a little bit away from the metal.

In the end, her hand dropped back to her side, and she shook her head. "No, it's fine. I just want ..."

He walked past her and finished her thought, "An explanation. I know, and I told you that I'm going to explain myself." Edmund unbuttoned his jacket and draped it on the coat rack by the left side of the door. "Take a seat in the kitchen."

"I ..." She was about to mention that she would be fine standing, but she would be lying. Given the circumstances, she needed a seat. "...Right." Elaine entered the kitchen as Edmund flipped on the kitchen lights. Grey metal pendant lights hung over the center of the space, but they were high enough up that no one accidentally could run into one of them.

Elaine pulled out one of the metal stools underneath the black granite countertop. She placed her water bottle on the counter before she seated herself. Her eyes scanned over the living room. Directly across from her was a large window with grey linen curtains pulled to the side. Another window was off to her left in the living room and had its curtains open too. Edmund was quick to untie and close them before he made his way into the kitchen.

Gaze shifting from the living room, she watched him open the black stainless steel fridge as he loosened his white tie. He was matching her again. Her eyes couldn't help but turn to his windows. He was right across the street from her. It was reasonable to assume that he could've been spying on her the whole time and seen her outfit choices before he had left his apartment each morning. An unpleasant shiver ran up her spine.

Hearing movement behind her, she couldn't stand having her back to him any longer. She shifted a bit so that she could watch him. He closed the fridge and grabbed a simple plastic blue cup from one of the cupboards. Edmund poured part of the bottle of sparkling berry water into the glass. "Would you like some?" he asked as his back faced her.

The question was simple, but there was too much tension in the air not to give her pause. "... No, I'm fine ... Thank you." Almost, she thought that she saw him chuckle, but she hadn't heard such a sound from him. He put the bottle away before he shortly joined her at the counter.

Again, she faced away from him. Her thumbs rubbed over the top of the bottle cap while she kept an eye on him out of the corners of her eyes. "Do you have anything specific to ask me, Elaine?"

"You already know what I want to know."

"And if Gerald hadn't called me, what would you have done?"

"Does it matter?" Her thumbs stopped, and she glared at the bottle, annoyed that he was switching topics. "I wouldn't have broken in if I had found your apartment. I simply wanted to know that I had seen you enter this place last week." She directed her glare to him. "And, it had been you. You had slipped up, hadn't you?"

Not shying away from her accusation, he remained composed. "Yes. In the past, I had looked up to see if you had been at either of your front windows. If you had been, I had stayed out of sight until you had moved. Then, I had hurried to the entrance. Last week, I had forgotten to check. The day had been stressful, and I had been more focused on talking to you." He took a sip of his water before he placed the glass down and untied his tie.

Harshly, she averted her eyes from him and back to the bottle. "You're putting the blame on me?" His movement halted. "It isn't my fault that you had been keeping a secret like this from me." She was ready to throw the bottle at him, but she forced herself to keep herself somewhat composed. "If I wasn't willing ..."

"I'm not putting the blame on you. I'm only stating why I hadn't been more careful. Me not telling you about this is my fault." His tone held no anger, but it was firm. "And, I have a reasonable reason for doing so." Her eyes diverted over to him, urging him to continue. "It's simple. Us both being at the same coffee shop, running into each other at the hospital, matching in colors, everything makes it seem like I've been stalking you."

"Have you?"

At that, his neutral expression and tone dropped. He sat up straighter. Abruptly, he faced her, and she scooted over on the stool. A heavy frown controlled his lips. "No. All of that just alarmingly worked out that way." His frown fell, and a sigh escaped him. "Even now we're matching, but that's all that it is. If anything, it shows that we like the same colors. You've even bought me matching clothes."

Combing his right fingers through his hair, he removed his tie from his shoulders and placed it on the counter. "Besides that, I had bought this place awhile back." He noted the accusatory gleam popping up in her eyes again. "Yes, it had been after you already had purchased your apartment with your ex, but we hadn't known each other back then."

"That's not reassuring. We may have not known each other, but you might've known me. Had you ..."

Roughly, he stood up from his stool. "Don't." His voice was piercing, and she almost fell off of the stool from its unexpected sharpness. "I'm not a killer, Elaine. I hadn't planned your ex's accident. I hadn't set him up with Gina so that you could hate him all the more." He spun on his heel and rubbed the bridge of his nose.

"Here are the simple facts." He started to walk away from her. Despite the situation, she wanted him back on the stool and close to her. Edmund was somewhat predictable then. Now ... Well, she didn't know. It had been wrong of her even to begin to think to ask that, but she hadn't been able to help herself. If he had been watching her for a long time, it had been a possibility beyond imagination.

"One." She broke out of her thoughts and observed him head into the living room. "I had bought this apartment because I had liked the design and affordability given the space within it, not because you had lived across the street. Two." He reached the couch. "After I had bought it, I had seen you leave your apartment, but I had recognized you from Bread and Books. I had thought that it would be odd to point out such a fact to you at the café."

Sitting down, he crossed one leg behind the other and stared to the drapes. "Three. After I had gotten to know you better, that fact had become even more awkward to point out. Then when we had started dating, it had grown worse." A slight growl-like sound passed from his lips. "That's all there is, Elaine. If it's that too much of a concern for you, you can leave."

His unpleasant tone froze her to her seat. "I'll even move if that's what you would like." Those words paralyzed her even more. Silence followed. Edmund was thankful that he had closed the drapes since his reflection couldn't be seen in the glass of the window ahead of him. A smirk tugged at his lips. Any moment now.

Metal sounded. Perfect. Light, almost inaudible steps followed. His smile fell and was replaced by a frustrated, yet pained countenance. She stopped in front of him. Steadily, his orbs looked up to hers. Hesitation was evident across her face, but her lips parted in the end. "I ... Well, I ..." Elaine took a breath before she exhaled. "I don't want you to leave. I just want to trust you again." How utterly exceptional she was.

Gesturing with her hands to the apartment, she continued, "The fact that you live across the street from me and could easily watch me in my apartment isn't easy to swallow." A look of offense crossed him, though; it was hard not to chuckle at the fact that she caught him dead on but didn't know it. "Can I ..."

"You can trust me."

## Chapter Thirty One: Doubt

*Light shone from the space, but it didn't touch the darkness where she was. She stole a glance before heat rushed to her cheeks, and she covered her eyes once more.*

Curled up on the large, plush couch, she pressed the cap to her lips absentmindedly. Her eyes stared forward to the television, which wasn't even on. Edmund was upstairs and taking a shower. She could leave and lock herself up in her apartment for awhile. There was enough food in her fridge, but he had told her that she could trust him like before. How she wanted too, but a nagging feeling invaded her mind and tickled her stomach dreadfully.

She had nodded her head to his statement, though, reluctantly. Her thumbs rubbed against the plastic as her thoughts further consumed her. He should've mentioned his apartment's location sooner even if she had reacted poorly. Maybe, she wouldn't be in his apartment presently. Perhaps, she would've parted ways from him and dealt with all of that drama from her ex by herself. Elaine didn't know. Those possibilities were gone now.

Again, all she had to do was exit through the front door, take the elevator down, leave, cross the street, enter her apartment and lock the door. It didn't consist of a few steps, but it was simple enough. Or, she'd like to think that. Since Edmund hadn't detailed his home location earlier on, she found that she couldn't. She just couldn't leave him. He had stolen her heart, and it was too tightly in his grasp for her to retrieve it back.

Elaine moved the bottle slightly away from her. Her eyes shifted from the blank television to the curtains. Slowly, she got to her feet. The bottle dropped from her hands and onto one of the couch's cushions. Both of her feet carried her over to the drapes, and she slipped them back. Across the street, her apartment remained.

Almost, she chuckled. Moving locations was a silly thought, but her home did look far away. The street transformed into a massive river, and the asphalt morphed into roaring waves. She shook her head a little before she leaned her forehead against the glass. If she was so worried, she should leave; she could ... she could ... she ... No.

A barely audible sigh parted from her. Her emotions were in constant conflict, but doubt was losing horrendously. Still, it struggled on. Elaine shifted her dark brown orbs to the stairs. Barely, she could hear the water running. He hadn't asked her to remain on the first floor. Suddenly, doubt discovered an opening. Quietly, yet swiftly, she progressed up the stairs. She could check around his bedroom. It was a clear indicator that she didn't trust him entirely, but he was in the shower. And, he hadn't requested that she stay out of his room.

At the top of the steps, she made a left turn. Light came from under the farthest door down the hallway. Water sounded. Good. His bedroom door was shut, which was a nuisance. She made her way over, and her hands rested on the knob carefully. Delicately, she turned it and pushed in. The door didn't squeak. That was a severe relief.

Entering the room, she closed the door softly behind her. Dull evening light drifted in through the window across from her and barely illuminated the space. She could make out the furniture in the room, however, but it was sparse. He only had a bed and nightstand, yet the room could fit so much more in it. There was a closet, which could prove very valuable to her investigation. First, though, she would check the easy places.

Going across the beige carpet, she stopped in front of the nightstand. Her hands rested on the metal handle. Elaine was about to tug on it when her ears picked up a worrying sound. The water stopped. Would he hear her if she opened it, and how long would he stay in the bathroom? If he didn't bring a change of clothes in with him, it wouldn't be long before he stepped into his bedroom. He wouldn't do that, though, would he? She was in his apartment, and he was courteous. Well not if he was spying, but she wasn't certain of that yet.

Her next fear occurred. She heard a door open. Immediately, her hands left the handle but gently. Metal slamming on wood wouldn't do her any benefit. Swiftly, she threw herself under the bed. It was obvious, but she doubted that he was expecting her to be hiding in his bedroom. "Elaine, please don't come upstairs! I forgot my clothes!" she heard him call out to her, but she couldn't answer. That would give her position away. Elaine placed her hands over her mouth as a further precaution. A chuckle hit her ears next. Maybe, he thought that she was sleeping.

His bedroom door opened before he closed it behind him. Water dripped down onto the carpet, and a towel soon met the floor too. Despite suspicion still residing in her, she couldn't prevent her cheeks from heating up. She closed her eyes tight and tried to remove the swarm of mental images from her mind.

Another door opened, and a light flicked on. Hesitantly, she opened her eyes. Her hands traveled from her mouth to her eyes, and she peaked in-between her fingers before she quickly covered her eyes. Almost, she had seen too much. Heat beat at her cheeks, but she had to concentrate on how to remove herself from her current predicament. He was in the closet, and his back was turned from the door. Perhaps, she could sneak out. If she didn't try it, she would be caught eventually. He most likely would head downstairs once he was dressed, and he would find her not to be there. Uncovering her eyes, she took a deep, but silent, breath before she exhaled as softly as she could. Edmund didn't seem to notice.

Shifting herself, she crawled out from under the bed. Thankfully, he had carpet. On her feet, she refused to look back in case he wasn't fully dressed yet. She tiptoed across the room and reached the doorknob. As she turned it, she cringed along the way. Fear ate at her, but she opened the door as little as she could before she managed to slip out. Once it was shut, all of her relaxed. Another door closed.

Instantly, her calmness transformed into panic. Steps neared her. She wouldn't make it to the stairs in time. Her head felt like a swivel chair as it glanced between the stairs and door. Trepidation gnawed at her, and her feet were frozen to the spot. His steps halted. Oh no.

Heart pounding and mind racing, she raised her right hand as if she was about to knock. The door opened. Edmund took a surprised step back. "Elaine?" He opened the door more. "I thought that you had fallen asleep." His eyes searched hers as an eyebrow of his raised.

Gradually, she lowered her hand and shook her head. "I had been drinking water when you had called." That was a reasonable excuse ... possibly. Suspicion touched his orbs. Rapidly, she added, "But, I wanted to check on you and see if you were done." She smiled a bit and held her gaze on his, which was becoming harder with each passing second. "And, would you like to watch a movie?"

Suspicion became replaced with slight laughter. "Yes, that would be nice." He leaned against the doorway and crossed his arms. "I did finish resolving that problem at work." Finally, her heart calmed down a little; however, it nearly leaped out of her chest when he rested his right hand on her left shoulder. Leaning down, his lips ghosted over the skin on her ear. A chill crept up her spine. "Did you see anything?" She felt paralyzed. Hesitantly, she turned her head towards him as she took a step back. Edmund stood up fully, and she pictured herself as a mouse caught in a trap.

"I ... I ..."

Lightly, a chuckle parted from him. "You had gasped. I don't think that you had even realized it. I hadn't checked under my bed, but I had heard your gasp from there." He appeared amused rather than mad before hurt traveled into his green hazel orbs. "You still don't trust me, right?"

That time, she couldn't lie. She was too much in the spotlight. Slowly, she nodded. Her eyes averted themselves from him. "Sor ..."

"Don't be. I'm not mad, Elaine. I want you to trust me again, and if you need to explore my room for that, you can." She met his stare shocked. Her lips parted, and he stepped aside from his room. "Go ahead. We can watch a movie afterwards."

"Positive?" She received a nod. Skeptical, she moved past him and into the room. He leaned against the doorway. "Anywhere?" Another nod. Elaine stepped forward again but paused. Her eyes examined his. "Did you move anything from the room before you took your shower?"

"No." She was tempted to narrow her eyes, but his eyes held only truth in them. Elaine diverted her attention from him and turned to the room before she started to explore for anything that might reveal that he had been spying on her.

Once she faced away from him, he sighed internally. Thankfully, he had prepared for such a situation. His binoculars were in a secure place that she wouldn't find, or she shouldn't. If she did, the situation would develop into something that he'd rather avoid. She checked the nightstand first and then the bed. "Anything in the mattress?" Elaine presently was examining it for any tears or sewn-up spots.

"No." She dropped it and fixed his bed for him before she ventured into the closet. Elaine was being far too thorough, but he believed that he had chosen the perfect hiding spot.

## <u>Chapter Thirty Two: Trust</u>

*Ice floated up to the top of the drinks, and a bowl of premade popcorn rested between them. They were a treat to top off an arrangement that had been made.*

Sitting on the floor of the closet, various organizers were lying around her, and the shelves above her were bare. Nothing. Absolutely nothing that could reveal that he had been spying on her. Edmund sat on the edge of his bed, though; he had searched through his organizer with his boxers for her since she had been too embarrassed to do that herself.

"Do you trust me now?" She peered over her right shoulder at him. His legs were crossed, and his chin rested on the palm of his right hand. A slight bit of amusement twinkled in his eyes, which caused a small pout to form on her lips. "Or, are you going to search through my whole home for something? I don't mind if you would like that."

Sighing roughly, she shook her head. "No, it's fine." She picked herself up to her feet and started to put the organizers back for him. As she slid one onto one of the shelves, she paused momentarily. "I didn't want to find anything, but I also did. I guess ..."

"You still have him in the back of your mind." Elaine slid the box back before her hands fell to her sides gradually. Steadily, she faced him. "You're worried that you'll find something about me that'll tear you apart again. You don't want to lose us, but you can't help but constantly question if I'm hiding something dreadful in my home. And, it doesn't help that we're matching colors every time we see each other." His black pajama pants and white shirt proved that further.

Words left her. All she could do was stare for a little bit. She looked over his appearance. Strands of his pitch black hair fell loose from the water trying to hold them back. His white shirt hugged his torso in all the right places while parts of it remained wet due to his skin still drying from his shower, yet his black pajama pants weren't too form fitting. Despite all of that, she met his eyes. His statements struck at her too strongly for her not to.

Those green-hazel eyes ... She couldn't help but get lost in them. Her feet moved across the carpet again before she stood right in front of him. His eyes continued to meet hers. Before he could utter another word, she allowed herself to fall forward. Both of her arms reached out and wrapped around his waist while she buried her head into his chest.

The fall caused him to lie back on his bed, and he embraced her. Her hands tightened on his shirt as she tried to get a better grip on his back. Edmund rolled over onto his left side, and her right arm moved to the front of him. Elaine placed the palm of her hand against his chest and felt his heartbeat through it. Doubt began to fade in her mind. She hadn't found anything; she could relax and toss away that worry. Both their home locations and matching colors merely were odd and surprising, but they were nothing more.

"I'm going to trust you." Her words were soft and gentle but muffled some a little due to his shirt. A smile formed on his lips as fingers pressed lightly into her back. The gesture made her cling all the tighter to him before a smile took over her lips. "But if you somehow know my neighbors, I may get suspicious again." She poked his chest as a playful warning.

"Well, some of them might've been my customers."

Instantly, she peered up to him. A glare set on her face, which earned a chuckle from him. Her hand felt the rumbling of his chest, and it really was a calming sensation. She couldn't hold her scowl for long, and a light laugh escaped from her before she rested her forehead against his chest.

"But if I do recognize your neighbors, I'll let you know. Still, you don't have to worry about that." Edmund sat up and brought her up with him. His left fingers gracefully slid along her jaw before they stopped on her chin and held it lovingly. Her cheeks heated up a bit at the action. "And, I'm sorry that I had troubled you. I won't harm you again."

Searching his eyes, she smiled. Her hands rose to his face and cupped his cheeks. "That's a tall promise to make, Edmund."

A slight smirk graced his lips. "And, do you think that I'm not capable of it." Her own smirk fell upon her lips, and her hands fell to his chest. He continued to hold her chin. "Well?"

"Like I had said, I'm going to trust you." She leaned forward and kissed his lips softly before she pulled back. His eyes stayed on hers. "Let's go watch that movie." Elaine moved off of the bed and grabbed his right hand. He stood up and followed her out of the room. Inwardly, he grinned. His hiding place had worked perfectly, and she was back in his grasp. No unpleasant measure would have to be taken.

When they reached the living room, he parted his hand from hers. "I'll work on the snack and drinks. You can choose the movie." Before he left, however, she grabbed his hand again, giving him pause.

"Thank you." She smiled up to him. "For letting me explore your room." He returned the smile and nodded. Her hand loosened its hold, but she didn't remove it entirely. "Though, I wish that you had told me about your location sooner." Elaine averted her eyes to her right and bit on her lower lip, wondering if she should speak her next words or leave them hidden presently.

Noting her change in mood, he stepped closer to her. "Elaine, what's wrong?" Had he miscalculated her behavior from before? No, otherwise she wouldn't be holding onto his hand.

Slightly, a pout met her lips. She was irritated but not mad. That relieved him a bit. A sigh parted from her, and she stared up to him. "It's just that we live right across from each other, yet you've been driving to my apartment." Elaine rolled her eyes. "It seems silly." Now, she removed her hand from his and walked over to the television before she picked up the nearby remote. "And, we just repainted my whole apartment!" Her hands threw themselves up.

Spinning on her heel, she pointed the remote at him. "If you had told me sooner ..." By a little bit, the remote lowered. "Well ... well ..." She crossed her arms, and heat tickled her cheeks. "Maybe, it's still too soon for that."

Catching onto what she was implying, he felt his fear about her behavior vanish. How truly extraordinary she was. First, she was investigating him. Now, she was indicating that. "Do you want to live together from now on?"

More heat enveloped her cheeks. "We just repainted my apartment, though. Painting it again ... seems ..." She hung her head a bit before she met his eyes. "I want to enjoy the work we did together a little longer, but if we're so close to each other anyway ... It just seems ridiculous if we're so close."

"A month." She raised an eyebrow. "One month. Then, you can move in with me if that what's you would like. Or, I can move in with you. Then, you don't have to worry about repainting your apartment any time soon."

Shaking her head, she folded her hands in front of her along with the remote. "I want to move in with you. Besides," she looked around, "you have more room here. It wouldn't make sense for the both of us to move into a smaller place when you already have this one unless you want to save money, which I don't mind."

"I already have my monthly savings deposits handled, but I appreciate your consideration." He smiled to her, having a hard time holding back his laugh. Tonight was taking a very pleasant turn. "In a month, then. We can go over details of when to paint again and the matter of furniture later this week." She nodded in agreement before she seated herself on the couch and faced away from him.

Turning the television on, she switched to a streaming service, and his account loaded up. She clicked on his profile and began to search through the various movies available. "Can I choose anything?"

"Yes, I'm not too particular about the movies I like." He grabbed a bowl and filled it with popcorn. Elaine glanced back to him briefly. His back was turned to her, and he was preparing a glass for her. There was still water in the water bottle, but she could finish that off in the morning or at another time. Movies required something else than water.

Facing the screen again, she recalled that they had watched the older versions of Roman mythologies movies, so maybe he preferred classics. She scrolled through the various options but didn't find anything that she particularly liked, and he hadn't given her any suggestions. Frustration began to set in when she again didn't discover something that she wanted to watch. "Can you choose?" she asked as he seated himself down on the couch. Edmund placed the popcorn and drinks on the coffee table before he chuckled a little and took the remote from her.

"Did you check all of the genres?" She shook her head. He started to scroll through some of the movies before he found the 1981 version of another movie based on a myth. "Will this one work?"

"I must've missed that one, but yeah. Can you hand me the popcorn please?" He set down the remote and did so before he started the movie. She moved a bit closer to him and placed the bowl between the both of them. Finally, she could relax for the evening.

## Chapter Thirty Three: Sleep

*Legs draped down while arms curled towards the chest. Steady steps traveled upwards, and pale evening light drifted in through the hall window ... how familiar.*

Colors shifted in the background, and noises accompanied them. Edmund did enjoy the movie playing, but he enjoyed something or rather someone more. The bowl of popcorn was barren and sat upon the coffee table while their drinks were mostly finished. Neither of those mattered either.

His left fingers drifted through smooth, dark brown and curly short locks while his right fingers traced over the delicate skin of her hands, which were up against the left side of his chest. Her eyes were closed, and her breathing was steady and peaceful. She was fast asleep and curled up next to him. How delightful.

Credits rolled on the screen. Barely, he registered them before he shut the television off. Carefully, he moved her off of him and put a pillow in his place. She snuggled up to it instantly. It made his heart skip a beat, and to think that she would be moving in with him in a month. He could dispose of his binoculars, then, and he would never have to worry about her finding them. Perfect.

He pushed back a few strands of her hair before he worked on picking up their movie drinks and popcorn bowl. His actions were quiet and mindful. If she woke up, she might decide to return to her apartment even if that was unlikely. Still, he didn't wish to risk that. Having her in his home was extraordinary. It made him grin like a boy when he discovered his first crush. Then again, she was his first crush and now his first girlfriend. Under his plans, their relationship would progress even more.

Finished with cleanup, he headed back towards her. As if she was a porcelain doll, he picked her up with extreme delicacy. A slight moan of discomfort left her before she readjusted herself in his arms. Her arms and hands curled up by her chest, and her head rested against his chest. Light puffs of air occasionally would hit his shirt as she breathed softly.

Being careful, he made his way upstairs and used the pale evening light to guide him up the steps. The less artificial lights that he had to use were for the better. Soon enough, he entered his room and placed her on his bed. She rolled onto her right side and let out a content sigh, which caused him to smirk. After he draped the sheets over her, he left his room and proceeded with his night routine.

Only when he completed it did he return to his bedroom. She remained asleep, though; she now was on her stomach. Her arms were wrapped around one of his pillows, and the sheets only covered half of her. Happy to find her so comfortable, he closed his bedroom door and made his way to the other side of the bed.

Once on the bed, he positioned himself on his left side and moved closer to her. He draped his right arm over her waist before he pulled her over to him. Her arms left the pillow, and her hands found his shirt. Elaine curled her fingers around the fabric and cuddled right into him. An almost inaudible sigh escaped her, and her lips remained partially parted afterwards.

Leaning his head down, he placed a kiss upon the top of her head, and she nuzzled her face into him more. Pleased with her reaction, he rested his head upon his other pillow and closed his eyes. Hopefully, he would wake up first in the morning so that he could spoil her with breakfast in bed.

~ ~ ~ ~ ~ ~ ~ ~ ~ ~ ~

A hand reached out. Fingers curled up in the sheets, but they didn't want to find fabric. They wanted warmth. A frown settled upon lips, and brows furrowed. Steadily, Edmund opened his eyes. He squinted as they adjusted to the morning light entering through the two windows in his room. Elaine wasn't there. His eyes widened, and he was about to spring up from bed before he heard noise behind him.

Rolling over, he peered up. A wonderful smile was sent his way. "Good morning." She picked the coffee mug back up and held it out to him. "I made you some coffee." Heat entered her cheeks by a little bit. "Thank you for letting me stay the night."

Sitting up, he returned her smile. "You're welcome. I didn't want to wake you." He accepted the coffee and took a careful sip. The entire time, she watched him, and he tried not to laugh. Once he swallowed, he reassured her. "It tastes delicious."

Across her lips, another smile formed. Her right hand rubbed her left arm. "Well, I might've asked Frank from Bread and Books what you've ordered there," she muttered quietly and didn't make eye contact as he was about to take another sip.

Pausing, he set the coffee aside and held out his right hand to her. Trustingly, she placed her hand in his. His fingers intertwined with hers before he pulled her towards him. Edmund's left fingers settled under her chin and held it affectionately before he closed the distance between their lips. The kiss was loving and gentle. It was appreciative too.

When he moved back, he smiled up to her as his eyes focused on hers. "You're truly my treasure." Heat danced upon her cheeks violently, but she didn't break their locked-together gazes. He gave her one more kiss, shorter and even more delicate, before he let her go. His hands retrieved the coffee once more. "Did you make some for yourself?"

At that, she brushed aside her embarrassment and nodded. "I wanted to try what you liked so much." She broke eye contact with him. "I like cappuccinos more." After another sip of his coffee, he placed it down and stood up from the bed before he kissed her on the left cheek. Elaine jumped a little before she smiled.

"I know. You order one every time you go into Bread and Books." He walked past her while she tried to calm down her quickening heart. He really knew how to strike the right strings.

"Are you going to eat breakfast?" He stopped. "I made some for both of us." Edmund stared back to her. "I hope that you don't mind that I used your kitchen or your food." She folded her hands in front of her and wrung her hands together. Elaine shifted her eyes to the carpet.

"And, here I thought that I was going to make us breakfast in bed." He chuckled and leaned against the frame of his closet. She met his eyes again, and her eyes widened slightly before she smiled. "I'll change and meet you downstairs unless you'd rather watch from under my bed again?"

Immediately, heat scorched her cheeks. "I had covered my eyes!" she exclaimed, completely embarrassed. "I hadn't seen anything! I swear!"

Laughing, he shook his head in amusement. "I know. I know. Under the bed isn't the best viewing point."

Heat reached her ears. "Edmund!" He chuckled and entered his closet, closing the door behind him. Her fists clenched a little before she hurried out of the bedroom in an embarrassed huff. When she entered the kitchen, she moved the eggs, potatoes and peppers off of the hot burner and onto a cool one. She was tempted to eat without him due to his comments, but she waited in the end. They were his ingredients after all.

Catching movement, she averted her eyes to the stairs. Edmund stood at the bottom of them. Black pants and a white button-up covered his form. His hair was still in its bed-head state, but it looked stunning regardless. The loose strands only highlighted his angled face more, but his matching colors stood out to her too. "I'm going to be changing later." She gave him an amused smirk.

"Well, you know what I'm wearing now. You can match me." She quirked a brow before she retrieved some plates from where she had seen them earlier in the morning. He walked into the kitchen, set down his coffee and scanned over the breakfast dish. "It smells amazing, Elaine. I'll get you a drink."

"Thank you." She placed the plates on the counter. "But in regards to clothes ... this is my only white blouse." Elaine grabbed a large spoon to dish out the meal. "I don't think that we'll be matching later."

While he worked on a new cup of coffee for her, he poured the kind she made into a measuring cup and covered it with a plate for later. "I should change my shirt, then. What will you be wearing later?" He started the coffee machine and leaned against the counter.

Thinking over the question, she furrowed her brows and set the spoon in the now empty pan. "Hmm, black and red?" She met his eyes for approval, and he nodded. "Then, will I be seeing you later on today?"

"Well, I don't have work today. You could change and shower if you would like before you come back here. We can watch movies and relax for the day."

That was a hard to pass up offer. Liking it, she nodded. "Do you want me to bring anything over?"

Shaking his head, he headed over to the kitchen counter and pulled out a stool for her. "No, we'll have everything here. For now, let's eat. And, your coffee should be done soon." She smiled to him before she grabbed the plates, some forks and rested them on the counter. Elaine took her seat and enjoyed her meal with him.

## Chapter Thirty Four: Watch

*Splashes of water sent delicate droplets into the air before they rained back down into the pool below. Arms leaned on wood while soft fabric blew in the slight breeze.*

Cars passed by, all in different colors. She didn't have time to observe further details as she drove along on the opposite side of the road. Her left hand held the wheel while her right fingers tapped her leg gently. A light tune played in the background. Elaine wasn't familiar with the song, but it had a nice, slow beat to it that fit with the soothing weather outside.

A few gentle clouds rolled by across the blue expanse, and the sun broke through their passing, but it wasn't scorching hot. She made a right turn and drove down the small, dirt road towards the parking lot. Tree branches shaded her car and gave off the effect that she was entering a hidden grove.

Her mind drifted from the road and to the fact that she was going to be moving in with Edmund in a few days. All of her apartment already had been repainted again. She had paid for the paint, but only because she had reached the register first and had left Edmund back with the paint cans. The cash register had given her a funny look since she had been out of breath from the swift run, but it had been worth it in the end. Or, that had been the outcome that she had been hoping for.

Elaine still couldn't quite figure it out, but he somehow had managed to replace her credit card with his while they had been retrieving the paint cans. In the end, he had ended up paying for all of it. A light laugh left her lips, and she shook her head before she made a left turn into the parking lot.

Turning the key and removing it from the ignition, she dropped her keys into her black leather purse. By a little bit, she leaned back against her seat. There was still her furniture and boxes to move into his apartment. Admittedly, though, the only actual furniture item was her nightstand since Edmund only had one in his room. All of her other furniture had been sold off. She hadn't minded since those pieces at one point had belonged also to her ex.

After a light sigh left her, she exited and pushed the lock button on the inner side of the driver's door before she shut the door. She shifted a bit in her black pumps and smoothed out the skirt of her short, dark blue dress, which had a black belt around the waist. When she was finished, she adjusted her purse on her right shoulder and headed down a dirt footpath.

She was at a new park, but she had examined some pictures online beforehand of it. There were several dirt paths throughout the area, and she could see some of them at the moment. One of them supposedly led to a quaint bridge over a stream, so she listened for the sound of water. Presently, she couldn't hear anything like water.

Chirps of birds and the rustle of leaves were the two noises that met her ears. She walked further into the park and made a right turn down a narrow path. It seemed like it didn't receive too much use, and she couldn't see anyone else down it; however, a peaceful atmosphere surrounded it.

Brushing a few strands of hair behind her left ear, she viewed the scenery of the various trees and hummed quietly to herself. She would've liked to walk the path with Edmund, but she also enjoyed it by herself. Besides, he was at work and finishing up paperwork for the week.

When she had learned of that, she had offered just to drop in and bring him a cup of coffee so that he could take a break in-between his workload, but he had reassured her that he would be fine. She did wonder why he didn't complete the papers at his apartment since she could stay with him that way until she realized that would probably be distracting. If she had editing to work on, she most likely wouldn't get it finished with Edmund right next to her.

Pausing, her eyes widened a bit before she hung her head down. Once she moved in with him, that was going to be a problem. Then again, he did wake up before her often and head off to work. She could finish up her job's duties while he was away. Her feet moved again. Things would be fine; she needed to stop worrying about such details even though there were many.

Several twigs snapped under her next step. Briefly, she glanced down to them before she looked ahead of her again. No matter how hard she tried to focus on the scenery, her mind brought up those details again. They would be sharing the same bedroom and bathroom. Beforehand, she had slept in the same bed as him so that wasn't too huge of a concern for her.

It was the closet that worried her. He accidentally had viewed her lace undergarments before, but he still didn't know exactly what she was wearing underneath her clothes. Since they would be living together, he reasonably and accidentally could sight what she would be wearing when she brought her clothes into the bathroom. There was also the issue of the laundry. Would they do theirs separately? If not ...

That thought, she couldn't finish. She rubbed the bridge of her nose, but she was tempted to rub her eyelids to remove any images from her mind; however, that action would've wasted the time she had spent on putting on her eye shadow and mascara. Her lips, painted in a matte burgundy, pursed in irritation.

Both of those problems didn't even reach, though, to the embarrassing possibilities of the bathroom. There was a lock on the door, and she doubted that he would peek at her. Still, that didn't ease her mind too much. A slight groan left her. She had been considering such things over the past month, but the thoughts only were growing stronger as the date to move in with him became closer.

Removing her fingers from her nose, she raised her head a little in awareness. Water. She heard water. A smile graced her lips. That would be sure to calm her thoughts, or she hoped for that to be the case. By some, her pace quickened, though; she remained careful of her steps due to her heels.

Making another turn, she heard the sound of water increase in volume. She moved further down the path and just could make out a bridge in the distance. A strong rustle of leaves to her left, though, halted her steps. Elaine stared over that way, and her eyes scanned over the area.

No person or animal greeted her eyes. Then again, the trees that way were dense, and the undergrowth was thick. Hopefully, that had been only a tiny animal. Just in case, she reached into her bag for her phone and pulled up her contacts. 911 was at the top and ready to contact. After she locked her phone, she made certain that her utility tool was in an easy to grab place.

Once reassured that it was, she continued on her way again, though, even more quickly than before. Her feet soon reached the wooden bridge. A steady stream carried on below it, and some fish swam underneath the surface. She stepped farther on and up it until she was at the center. Elaine leaned forward on the wood railing after she had checked its stability and had been satisfied by it.

Slightly, she could spot her reflection in the water. A fish swimming by broke it, and water droplets lifted into the air before they dropped back down. She rested her chin on the palm of her right hand as a light breeze came through and cooled her off from her walk more. The trip had been worth it, though; she did keep a listen out for anything in the woods around her.

While she continued to observe the water peacefully, Edmund avoided anything that might give him away again. Luckily, he had hidden himself before she had seen him. Otherwise, he might've not been able to pull off a reasonable explanation. Doing paperwork in the woods close to where she was in the park didn't seem like it would go over well.

He had finished his paperwork, though. It had been quicker than he had expected, so he had decided to travel to the park that she had told him that she would be going to. Edmund could've called her and asked her to wait, but he couldn't deny that he liked watching her from afar at times. Now was one of them.

Undeniably, she was picture perfect. A fragile smile graced her burgundy-painted lips, and her dark brown eyes sparkled next to the shimmering water. Her dress hugged her form in all of the right places, and her hair was brushed to an ideal shine. To make matters all the better, she was his. Every last fiber of her being was his, and that caused his heart to soar and his lips to form a pleased smirk.

His treasure changed positions to the rocks by the bridge. She crouched on a few and glided her fingers across the water. A fish swam up to her fingertips before it quickly went off in fright. From her mouth, a light, heartbeat-skipping laugh emitted. Almost, his eyes didn't notice her next action since he was so distracted by the delightful sound.

Beginning to stand fully, she miscalculated her balance, and her left heel slipped out from under her. She landed on her bottom and slid into the stream. A loud splash erupted throughout the area, and he was tempted to run out and help her, but he remained hidden. He could aid her in another way. Silently and swiftly, he headed back to his car. Elaine would need something to dry off with. Edmund didn't know if he had anything that would be suitable for drying her off, but he probably would give her his suit jacket.

Passing by many trees, the sound of the water grew faint before it disappeared. He couldn't hear her anymore, but he didn't slow down. His phone ringing, though, gave him pause. Edmund stared to the number and held back a chuckle. Elaine.

## Chapter Thirty Five: Dry

*His jacket was wrapped around her waist. Shivers ran up her legs, and her hands tightened the jacket before they parted ways.*

"I'm already in the parking lot." He leaned against the front of his car while a light chuckle past his lips. Her slight gasp on the other side of the phone was entertaining. "I finished early, so I decided to stop by. Do you want me to head in there or wait here?"

"Wait there. I should be there shortly ..." He heard her grumbling about something, but he couldn't make it out. "Sorry, my shoes are soaked, and water got under the padding." She released a rough sigh. "I hate wet shoes."

A slight smile hit his lips. "Will you be alright driving home?" He wouldn't mind taking her home. It would be better if they did only have one car. Besides, she worked from home. She didn't have to go out often, and if she did, he could take her.

"Yeah, I'll just take the heels off." He raised a brow even though she couldn't see it, but his silence was questioning. "I'll be fine. I've done it before."

Before he could respond again, he heard footsteps approaching and looked up. From the waist down, she was drenched. He hung up on the phone and quickly pushed himself off of his car. She hung up her phone too and put it into her purse. A hopeful look was in her eyes. "Please tell me that you found a towel or something since I last had asked you."

"Unfortunately, I didn't, but I do have tissues. Some of that water at least can be wiped off of you." Her head hung before she met him at his car. She set down her purse on the hood and glanced down to her feet. It was clear that she wanted her shoes off.

Edmund opened the passenger door and signaled for her to take a seat. "You sure? I'll get the seat wet."

"I don't care about that, Elaine. Take a seat. Those heels probably are like little lakes, right?" A smile graced her lips, and she chuckled softly before she nodded her head. He moved aside some more and allowed her to seat herself down. Edmund was about to walk over to the driver's side to retrieve the box of tissues, but Elaine reached behind her and grabbed them before she held them out to him.

"Here." He stopped in his steps. "There's no need for you to walk around. You could've asked me." Edmund took them from her as she smiled and laughed a little. "Just because I'm soaked in water doesn't mean that I'm incapable of helping out."

Returning her smile, he pulled out a couple of tissues and crouched in front of her. "Yet, you're still wanting me to wipe your legs and feet off?" A light chuckle escaped him. His eyes peered up to her briefly, and she was averting her eyes in slight embarrassment while a pout formed on her lips. Edmund smirked before he returned to drying off her right leg.

"Well ..." She crossed her arms and huffed. "It'd be hard to wipe off my calves and feet without my dress sliding up awkwardly." Edmund forced himself not to think of that mental image, but it was incredibly difficult. Elaine, however, noted his furrowed brows and gave him a tiny glare. "I shouldn't have said anything."

At that, he laughed again and finished drying off her right leg. "That probably would've been best." He started to dry off her left foot. Remaining embarrassed, she kicked her foot up slightly and just missed his chin. It wouldn't have been a hard impact if it had hit him.

Quirking a brow, he grabbed her foot again and held it tightly. He raised it a little, and she tried to pull it back. "Edmund, what are ..." His lips touched the top of her foot, and heat rapidly invaded her cheeks. Once his lips parted from her skin, he stared up to her amused. She couldn't break her eyes away from his despite her warming cheeks.

"Should I continue?" His hands slid up her leg slightly, and a chill coursed through her body before a warmth started to form. He dried off her calf during her silence. Once done, his lips drew closer, and she was at a loss for words. She'd be lying if she said that she wanted him to stop. Since she didn't protest, he pressed delicate kisses upon her skin.

Her hands dug into the seat a little as she supported herself up, and her cheeks were burning. They had shared many intimate kisses in the past, but the slow, methodical kisses were like little buds of flame biting into her skin. They didn't produce a continuous soothing flame. Rather, they were like a light flickering on and off but brighter each time that it came on.

Stopping at her knee, she felt herself hold a breath. Her dress when sitting stopped a little above her knees. Would he continue up her whole thigh? Elaine's heartbeat picked up. "Did you want me to dry off your thigh since part of it is covered by your dress?" She parted her lips to speak, but words failed her. Instead, she closed them and swallowed as unnoticeably as she could. "I didn't dry off the other one."

Still, she couldn't speak. A smirk graced his lips. Her fingers gripped the seat more. "Maybe, I should've given you kisses here sooner." He chuckled. His fingers rested on the skin just above her knee. She curled her toes a little to try and calm her body down, but it barely helped.

The sound of a car met both of their ears. Edmund diverted his eyes behind him as the sound became louder. He felt Elaine's leg relax under his touch. Almost, he chuckled. He turned his attention back to her, and he easily could tell that she was disappointed.

Picking up the tissues, he deposited them in a nearby trashcan before he returned to her. The car pulled up into the parking lot, but Edmund didn't focus on it for that long. When he looked back to Elaine, she already was getting ready to slip her shoes back on. "Those are still wet, and I just dried off your feet," he pointed out before she nodded her head briefly.

"I know ... Thank you." Her cheeks remained quite warm. "But, I don't want to walk barefoot to my car. I can dry them off again on the carpet in my car."

"Then, what was the purpose of me drying them off?" An amused gleam entered his eyes as he leaned on his car door. "Or, are you asking me to dry them off again?" Instantly, she froze, and a series of stutters left her.

In the background, there was the sound of children along with a man and a woman. It sounded like there were four kids along with the two adults. When she glanced back, she noted the family taking a different trail into the woods. She focused her attention back to the front of her and noted that Edmund was watching the family too. Her cheeks still getting tickled by warmth, she asked, "Edmund, do you want children?"

"No." His answer held no hesitation, and it shocked her to a slight degree. As she was about to question him again, he responded, "When I get old enough to retire, I'll sell the business." Edmund met her gaze, and his eyes softened a bit. "I have you. That's enough for me." She couldn't help but smile at that answer. "Did you want children?"

Diverting her eyes from him a little, she bit the inside of her lower lip a little. "I'm not sure." She locked her eyes with his again and smiled. "But, I want to support your decision." Goodness, she was wonderful. Not being able to help himself, he reached forward and scooped her up into his arms. A surprised yelp escaped her before her hands clutched to his jacket and dark blue button-up. "Edmund, I can walk."

"I know, but I want to carry you." He quirked a brow. "Don't you want to support my decision?" Her brows furrowed before she chuckled and shook her head. "Then, I'll take you to your car." Edmund grabbed her purse along the way, and she grabbed it from him so that she could fish out her keys.

After she unlocked the driver's side, Edmund managed to open the door, and he placed her down onto her seat. "I'll go get your heels."

"Don't bother. Just throw them out. They're ruined."

"And, what about when you reach your apartment? Are you going to walk barefoot across the asphalt?" A look of embarrassment crossed her countenance. "Oh." He smirked. "Are you wanting me to carry you again?" Her eyes diverted away from him.

"Yes," she mumbled almost inaudibly. She set her purse down on the passenger seat before she glanced back to him shyly. "Since you're done with work, I thought ..."

"I'm fine with that." He leaned down and kissed her left temple. Before he closed the door for her, he unbuttoned his jacket and wrapped it around her waist. She tried to ignore his fingers brushing across her, but her toes curled into the carpet. Once he was happy with the jacket's arrangement, he mentioned, "I'll see you soon." Edmund closed the door and headed back to his car.

Before she started her car, shivers ran through her legs and up her torso. The memory of his lips upon her leg really knew how to distract her. She tightened the jacket around her and forced herself to focus on driving home.

## Chapter Thirty Six: Switch

*Blankets were laid out across the floor, and two pillows joined them. Food and cards accompanied the soft items, and pale, artificial light shone onto them from the kitchen.*

Tying the belt around her bathrobe, she sealed off her thulian pink cotton nightgown. Only the pink neckline of it could be seen. Elaine pushed several wet strands of hair behind her ears and looked over her attire. She couldn't wear her pink nightgown every night. It would wear out with time with all of the washing that would come from that. Eventually, she would have to wear her olive green or blue satin one around Edmund. Or, she could buy new ones. Already, she had to purchase new blue heels since her other ones had been ruined by the water.

Maybe, a minor shopping trip was in order. Then again, she had worn both nightgowns around her ex ... Yes, a shopping trip definitely was in order. She wouldn't change her whole wardrobe since she didn't want to blow an entire paycheck or two on clothes and shoes, but she could at least switch out her nightgowns, including her pink one.

Opening the bathroom door, she shut off the light and stared at her room for a moment. Once again, the walls were white, but the room itself was empty. Tomorrow, she would be moving in with Edmund. Perhaps, he would carry her into their now shared home like he had brought her into her apartment a few days ago. Her cheeks heated up slightly at the thought.

A pop of a bottle caught her attention. She glanced down the hallway and noted only the kitchen light on. Elaine smiled. So, he had brought wine over. Most likely, it was another brand of pinot noir since that was his favorite type of wine.

When she entered the kitchen, Edmund was pouring the beverage into two wine glasses, which he definitely had brought over with him. Most of her glassware except for a few mugs had been sold or moved to Edmund's. The same went for her dishware.

He smiled over to her and held out a glass. Her eyes drifted to the bottle: another pinot noir. She never had tried the brand before. Elaine swirled her glass, and an aroma of black cherries, marion berries, ripe plum and a bit of anise came through. Edmund sipped at his wine, and a satisfied smile overtook his lips. A chuckle couldn't help but escape her.

"What is it?" he asked, lowering his glass.

"It's cute how you enjoy your wine so much." She leaned forward a bit and rested her chin on the palm of her right hand as she set her glass down. By a smidgen, she noticed him grow embarrassed. "And on top of that, you forgot to match." Elaine pointed her other index finger at his clothing: a black t-shirt and pants.

Briefly, he glanced down at his attire before over to her. "Well, I don't have that pink color unfortunately, but I'll go buy a shirt soon." He took another sip of his wine while a frown adorned his lips.

"It's fine. I'm going to replace my nightgowns anyway." Edmund made no comment and took another sip of his wine. Inwardly, though, he was quite pleased by that news. Pushing herself up, she took a sip of her wine. As the taste lingered in her mouth more, a woody, cacao and vanilla flavor tickled her tongue. She hummed in approval, and she noted that Edmund glanced over to her out of the corners of his eyes. At that, she couldn't help but laugh again. "Are you that embarrassed by me calling you cute?"

Quietly, a sigh escaped him, and he placed down his glass. "I was caught off guard is all." A smirk slowly formed on his lips, and he peered over to her. "But, I think that I've caused you to be embarrassed more times." He moved around the counter, and she watched him carefully.

After he took the wine glass out of her hand and set it aside, his left fingers slipped under her chin and lifted it slightly. Warmth began to invade her cheeks. "Like right now." His lips moved in closer. "You just freeze up for me. That's truly cute."

Gently, he placed a kiss upon her lips, and she returned the soft sign of affection. Her hands rested against his chest before they slid up and around his neck. His fingers continued to stay under her chin while his other hand slipped around her waist. Carefully, he pressed her up against him.

Needing air a few minutes after, she pulled back as her chest rose and fell with a slightly quicker rate than before. Her arms remained wrapped around him, and her head soon leaned against his chest. From that position, she noted her living room. It wasn't empty, but the blankets and her pillow that had to be moved over to Edmund's were all laid out on the floor. Another pillow was among the comfortable setup, which she assumed to be from Edmund's place, soon to be their place.

In the center of it all, there was a plate with cheese, crackers and fruit. She smiled before she buried her head into his chest. "You like it?" Elaine nodded her head to his question before she looked up to him and pressed a kiss to his right cheek.

"But, how did you bring it in without..."

"Without you noticing?" She nodded. Edmund slipped away from her before he walked over to the wine bottle and his glass. Picking them up, he headed over to the blankets. After he set them down, he seated himself. "While you had been in the shower."

"You had left my door unlocked?" she questioned, pretty shocked if that was the case. She grabbed her glass and joined him on the blankets.

"No, you had left your keys on the kitchen counter. I had locked the door while I had gone to my apartment and brought the items over." He pointed over to the keys atop her counter once more. "You didn't have anything in your fridge since we had eaten out today."

"Right ..." She chuckled. "We probably should have left a few things in there." He shook his head before he took a sip of his wine. Elaine's attention, though, focused on something else: a deck of cards. "What game are we playing?"

"You're welcome to choose." He plucked a grape off of the plate and popped it into his mouth. After he swallowed, he mentioned, "Or, we could try and build a house of cards."

"... That might be ... I'm terrible at those. And on blankets?"

"It gives us a challenge." She raised a brow at him and placed down her glass. He chuckled at her expression and removed the cards from the holder. "If it's any consolation, I've never been able to build one either." Doubt met him, and he laughed. "It's true. I can never position them right."

"Then, why suggest it? Because, it gives us a challenge?" She crossed her arms, her tone mocking.

"Exactly." He split the deck into two and handed her one half. "We can race to see who builds the first level successfully. If we both finish at the same time, we move onto the second level."

"Is this why you brought the wine and food out?" She smoothed the blanket out as much as she could before they started. "So that you get an edge up?" Elaine stared to him out of the corners of her eyes.

"I would never play like that, Elaine." He placed some cheese on a cracker and ate it just to prove her wrong. Once he swallowed, he held his left hand out to the meal. "It's simply dinner. Please help yourself."

Narrowing her eyes at him, she ate a grape before she got her cards ready. "Let's start." She received a nod from him, and they swiftly began. As the competition carried on, Edmund did prove to be quite awful at card house building. Several times, she kept being ahead of him before she would make a mistake and have to start over. His seemed to be falling over constantly.

An hour passed, and Elaine took another sip of her wine. She was on her second glass by that point, and her cheeks felt a little flushed; however, she was close to finishing the first level. Elaine concentrated heavily on the final card. Just as she was about to place it, Edmund reached for a grape. His slight movement caused a tiny breeze to knock over a card. Before she could even place the final card, her first level collapsed.

"You did that on purpose!" she yelled, completely frustrated. Her eyes turned sharply to him as a pout formed on her lips. Her shout did sound somewhat childish, like someone had stolen a doll from her when she had been a child.

"I was hungry." He popped the grape into his mouth, and she glared at him, but it soon became playful. Edmund noted her expression, but he made no motion to stop what she was planning. Her eyes shifted to the few cards standing up by him. Rapidly, she leaned towards them and knocked them over.

"There, now we're even!" She leaned back and crossed her arms triumphantly.

"Even?" He took a sip of his wine and finished off his second glass. "Hardly." She diverted her eyes to him curiously, only to soon find herself being tugged towards him. A surprised cry left her. Elaine landed on his lap and felt heat rush to her cheeks. Her eyes met his. "We still have more rounds to go."

## Chapter Thirty Seven: Attain

*Locks clicked, one sealing and another opening. Things were forever moved, and smiles and smirks ruled the morning hours.*

A clicking sound resonated throughout the apartment, which caused Elaine to stir in her sleep. From her lips, a light moan escaped, and she rolled more into the blankets. Her head moved off of the pillow and onto the other blanket. Due to the change of surface, she steadily opened her eyes before she groaned at the light coming in. Soon enough, a shadow blocked her from it.

Looking up, she spotted Edmund crouching in front of her. "Good morning, Elaine." He reached forward and brushed back some locks of her hair. His fingers twirled a few strands between them before he dropped them. "Do you feel alright?"

She leaned into his touch and tugged on his hand when he started pull away. A chuckle emitted from him before he took a seat next to her. Elaine moved her head onto his lap and mumbled out, "I'm fine. I only had two glasses." Her right index finger poked him lightly in the side. "You finished the bottle." Now, all of her right fingers moved to his side before they played with the fabric of his black jacket ... Jacket? He wasn't wearing one last night.

Lifting her head up, she noted that he was in his day clothes. She furrowed her brows and sat up fully, much to Edmund's hidden disappointment. "When did you change?" A yawn past her lips, and she covered her mouth before she blinked some sleep out of her eyes.

"While you were sleeping. I woke up early," a small smirk touched his lips, "as usual." A pout formed on hers, and she crossed her arms, letting the blanket slip down her form more.

"I had woken up before you when I had spent that first night at your apartment." He was about to speak, but she beat him to it. "But, you have woken first the rest of the times when either of us have stayed over at the other's." She rolled her eyes. "Maybe, I'll get lucky tomorrow morning and be able to make you a surprise breakfast."

"Dinner might be better," he joked, and she threw the nearby pillow at him afterwards. Of course, he caught the flying object, causing her to roll her eyes again. That was when she noticed something else peculiar. All of her things were gone, except the blankets, pillows and one of her outfits.

"I had moved everything while you had been asleep too." She stared to him. "And, I had locked the door after me. I would never leave you so vulnerable to others." Her lips parted, but he shook his head. "I wanted to, and I have to head out to work here soon." A frown appeared on his lips, and a rough sigh parted from his mouth.

"It isn't that seller from before, is it?"

Edmund shook his head. "No. I'd never do business with him again after those frames. I have to have a word with the security at one of my stores after I check video footage. Someone might've stolen several hundred dollars worth of crystal beads." She raised a brow at how that could've gone unnoticed. "I don't know how the guard missed that footage, but a worker called me this morning and said that two whole rows of crystal beads were missing and none had been sold the previous day."

"Wouldn't that have been noticeable, though, if someone was trying to leave the store with them?"

"Not if they had a purse or bag of some sort that didn't look too suspicious. Two rows of beads could easily fit in there, and those particular beads are twenty dollars per string, and there are ten strings per row." He rubbed his temples. "I apologize that I have to leave you so soon in the morning, but I'll drop you off at our apartment before I head out. There is some breakfast already prepared for you there."

Softly, she emitted a sigh of her own before she smiled to him. She reached up and held onto his hands, rubbing her thumbs over the tops of them. "Don't apologize. You didn't know that would happen." Her brow furrowed, though. "But, how long had I been asleep for?"

At that, he chuckled loudly. "Several hours. It's eleven now." Her eyes widened before a little bit of heat touched her cheeks. She rarely ever slept in that late. Maybe, the wine had affected her more than she had thought. A kiss to her forehead drew her attention back to him. "Don't worry, Elaine. We did stay up late." Briefly, his eyes shifted to her neck and collarbone.

Heat burst into her cheeks when she followed his eyes and noted the bruises forming there. She retracted her hands from his and adjusted her bathrobe collar. Another laugh hit her ears. "You left one on me too." Elaine broke eye contact with him and averted her eyes to his covered neck. About to reach her hands up, he caught them. "I have work remember." By a little bit, a frown greeted her lips. "You can check when I get back. Don't you have your own work to do?"

"You have to drive me there first," she argued back, her frown being replaced by a small smirk.

Amusement filled his green-hazel orbs before he stood to his feet and lifted her up with him. "I suppose so." He retrieved the blankets and pillows while she looked to her stack of clothes. Elaine decided to pick them up but not change into them. She could do that later when Edmund wasn't a few feet from her. Besides, she wanted to relax in her pajamas a little bit more. After she put on her slippers, she looked to him. "Ready?" She nodded and followed him out.

Once the door was locked, they headed to her car, not bothering to leave the key since the locks would be switched. He set the items in the back after he had opened the passenger door for her. "I can drive my own car, Edmund," she teased, but she got into the passenger side regardless. The trunk slammed, and he seated himself on the driver's side soon after.

"I know, but you're in slippers." She was about to argue, but he shook his head. "I'm not having you drive barefoot when I easily can prevent that."

"You didn't leave me any shoes but my slippers." Her left index finger rose accusingly as she raised a brow at him. Edmund shrugged his shoulders, but a smile was clear on his face. "I hope that I wake up before you tomorrow," she grumbled to which she earned a chuckle from him.

Arriving at the apartment, she watched him pull right next to his car. A smile formed on her lips. "Want to move any closer?" she joked as she diverted her eyes to him. He didn't answer immediately. Rather, he unbuckled his seatbelt and leaned over to her. His lips met hers in a brief kiss.

Moving back, he whispered against her lips, "You already know that answer." Her cheeks warmed up significantly, and she simply watched him leave the car and close the door behind him. She attempted to remove his words from her head as she left her car too, and her mind shifted to her attire. Maybe, she should've changed. There was still the guard on the first floor, and Gerald didn't work late morning shifts.

Elaine tried to remember which guard was on duty, and she hoped that it was the female guard she had seen there before. That would make her pajamas a little less awkward to be walking around in. Maybe, it would've been better if she had switched clothes. The trunk closing caught her attention, and he signaled to her for her to follow.

Stepping up beside him, she entered the building. To her left, she saw the female guard, much to her relief. "Good morning, Mr. Fex and Ms. Margarit." She smiled to both of them, and it was out of genuine niceness, which was refreshing to see; though, the woman did remain a little bit intimidating, but that was part of her job. The woman had to be at least 5'8, and her muscles flexed a little under her blouse, but she wore bright pink bows in her honey blonde hair, which gave her a softer look too.

"Good morning, Kate," Edmund greeted, and Elaine followed with her own greeting. Kate watched for a few seconds before she shifted her light blue eyes down to her desk and carried on with her other work.

Entering the elevator, Edmund pressed the third floor button. It wasn't long before they were there; however, when the doors opened, her feet were swept off of the ground. Instantly, her hands clung to him so that she wouldn't fall. Luckily, her clothes fell onto her midsection and balanced there. "Why ..."

"It's the day that you're officially moving in. Of course, I should carry you."

Some heat hit her cheeks. Just like when she had been soaked from the stream, he was carrying her again. Her secret wish had been granted, though; her mind traveled to another thought. More heat met her skin. "You're making it sound like we just got married."

Pausing, he glanced down to her and quirked a brow, but he didn't say anything. Instead, he looked forward again and continued towards his apartment door. His silence only made her heart increase its beats, and she couldn't find it in herself to break it. She did desire to marry him, but it only had been around two months of knowing him. That seemed awfully fast, yet her heart was about ready to race off in joy at the implication of his silence and quirked brow.

Keys jangling hit her ears, and a lock clicking sounded afterwards. The door opened and revealed her new home. Edmund set her on her feet and placed the blankets and pillows on the couch before he faced her again and smiled while inwardly smirking. "Welcome home, love."

## Chapter Thirty Eight: Live

*Across the street, the door was locked, and the space empty.
One home was gone, and the next was up: what a quick move.*

Sipping at a cup of coffee, Elaine moved the mug to her lips
and took a sip or at least tried to. When no coffee touched her lips
or tongue, she pulled the mug back and noticed that there was none
left. She turned a little on the stool towards the coffee maker, and
the pot was empty too. A slight sigh left her. Her eyes glanced to her
laptop. Almost, she was finished with her editing.

After she set down her mug, she made the last few edits
before she saved her work, sent it off to her employer and closed
the laptop. Once she stretched her arms and legs, she hopped off of
the stool, put her coffee mug in the sink and headed upstairs for a
shower since she hadn't taken one the previous night.

Currently, her bathrobe and nightgown were still on, and she
wondered if she just should change back into them after her shower.
It was early afternoon already. Then again, she wanted to be dressed
nice when Edmund arrived. Her cheeks heated a little at the thought
as his nickname tickled her ears' memory again. *Love.* He hadn't
called her that before. Edmund had nicknamed her his treasure
before, but love stuck with her more. The name was simpler, yet felt
more impactful.

Entering the ... their bedroom ... The thought was still so new
to her, and the words in her head seemed like loud booms. She
rested her face in her right hand, embarrassed by how she was
acting. At least, Edmund wasn't there to tease her about it or cause
her thoughts to become worse. Her mind traveled back to
Edmund's possible implication of marriage. If that happened, the
present would be her entire life. Elaine couldn't hold back the tiny,
shy smile that graced her lips.

She removed her hand from her face and reminded herself to
calm herself a little. Otherwise, her mind rapidly would spiral down
a whirlpool of thoughts about the future with him. That wasn't a bad
thing, but it would keep her from getting her shower.

As she stepped across the beige carpet, she noted her alarm clock and bouquet of lavender roses placed on her nightstand, which was on the other side from Edmund's nightstand. The flowers looked odd among the room's more natural tones of beige and grey; however, they also added a softer touch. They gave the room a bit of a feel of her old one when it had been painted lavender.  He had been sweet to put them in such plain site. Then again, he had given her them.

Drawing her attention away from the flowers, she walked into the closet after she flipped on the light switch. Her boxes of clothes remained closed and rested on the floor next to empty racks, drawers and shelves. He even had cleared space for her already. She shook her head in disbelief. How had she been so lucky to meet him? What a cliché thought but she honestly didn't know. If he never had given her his number, she probably never would have spoken to him. Most likely, she would be in her apartment and living a shell of what her life could be.

Opening the boxes, she took out the clothes and undergarments she wanted for the moment before she closed them back up. If she finished her shower and Edmund wasn't home, she would unpack them. Elaine soon made her way out of the bedroom and headed for the bathroom. She pushed open the door with her free hand and flicked on the light.

All of her bathroom supplies were placed neatly on the white marble counter by the metal bowl sink. She set down her clothes and found a note on the same side of the sink. *If you don't see the items on the counter, they'll be in the drawers. Everything of yours is on the left side.* Maybe, sleeping in hadn't been so bad. Either that or he wanted to avoid the possible argument of where she could put her things. A mental sweat-drop formed. Elaine would go with the first option.

Locking the grey bathroom door, she slipped out of her clothes and kicked her slippers aside before she stepped into the brown, beige and red wood-like, tiled shower. She closed the glass sliding door, which made her a little nervous since if she forgot to lock the door at one point, Edmund easily would be able to view her whole form. Still, he would be able to hear the water and hopefully would have the decency not to walk in.

Switching on the water, she pushed such thoughts aside and enjoyed the water. Her shower didn't take her too long, and when she was finished, she smelled of honeysuckle. After she dried off with one of the white plush towels, she changed into her clothing and nuzzled her feet into her slippers. Normally, she would've worn heels, but they were sharing an apartment now. Elaine didn't desire to wear heels the entire time that she was home. The black button-up dress, with a plum-colored ribbon around the collar, would be enough.

Elaine fixed her hair with a blow dryer and hairbrush before she was satisfied with its look. She forwent makeup since she didn't plan on going out later and Edmund had seen her plenty of times without it by that point. Leaving the bathroom, she headed back downstairs. No sound came from the kitchen or living room, nor did she sight him down there. The problem he had to deal with, though, sounded far from simple, so she wouldn't be surprised if he didn't show up until the evening.

Making her way into the living room, she headed for the television remote, but she stopped midway. Her eyes stared over to the nearby window and across the street towards her old home. It was now empty and locked. The locks would be switched soon, and someone else would live in it. Earlier that day, she had been its resident. Now, that was no longer the case.

The move had been so swift. Only about two months together, and they were already living with each other. It seemed hard to believe, yet she wouldn't change her decision; however, something in the pit of her stomach felt off. She had no clue why, except maybe the quickness of it all.

Her eyes caught sight of someone that pulled her from her thoughts. Edmund was walking on the sidewalk below. He was on his phone and seemed less than pleased. His steps paused, and he looked like he groaned. Was he being called back into work?

Edmund diverted his eyes up momentarily. That had been long enough for him to catch her staring. Their eyes locked, and she was tempted to close the curtains out of embarrassment. Instead, her right hand merely clutched the drape from surprise. His eyes softened, and he smiled up to her before he broke his gaze with her and continued to walk. Despite that look from him, her heart still was pounding a little fast. Calming herself down a little, she hung her head. She really hadn't been expecting him to glance up like that. If he had been a stranger, she would've jumped, closed the drapes and checked all of the locks. Luckily, that wasn't the case at all.

Breaking herself away from the window, she retrieved the remote and placed it on the couch, but she didn't turn on the television. She would wait to find out what had happened at his work, so she simply seated herself on the couch. When the door unlocked and Edmund entered, he was no longer on his phone.

Rather than upset, he looked exhausted. He unbuttoned his jacket and hung it on the coat rack for the meantime before he locked the door behind him. "What had that call been about?" Her question caused him to stare over to her. He combed his right fingers through his hair and made his way over to the couch. "Had it been that possible theft?"

Seating himself beside her, he leaned back against the couch and relaxed. "No. I had resolved that after an hour of video footage and had reported the details to the police as well as notified my other stores of the woman. She had been fool enough to try and rob another one of my stores, so she was caught."

"And, the guard?"

"Suspended for two weeks. He will receive another chance after that. If he messes up again, I'll fire him. Hopefully, there won't be a second time." Edmund reached up and undid his tie before he removed it from his neck; however, his attention soon was drawn to delicate fingers sliding along the right side of his jaw. Elaine turned his face towards her before her fingers pushed back loose strands of his hair.

"Then, why had you seemed so upset out there?" She moved a bit closer to him, and her eyes analyzed his carefully. It was as though that strange feeling in the pit of her stomach vanished when she was so close to him. His new nickname for her rang in her ears, and she couldn't help but glide her fingers across his well-defined face and smooth, gelled-back hair.

Lifting up his hand, he intertwined his fingers with hers and brought their hands down to his lap. His other hand wrapped around hers, and his thumbs smoothed themselves over her soft skin. "A trouble with an order, but I settled the issue. It won't happen again." He gave her a reassuring smile, and she overlooked the vagueness of his statement due to it.

"There's something else, though, that I want to talk to you about." She hummed to motion him to continue on. "You had mentioned that you were going to go shopping. Let's go together in a few weeks on a weekend trip to the mall by the ocean. What do you think?" An appreciative smile touched her lips, and she kissed him on the left cheek in thanks.

## Chapter Thirty Nine: Infuriate

*Heels clicked, and the sound grew in volume as it grew nearer and nearer. Something felt off before an unwelcome presence spoke too close for comfort.*

A nice cool air entered the car since the windows were down. No music was on, and the both of them just enjoyed the peaceful silence of the drive and the beautiful scenery to accompany it. To their right, there were a variety of trees nestled together to create a thick wood. In some places, there were parking lots and trails so that people could walk through the forest if they wanted to. On their left, grasses and bushes grew on rocky land and spread out to the edges of cliffs, which overlooked the ocean.

In the air, there was a smell of the sea, but it mixed in with that of the woods. It was a relaxing scent, and Elaine almost fell asleep a few times. Edmund and she had left their apartment early in the morning, and they had been on the road for a few hours, but they appeared to be getting close to the mall. A welcome wardrobe change for her nightgowns and a pair of shoes awaited her since her pink nightgown was her constant bedtime wear, and Edmund had been polite enough not to tease her on it.

Elaine covered her mouth with her right hand, a quiet yawn leaving her. Her eyes closed slightly, but they opened again when fingers intertwined with her other hand. "We're almost there, Elaine. Another ten minutes, but you can sleep if you want."

An appreciative smile fell on her lips as she kept her fingers wrapped around his. "Thank you, but I should be fine." She sat up a little more, and her eyes glanced around him to the ocean momentarily. "Will we be able to go to the beach while we're here?" Her eyes focused on him, and he nodded.

"Yes, we'll do that tomorrow. I did book us a hotel room for the weekend, so we'll have plenty of time. We can even go tonight if you would like."

Eagerly, she nodded. She hadn't been to the beach in quite awhile. It hadn't been like she had been far away. The drive was only a little over two hours, but her ex hadn't cared for the beach too much, so they never had gone. "That'd be really nice."

"Then, that's where we'll go in the evening." Quickly, he raised her hand and kissed the back of it before both of his hands returned to the wheel. Elaine's cheeks heated a little bit as she leaned back on her seat. "Our check-in time, though, at the hotel is 2pm, so we'll have to leave the mall a quarter of, but we can come back later if you want."

"No, it shouldn't take me too long to find some things that I like." Her hands folded on her lap before she wrung them a bit together. "But," her cheeks heated up, "can you go to a different section while I look at the nightgowns?" She stared to him out of the corners of her eyes. Edmund released a chuckle, which caused her to pout a little. "Well?" she asked with a little harshness in her tone.

"I'll go somewhere else. Just text me when you're done in that section, and I'll meet you in the shoe section." Inwardly, she sighed in relief as she nodded in response. Elaine relaxed in her seat again and waited for them to arrive at the mall.

When Edmund parked the car, he unlocked the doors, and she stepped out. Elaine closed her door afterwards and adjusted her purse on her right shoulder. Her left hand smoothed out her black chiffon skirt before she tugged on the sleeves of her red blouse, with ruffles around the collar and sleeves. A red bow tied back several strands of her dark brown locks, and red matte lipstick covered her lips. On her eyelids was a medium dark smoky eye look.

After he locked the car, Edmund waited for her by the front of it. Her red Jeannie pumps, with small black bows, clicked on the asphalt as she made her way over. Reaching him, she intertwined her left fingers with his right, and they headed over to the mall, which, since it was a weekend, was busy.

Entering the store, she looked over a map of it and saw that she needed to head to the upper floor. "Is there something that you're looking for too, Edmund?" He glanced to her briefly before he smiled and kissed her left cheek. His hand left hers, and she stared to him suspiciously. "Edmund?"

"Just something that I need to check out." She narrowed her eyes at him and crossed her arms. "If I like what I see, it'll be a surprise." Elaine raised an eyebrow. "A good one, Elaine. Trust me." A sigh left her lips, and she nodded reluctantly. He smiled and kissed her this time on her forehead. "I'll see you later."

"Yeah, I'll text you when I'm ready." He nodded and headed off. She watched him for a bit, half-tempted to follow him. Elaine bit her lower lip and forced herself to look away from where he had gone. No, she would trust him. Another sigh left her before she made her way to the woman's sleepwear. As she headed there, she received a few stares from people. Then again, Edmund and she probably looked overdressed for a shopping trip, but she walked with confidence regardless.

Once at the sleepwear department, she glanced around, wondering if Edmund was somewhere nearby. Elaine doubted that he would break his word, but it was a precaution. Thankfully, she didn't spot him, and he couldn't hide easily since there weren't any men in the particular section of the store. Honestly if there was a male stranger walking around the department and alone, she definitely would feel awkward and probably would text Edmund to come over. Luckily, she didn't have to worry about that scenario. She stepped over to the back corner where the selection of nightgowns was and looked over the selection; however, a click of heels that wasn't from hers caught her attention.

It sounded like they were headed straight for her direction. That wouldn't be odd since she was in a department store; however, something simply felt off about the person's presence. That feeling was confirmed when she heard the individual speak. "You wear nightgowns for him too?" Elaine froze and hoped that she just was hearing things, but that theory fell to pieces when the woman stepped up next to her: the nurse.

The nurse lifted her right fingers up to a nude and red see-through nightgown. "Maybe, you should get one like this?" She chuckled bitterly. "Oh wait, you wear lace undergarments a lot, don't you? At that point, you might as well wear one or the other." Elaine furrowed her brow as a scowl set on her lips. "Reginald had told me." Her fingers dropped from the clothing item. "He'd say how he had hated how you had teased him with those undergarments only to wear a nightgown over them." Gina faced Elaine fully. "Maybe, that's why he had an easier time coming to me."

"What do you want?" Elaine spoke harshly, suddenly regretting to come to the store. Then again, the chances of running into the nurse there were incredibly low.

"Can't I shop over here? It's a public place, Elaine." She smirked and focused her eyes on the clothing.

"I have a hard time believing that after the last time we had seen each other."

"Oh, trust me, Elaine. I only had come here to shop and enjoy myself. I hadn't planned on running into you, but I suppose that I had walked over here because I had seen you." Gina smirked, but it wasn't a pleasant one. No, it was far from it. "I know that you know about his threat to me now."

"He didn't threaten you. He gave you a choice." Elaine stared away from her and to the clothes on the wall. "You already know about what had happened at the Fox's Garden if you know about that."

"Yes, yes, a choice." She made air quotations. "My other choice was to be thrown out on the streets. Not much of a choice." Her tone was bitter, but her smirk remained on her lips. "However, you're still in the dark about something. Is he here with you?"

Reluctantly, Elaine shifted her eyes to the nurse. "Yes, why does it matter?"

"Oh, it matters, but it looks like he isn't in the vicinity." Gina didn't get a chill like the last time. She felt safe, and there were plenty of people watching if that man tried to threaten her again. Elaine could inform him of what happened, and she probably would, but she was established in her new nursing job and an excellent addition to the team. That man couldn't threaten her job again, especially since she knew the chief nurse well enough now and he had his own connections in the hospital.

Facing Elaine again, she grinned maliciously. "So, I'm going to share a little secret of your boyfriend's with you. Whether you believe me or not, your choice, but it'll sink into that awful little head of yours." Elaine was tempted to walk off. The nurse's words would be lies. "..." Gina, though, never got a word out.

"Elaine, I know that you had asked me not to come over here, but I need your opinion ..." Edmund stopped partway. Both Elaine and Gina averted their eyes over to him. Hatred bubbled up within him. What had she told his treasure, and why was she at the same mall? Inwardly, he wished to tear that woman apart. Outwardly, he diverted his gaze to Elaine as he headed over to her. "Are you alright?" His hands rested on her shoulders. Gratefully, she rested her hands over his and nodded, which caused his eyes to meet Gina's next. The nurse noticeably gulped.

## Chapter Forty: Scurry

*Heels nearly failed to support trembling limbs, and they took a step back, which almost caused the woman to fall. All the while, too protective of an embrace ensnared another.*

"... Ge-George," Gina stumbled out, her body beginning to quiver. "I-I-I ..."

"What are you doing here?" His tone was harsh, and his hands gripped Elaine's shoulders a little tighter as he pulled her back towards him more.

"It-It's a ..." She took a deep breath in before she exhaled. "It's a public place. I have every right to be here." Her tone was steady, but it was near to shaking again. Elaine might've been concerned by the fear rising up in the nurse's eyes if the nurse hadn't slept with her ex and insulted her prior to Edmund's arrival.

"I know that." The sharpness of his words cut through hers like an axe slicing through wood cleanly. "But, I was hoping that I wouldn't have to explain myself." He stood taller, and his green-hazel eyes could've incinerated the nurse's form if that was possible. "What I mean is what are you doing here harassing Elaine?" His eyes narrowed into murderous slits, and Gina stepped back and almost tripped on the bottom of a clothes' rack. Unfortunately for the couple, she didn't fall over. "That, you don't have a right to."

"I wasn't ..."

"Don't lie." The command was simple but powerful. Gina visibly gulped and glanced over to Elaine as if she would mention the secret from before. Elaine wouldn't give her the satisfaction of that. "Don't look at her. I'm talking to you." Edmund's hands moved down to Elaine's upper arms and gave them a reassuring squeeze.

"I-I ..." The nurse's brown eyes were wide as saucers, and she nervously shook her head. Her behavior did cause Elaine to question what secret the nurse had been about to tell her, but Elaine wouldn't ask Edmund until the nurse was gone.

After Gina shook her head more, she stepped back again. Barely, her heels were giving her enough support to stand upright. It was surprising that she wasn't toppling over. "I-I ..." Gina gulped before she turned to run off. A loud cough interrupted her escape. Hesitantly, she shifted her orbs back to Edmund. Elaine couldn't view his eyes from her perspective, but his stare must've been incredibly deadly by the way that terror grew alit in the nurse's orbs. If Gina didn't answer, Elaine didn't know what Edmund would do, but it probably wouldn't be something subtle.

Only one word past her lips. *Secret.* She was off. Her ruby red stilettos clicked against the tile in hurried succession, and her dirty blonde hair flicked back and forth as though its owner's life depended upon it.

Edmund's hands slackened their hold on her, and a long sigh past his lips. Elaine turned in his arms and noticed his countenance was one of irritation, yet calmness. "I apologize that I hadn't gotten here sooner. I ..."

A finger pressed to his lips. Elaine shook her head and moved her appendage back to the handles of her purse. "You didn't know. I'm just happy that you showed up, though," her eyes glanced over to the nightgowns, "I don't want you to look when I'm picking them out." He quirked a brow. "I know that you'll see them, but I ..."

"I understand, Elaine. It's fine. That had been my promise originally. I'll face the other way." He leaned down and placed a kiss upon her forehead. She smiled before she tilted her head back and pressed her lips to his. Edmund's eyes nearly closed before she stepped back and broke the kiss. His eyes followed her movement as he stood back up fully. "Elaine?" A more serious, and worried, expression touched her face.

"Before we continue, though, I just want to know." He had trouble keeping a frown off of his lips. "She obviously had been scared of you, and she had mentioned a secret before. Based off of what I just had witnessed, those two have to be connected." Edmund bit the inside of his right cheek to keep a neutral expression on his face. "What was that secret?" Immediately, he didn't answer, which gave her all the more concern.

Almost, he combed his left fingers through his hair but stopped himself and placed his hand back at his side. His eyes searched the area before he found a chair by the entranceway to the dressing rooms. Edmund moved over to it before he took a seat. He leaned forward and intertwined his fingers in front of him. Meanwhile, nervous tugs met her stomach. "Edmund?" She moved closer to him.

Looking up slightly, a barely noticeable, bitter smile touched his lips. "I don't want to say." His eyes broke their gaze from hers, and her heart skipped a troubled beat. Edmund's gaze met the floor. Silence dominated the two of them. He looked ashamed.

An idea of what the secret was ate away at her, and she thought that she might faint. Her words were barely audible. "Did you cheat on me?" Maybe, it was unreasonable given how much time they had spent together and having just moved in together a few weeks ago. To her anxious mind, however, it seemed to be a very plausible explanation for his current behavior.

Instantly, his head sprung up, and his eyes went wide. "No, that isn't it at all!" Quickly, he grabbed her hands and tugged her nearer to him. She was almost reluctant to stand so close. Isn't that what all cheaters say? "I would never do that, Elaine!" His hands pulled on hers more, desperately. That had to be another line of a cheater, and she could feel tears forming.

"I'm sorry for worrying you." Her eyes averted from his. "Remember why I had come over here?" Slowly, she nodded. "Well, I still need your opinion on something. I was angry because I feared that she would ruin the surprise, though; my question might've revealed it already." Steadily, her dark brown eyes shifted back to his green-hazel ones. Reason began to enter her mind again.

"When I had met with that vile woman before, she had figured it out. She had discerned that I was in love with you." Her heartstrings were pulled, but her worry didn't vanish entirely yet. "Before I even had given you my number." Now, she froze, and a slight bit of fear began to creep into her veins. "And, no. I already had told you when you had discovered where I had lived, where we now live." He held onto her hands tightly. "I didn't plan his death. Everything just worked out this way." His eyes were pleading her to believe him. "I swear."

"Edmund, I ..."

"What I'm saying Elaine is that I had seen you hurting back before he had passed. I had wanted to help. That's why I had given you my number. Even if we never had gotten together, I would've been happy just to help you work through all of that." He released a bitter chuckle. "That probably sounds suspicious, and she had known that. If she had told you, it would've ruined ..."

Shifting his eyes from hers, he loosened his hold on her hands before he dropped them to his lap. "I understand if you want to leave and have some time to yourself." Her hands didn't go back to his, but she didn't move from her spot either. She lifted her hands up to her eyes and wiped some of the tears that had been there from before.

"What would it have ruined?" Her words were soft and slightly scared. She was losing her trust in him again, but he knew that he had her on a hook. All he had to do was reel her in, and it would be perfect.

"You know what it is now, Elaine." His eyes met hers again, and there was yearning in them. "I can see it in your eyes. You know, but this has gone all wrong." Edmund stood up from the chair. "Things are starting to turn against me, and my image in your eyes ... Well, it's ruined, isn't it?"

Wringing her hands together, she bit her bottom lip before she shook her head. "It's just that it worked out so well for you." She looked up slightly to continue to hold his gaze. "But, it worked out well for me too. I thought that you had cheated, but it had been that instead." Slightly, a smile touched her lips. "That's much better. But, first the apartment, now this." A sigh parted from her. "It's hard simply to accept it, but I want to."

Reaching forward and up, her hands cupped his cheeks. Her eyes examined his, and they saw only hope and love. It melted away her doubt, but she needed to confirm that she was making the right decision. "Please, tell me one more time that it's just how things worked out, that I can trust you. I need to hear you say it again before anything else."

Raising his hands up, they rested over hers. "I promise you, Elaine Margarit, that all of this has simply worked out for the two of us. You can trust me." Her eyes searched his for any sign of falsity before more tears greeted the corners of her eyes. A smile graced her lips. He wasn't lying. His eyes bore only the truth. Edmund wiped away her tears before she leaned her head against his chest and moved her hands to his back. All of her fingers clutched at his jacket. "Tonight." Elaine's heart skipped a beat, and Edmund smirked on the inside. Once again, his treasure was back in the palms of his hands, and his plans were even moved up in the process. How delightful.

## Chapter Forty One: Stroll

*Water tickled toes, and soft sand brushed against skin. Pieces of seaweed and seashells washed up on the shore, and the background noise of others was drowned out over time.*

Arms leaned on the wrought iron railing, and a gentle ocean breeze blew by. Both her chiffon skirt and strands of her dark brown hair swayed back and forth before they rested again against her. The sun was setting over the water, which made the waves sparkle in the red, orange and yellow light. A few people below walked upon the sand, enjoying the quiet and peaceful air of the place.

Off to her right, there was a restaurant with seating near the pale sands. Sounds of conversations and music traveled up to the balcony, though; she couldn't pick apart the words of the people, but she didn't mind. They were none of her business. Besides, she'd rather enjoy the last rays of the sun than focus on their conversations. Edmund was missing out, and she wondered how long it took to get towels for the bathroom since the hotel staff had forgotten to put new towels in.

When the last rays faded past the horizon, she smiled a little. That had been relaxing, and the soothing breeze still continued. Her limbs felt light, and her mind cleared. Honestly, the trip had been an excellent idea minus the incident from earlier. Elaine pushed back some strands of hair behind her left ear and faced the room.

A few shopping bags were on the white desk chair in the room. New nightgowns and a pair of blue heels were in them. He had kept his promise and hadn't looked at which nightgowns she had picked out, and he had been kind enough to scout out the whole shoe department, making sure that the nurse hadn't been anywhere in the vicinity. Another encounter with that woman would be a nightmare. Almost, she had lost her trust in Edmund again.

Entering the room more, she seated herself upon the plush bed and kicked off her black fuzzy slippers. She kicked her legs back and forth lightly as she leaned back on her hands. A soft sigh parted from her lips. What had happened back in the mall played again in her head, and her fingers curled around the turquoise comforter.

Tonight, she knew what was going to happen, and her heart beat fast at the prospect of it. It almost erased her memory of what else had been exchanged in that conversation at the mall. For longer than she had expected, he had loved her. It still tugged at her stomach a little in a negative manner as she thought over his words more, but, at the same time, she trusted him. Perhaps, that was foolish, but she had seen only truth in his eyes when he had stated that promise to her and that she could trust him. She had to believe him. Her heart didn't want to accept an alternative.

The click of a door caught her attention. She peered over her right shoulder. Edmund closed the door with his foot and set a stack of towels on the bathroom sink. He exited the bathroom soon after, and she faced him fully on the bed. Elaine smiled to him, and he smiled back; she just had to trust him. "What had taken so long with the bath linens?"

"A shortage. This is a popular hotel, and some guests have been requesting more than the usual amount." He stood near her. "Probably, they'll order more in." His eyes shifted to the balcony. "Should I order dinner in before we head out, or would you like to stop by that restaurant one building over?"

To both options, she shook her head. "We can order in food later. Have a midnight snack." She smiled up to him again. "This is our vacation. Let's sit back and watch movies later while loading up on junk food. I think that would be better than a loud restaurant, and we get comfier seating here."

Chuckling, he smiled back to her once more. "I can't argue with that, though; are you wanting to skip dinner now for another reason?" A playful tone hit his voice, and she broke eye contact with him while a little bit of heat hit her cheeks.

"Well, I ..." She pouted and crossed her arms. Her eyes looked back to his. "I just don't want to be in a slight food coma when I'm on the beach with you." Almost, she nodded her head firmly like a character would in a television show.

"Is that right?" he teased before he held out his right hand for her to take. Reluctantly, she took it, and he lifted her up from the bed. His eyes peered down to her feet. "Are you going to wear any shoes, Elaine?"

"No." She intertwined her fingers with his. "I'll be taking them off anyway once on the sand, and the hotel is right on the beach." Her eyes moved to his feet. "You should take off your shoes and socks." A light chuckle left her. "Maybe, roll up your pants." Elaine proceeded to point to herself. "Even I'm probably overdressed for going on the beach. We tend to be overdressed for a lot of things it seems."

"Or, everyone else is underdressed." He smirked to her, and she couldn't help but laugh in return.

"Your choice. It's your shoes, socks and pants." He quirked a brow back to her, and she returned to him a cautious stare. "Edmund?" Slightly, her fingers loosened their hold on his. Most definitely, he was planning something.

"And, what about your clothes?" He leaned down towards her, and she parted her hand from his. She took a few steps back and gave him a questioning look. Edmund wouldn't throw her into the water, would he? "You might not be standing for long." His right fingers slid under her chin and tilted it upwards. "I might just knock you down from your feet." A smirk decorated his lips.

"And if I land on you?" she challenged back, standing a little on her tippy-toes so that his fingers would no longer touch her chin and she would appear more intimidating. Elaine doubted that she did to him, but it was the thought that counted. "Then, you'll be more drenched, and I'll stay dry."

"Depends on how deep we are in the water, doesn't it, love?" The nickname caught her off guard. Her lips parted, but no words came out. She closed and pursed them as if she was about to scold him for his comment. Before she could react, he grabbed her hand again and spun her around him. Elaine impacted his back while his hands gripped her thighs.

Instantly, heat took over her cheeks, and she was thankful that her skirt was somewhat long. He lifted her up before he held her to his back. To support herself, she draped her arms over his shoulders and hanged onto him. "Edmund, you don't ..."

"How else will I drop you into the water?" He peered back to her and smirked. A frown set on her lips. "I could carry you bridal style too," her cheeks remained heated at that, "and then throw you in." Her frown stayed.

"If you do that, I'm taking you with me, and I'll ruin your entire suit."

"Good thing that I picked up towels, then."

Not being able to help herself, her ears burned at that statement. She rested her head against the back of his neck. "Let's just go to the water." Her voice grew a little quieter. "Just please don't drop me in. The breeze outside is nice, but it easily can become cold." Edmund leaned back into her as a gesture that he wouldn't, and she smiled lightly against him.

After he locked the balcony doors, he left the hotel room with her and headed down towards the water. A few people in the halls stared or whispered while others smiled a bit along with one of the other actions. Elaine simply dug her face more into the back of him, too embarrassed to watch the reactions of others.

Once a dash of wind touched her skin and her hair blew back a little, she knew that they were outside. She lifted her head up and watched the water approach as Edmund stepped towards it. His shoes sank into the sand even as he got closer to the water. He made no motion to take them off. In fact, he didn't seem bothered by the fact that they would get ruined at all. Such a gesture tugged at her heartstrings, and it did all the more for the maintenance of her trust in him.

Waves rolled up to the shore and nearly touched the tips of his shoes. His hold on her loosened, and he gently placed her down on the sand. Her toes curled into the soft ground before she stepped forward and permitted the water to greet her skin. Its cold touch gave her a slight shiver before it became pleasant a little while after. Elaine watched seaweed roll onto the sand while seashells revealed themselves when the water pulled back.

Lights from the restaurant and hotels glowed at the back of them and illuminated some of the ocean before them. Voices sounded in the background, but they were soon drowned out to Edmund's ears as well as hers. His left fingers connected with her right ones. She could feel her heartbeat picking up, and she hoped that her palm wouldn't become sweaty. No words left her; she waited for him.

Giving her hand a tender squeeze, he moved her closer to him. A tiny wave crashed at their feet, and Edmund's shoes were now wet. He didn't give them a glance. Rather, he turned and faced her before he held her other hand in his. Edmund tightened his hold on her before he loosened it. His fingers glided under hers before only their fingertips were touching. Upon his lips, a smile grew, and he made his next move.

## Chapter Forty Two: Kneel

*Waves splashed upwards, and the term soaked was an understatement. Neither party cared, however, since the other was overjoyed for that time.*

Their fingertips no longer touched. Rather, Edmund kneeled down on one knee. His one pant-leg became coated in sand before water washed up against the edge of it. From his back pocket, he removed a small, black box. Elaine recalled him asking her opinion on the matter of what metal she liked most, but that had been all. She had answered gold.

He snapped the box open before a gold engagement ring displayed itself. The top part of the ring was shaped into a rose, and she smiled at the thoughtfulness of the design. In the center was a single diamond. It was simple but sweet and elegant; it was ideal. Her eyes, though, soon moved to his. "Will you marry me, Elaine?"

A larger smile hit her lips. Maybe, it was foolish to agree to an engagement after only about two and half months of knowing him. Perhaps, it was even more so since he had been in love with her before she ever had spoken to him. Her heart ached, however, and the cautions in her mind were thrown into the shadows. Like she had told herself before, she had to trust him. An alternative just wasn't acceptable, especially in the current moment.

"You already know the answer." A smile caught his lips. Elaine leaned down and cupped his cheeks before she kissed him gently. Her heart was swelling at that point, and she couldn't help but grin into the kiss. Edmund smirked midway through as his right hand grabbed her left. She felt the metal slip onto her ring finger, but she didn't cast a glance towards it presently. He was more pressing.

Edmund slipped the box back into one of his back pockets, but the slight focus on that action caused him to lose concentration on his one knee, which was sinking into the wet sand. His knee slipped when he applied too much pressure to it, and his balance became off. Instantly, his hands gripped the sides of her waist as he toppled to his right side. A slight yelp of surprise left her lips before water crashed around and over part of them.

Her head wasn't under water for long since he lifted both of them out of it. Both of them coughed simultaneously. She repositioned herself beside him, regaining her breath, before a smile and then laughter broke out from her. Elaine pushed strands of hair back from her face and shifted her eyes to his. "Looks like we both got drenched after all."

Another wave came up and crashed against them. She closed her eyes momentarily before she wiped the new water off of her and opened them again. "We should probably move, though." Elaine went to get up, but Edmund pulled her down. Her hands ended up grabbing hold of his shoulders while her legs straddled his hips.

An amused smirk coated his lips. "Like you had said, we're soaked already. We might as well enjoy the water some." Water splashed against his back, and she used his chest as a shield to her face. When she peered back up at him, mirth still covered his countenance. His expression caused her to shake her head in slight laughter before she sat up a little on him.

Gently, her fingers combed through his pitch black hair, but as usual, a few strands remained at the front curled. "The water does help hold your hair back." He leaned into her touch, and she tilted her head down and closed her eyes when more water came up. Before she reopened them, her lips were pressed against his. Her fingers slipped down from his hair to his chest.

As the kiss intensified, she pressed her hands against him too much. Effectively, she pushed them both back. Edmund lost his balance once more and coughed up water when he lifted his head up. Elaine brought herself up too and wiped water from her face. He supported himself up on his elbows while her hands held her up. When Elaine opened her eyes and noted their position, a slight bit of heat touched her cheeks.

"We really will need those towels," he teased, quirking a brow up to her. Her cheeks instantly burned due to quite a detailed image forming in her mind. Before he could make another embarrassing comment, she shoved her hands against his chest and proceeded to get off of him. A chuckle escaped past his lips as he sat up fully. Elaine was on her feet again and walking out of the water, wringing her hair out in the process.

His eyes followed her movement the entire time before they landed on the ring. Inwardly, his smirk stretched wide across his lips. Soon, that seal would be made permanent. She was blossomed, and he wouldn't let that bloom fade ever.

Picking himself up, he caught up to her and noted her shiver. The night air was a biting cold given their state. His hands rested on her shoulders, and he kissed her left cheek tenderly. Her eyes stayed off of him, and his lips could feel the heat in her face.

Keeping his lips close to her skin, he asked, "Should I carry you back and keep you warm?" She tensed and crossed her arms as though such a question brought about the internal debate of the century. Elaine, though, soon leaned back into his hands.

"I suppose." A cute, playful pout greeted her lips as she spun around to face him. "I'm taking a shower first, though, and separate." He quirked a brow. "And no, you don't get to see me in one of those towels." Amusement continued to decorate his expression, and heat remained in her cheeks. "I don't want to see you in one either."

"Then, you want to view me nude, Elaine?" He chuckled, and her eyes widened at how her statement had sounded. Hurriedly, she parted her lips, but he pressed his right index finger to them. "It's fine. I had understood what you had meant." Edmund moved his lips closer to her left ear and whispered, "We can leave that for our honeymoon." Now, her ears felt like they were on fire.

Moving away from his touch, she positioned herself behind him and patted him on the back. "We can talk about that later. I'm cold," she mumbled as she climbed onto his back and he lifted her up. Her arms draped around his shoulders like they had earlier, though; now, a ring sparkled under the artificial light.

Briefly, Edmund's eyes glanced to it. It suited her perfectly. He would've customized the diamond to be a light purple, but he felt that the regular diamond would match her various outfits more. Besides, he could buy her more lavender roses that wouldn't fade. His attention focused on her when she nuzzled her face into the back of his neck. Her breath hit his skin lightly and warmed it up.

Truly, her warmth was all of the warmth that he needed. He would be lying if he said that he wasn't looking forward to cuddling up to her that night. His mind did wonder to what nightgowns she had picked out.

Back in the store, he hadn't peeked, but he had wanted to at several points. Even if he hadn't seen what she had selected, he had viewed the choices beforehand. Some of them certainly had been more revealing than others.

Entering the hotel, he headed for the elevator and ignored any stares that they received. His mind was more focused on the future of the evening along with the present action that Elaine was committing. He could feel Elaine's lips up against the right crook of his neck, and her left hand absentmindedly played with the knot of his tie. She had no idea the present effect that she was having on him. If they were at home, he wouldn't be able to resist the idea of setting her on the nearby couch and planting kisses all along her lips, jaw, neck and collarbone.

Elevator doors opening, he headed in and was thankful that there was no one else in it when the doors closed. Some song sounded in the background, but his ears were more in tune to her voice. "Edmund?" she spoke quietly and gently.

"Hmm?" he hummed, barely watching the light move up the floor numbers.

"Can we stay an extra day?" A soft chuckle left him, and his slight shift of movement indicated for her to continue. "I'm just enjoying our time here. I want it to last a little longer." That caused his heart to skip a beat, but other plans needed to be dealt with. He would've stayed, but he had to finish arranging that project. It was vital before they proceeded to the next step.

"I can't, Elaine. You know that I have work on Monday that I can't miss." A sigh left her, and her arms slackened a bit on him as the elevator doors reopened and he stepped into the hallway. "Tomorrow, though, we'll relax in bed and enjoy the beach as much as you want. Whatever you want to do tomorrow before we leave, we'll do. But, you know that I would accept that offer if I could miss work on Monday."

"I guess that'll be fine." She moved forward a bit on him and kissed him on the right side of his jaw. "Still, you get to choose one activity tomorrow. It's your vacation too."

"Only one?"

Nodding her head, she laughed and repeated. "Only one."

## Chapter Forty Three: Formulate

*Crinkling resonated around the room as movement occurred under fabric. Some crumbs decorated the floor and sheets, and empty dishes were stacked atop both nightstands; it was lovely, then.*

Like on mornings past, Elaine reached out her hands towards the source of warmth that she adored so much; however, her right hand never found him. Rather, it slid into an opened bag of finished barbeque chips. She furrowed her brows as her hand moved around in the wrapper. Confusion covered her expression, and laughter awoke her mind. It tickled her ears, and her hand was freed from the food-packaging prison.

"Still hungry?" a voice chuckled out melodically.

She steadily peeked open her left eye. Perplexed sleepiness dominated it. "Wh-what?" she asked groggily, her eye searching for what he was referring to. When both of her eyes landed on the empty bag, a slight hint of heat greeted her cheeks before she couldn't help but laugh tiredly. "I guess so. Any left?"

Playing along with her, he tilted the opening towards him and pretended to examine the inside thoroughly. "A crumb or two." He pointed the bag towards her. "Interested?"

Slightly, she leaned up on her right elbow and investigated the internals of it. Two small crumbs were left. "Why not," she mumbled, amused. Her hand reached in and grabbed the tiny pieces before she ate them; her tongue ran over her bottom lip afterwards out of instinct more than anything else.

Edmund moved the bag back, crumpled it up and threw it into the waste bin. Elaine fell back onto the bed, but she moved closer to him so that she could rest her head on his lap. "How long have you been up?" Her fingers smoothed out some of the sheets absentmindedly.

"Ten minutes about." His fingers reached down and combed through her locks soothingly. She instantly relaxed under his touch. "Though, I think that we should skip breakfast." Her eyes scanned over all of the empty dishes and a few other chip bags before she laughed in agreement.

"Let's just relax in bed for a bit longer." A small yawn followed, and his fingers paused as he admired the cuteness of it. "I think that I'm still in a food coma." She cuddled more into him.

"Well, I did say that we'd do what you want to do today." A soft smile greeted her lips. "While we're relaxing, though, I'd like to discuss something with you." A hum from her indicated for him to carry on. "Our wedding, are you fine keeping it small?"

"I wouldn't mind. My parents are off on a tour of the states for a year right now as part of their retirement plans." She rolled over onto her back and stared up at him. "Besides, I take it that you don't want to wait a year." Elaine laughed a little. "It did only take about a few months for you to propose after all."

"You caught me." He held up his hands teasingly, and she shook her head at the gesture in mirth. "But, I was thinking that it could be just the two of us and the officiant. It could be in another month." Momentarily, she froze. Elaine had been thinking at least two. Then again if it would be just the two of them, planning wouldn't be quite as complicated. It probably was manageable.

Noting her look, he reassured, "I already know who to contact and how to make it happen. I just need you to trust me."

Gently, she smiled up to him. "You already told me to trust you, and I do." A chuckle escaped her. "And, you own a chain of art stores. You're sure to come up with something that'll stun the both of us." Her hands reached over to his, and she ran her fingers along his palms tenderly.

"Thank you, and I will. It'll be a perfect celebration for two."

"What about your aunt, though?" Her eyes scanned his cautiously. Rarely, he had brought up his family before, but, during the last month, he had confirmed that she was still living. That had been it, and she hadn't pressed more on the topic. Back then, he had seemed like he had wanted to change topics as quickly as possible. Now, there was a flash of hesitance in his eyes.

"She won't be able to make it. She'll visit you before the wedding, though, so that she can meet you. After that, however, she'll need to head back to her work and tend to her gardening business."

Something seemed off about his wording. Elaine removed her hands from his and sat up straight on the bed. She crossed her legs and faced him again. "Visit me?" Her words were slow, and her tone questioning. "What about you?" Edmund didn't answer immediately. "Edmund?" she questioned, worried.

"Unfortunately, the reason why work on Monday is so important is because I'll be heading out of town. I have a project that'll take the month to complete, but I'll return for our wedding of course. And, my aunt can take you shopping for your wedding dress."

Eyes widening, she pressed her hands into her knees. "What?!" she yelled quietly. "Shouldn't we wait, then? Even if you're planning it, and I do trust you with that, I still want to help out with our wedding besides my dress."

"Any idea you have, you can tell my aunt or me still. I do plan to call you, Elaine, while I'm away." His left hand rested on her right cheek. Part of her wished to move away so that she could appear more agitated by the news, but she couldn't. Edmund's hand felt so nice against her. She could melt into its light and caring touch.

"It won't be the same." A sigh parted from her. "Can't you work on this project afterwards?"

"And, have it possibly compromise our honeymoon?" He raised a brow to her.

At that, she couldn't argue. "And, you can't move it out till later than that?" He shook his head, and she hanged hers a bit. "Well if it's that important ..." Suspicion started to creep in, and she narrowed her eyes at him. "The timing is rather ... odd. Is there something going on besides work?" She leaned forward more. "Are you going to meet directly with some of those contacts?"

Entertained, he smirked some. "It's a possibility." Edmund tapped her on the tip of her nose. "Now, do you understand why I can't move it?" She didn't nod her head yet. "Yes, I do have work that I can't miss on Monday, but I also want to work on something for our marriage. If I wait, the honeymoon gets pushed back, and the effect won't be as grand." Her lips parted, and he pressed his right index finger to them. "And, yes. It'll take a month. I can't shorten it."

Slightly, a pout fell on her expression before she relaxed her shoulders and gave in. He removed his finger and pressed a quick kiss to her lips. Elaine smiled some against it before he pulled back. Meeting his eyes, she agreed, "Fine, I understand. Just make sure to call." Her hands gripped the fabric of her long, midnight blue and cotton nightgown, which Edmund thought was modestly adorable and suited her.

"Of course." He reached his right hand forward and moved back strands of her hair. "Even though I'm looking forward to this project, I'm going to miss you immensely." A slight smile fell upon his lips. "Think of it this way, though. We'll really be sticking to the tradition of me not seeing your wedding gown before the ceremony."

An appreciative smirk graced her lips. "Yes, it does seem like that'll be the case." Her smirk gradually morphed into a grin. "Though, this means that we really have to enjoy today. And, I have planned what we should do next." He quirked a brow. "You can bring us coffee, and we can sit on the balcony." She crossed her arms. "It's only fair that you get it after what you just pulled."

Chuckling, he complied. "Well, I doubt that they'll have anything as good as Bread and Books, but it should be suitable. Cappuccino?" She nodded, and he got out of the bed. "I'll change and be on my way, then. I shouldn't be too long." Edmund headed off into the bathroom, and she slackened her shoulders once he was out of sight. Him being gone for a month and right before their now agreed upon wedding date didn't sit right with her, but she would trust him. He simply was throwing a massive surprise for her, and she would get to meet his aunt finally. There were positives to his absence, though; she wished that there wouldn't be any negatives, but that was unrealistic.

Thankfully, a cup of coffee was on its way, which would clear her head for the day. If they got lucky, it would be similar to their favorite coffee shop. After all, they hadn't been able to frequent the café quite as much as they had used to, but that had made it all the more of a treat when they had gone.

Pushing back some strands of her hair, she moved off of the bed and started to pick up any crumbs or wrappers that had fallen on the floor before she deposited them into the waste bin. The bathroom door was closed as she past by it, and her cheeks heated up. In a month, there really wouldn't be a reason to keep it closed. Quite a few images that were worthy of volcano-level heat to her cheeks appeared in her mind, and she forced her eyes away from the door.

Her feet turned away, and she headed for the balcony. She opened the sliding door and stepped on out. The morning breeze was cool and welcoming. Leaning on the railing, she told herself that the wedding would be perfect for them and that Edmund's absence wouldn't be too long.

## Chapter Forty Four: Welcome

*Navy blue and white cushions seated their guests comfortably while the smell of potted plants and herbs greeted their noses. Colorful juices rested in glassware as two finally met the other.*

Two weeks had gone by since Edmund had headed off for his massive surprise project. The apartment was admittedly very lonely, but they had called each other every other day, and she had visited Bread and Books more, which had distracted her mind from his absence to a degree. Today, she was leaving the house as well but not for the book and coffee café. Rather, Edmund's aunt was in town, and Elaine was going to be meeting up with her for lunch and dress shopping, which was going to be ... interesting given the time limit before the wedding.

Elaine had offered for his aunt to stay in the apartment while she was there, but she had insisted on staying at a hotel. His aunt hadn't given her too much reason as to why other than she didn't want to be an inconvenience. Even when Elaine had assured her that she wouldn't be, she still argued that it wouldn't be right. After she had realized that she wouldn't make any progress on the argument, Elaine had given up on trying to persuade the woman to lodge with her.

For lunch, though, they were meeting at a small restaurant that was known for its outdoor seating and juices: Herb Grove. It supposedly was a peaceful setting and delightful for casual conversation. Elaine, though, had no idea what Edmund's aunt would be comfortable talking about. She desired to hear more information about Edmund, but his aunt might not be amenable to that. Rather, his aunt just might wish to learn more about her. Maybe, however, their meeting had an implied negotiation: fifty-fifty for each.

Turning her attention from her thoughts to the full-length mirror in the closet, she double-checked her appearance. She didn't wish to wear anything too complex since she was going to be trying on dresses later, and fitting rooms always were a hassle in her opinion. Her hands smoothed out her red pleated skirt, which went down to her knees, before she adjusted the chiffon sleeves of her white blouse. Elaine shifted her feet a little in her black pumps before she nodded her head in satisfaction. It would do nicely.

Leaving the closet, she flipped the light off and headed into the bathroom. Once done, matte red lipstick, a light bit of eye shadow and mascara decorated her face. Her dark brown locks were pulled back by a simple red hair tie. Anything more complex might just get ruined from the dresses later on. After she made sure that all of the lights were switched off and that the front door was locked, she went off to her destination.

The drive there was relaxing, though; she missed having Edmund's company in the car. After she had moved in with him, she hadn't driven around too much on her own since they had gone on their errands together. A slight frown met her lips, and she told herself that there were two weeks left before he would be back. And then, they would be tying the knot. At that thought, her frown morphed into a small, shy smile while a girlish giggle escaped her. At that moment, she was happy that he wasn't in the car to tease her about the action.

When she pulled into the parking lot of the restaurant, she left her red mini cooper car and locked the door after her. The place was small, but it most certainly had an inviting feel to it. Vines worked their way up grey wooden posts and hung from the overhang above the entrance door. Light blue and white striped curtains covered the inside of the window in the wooden door, and potted plants lined the steps up to it. She turned the doorknob, and a bell rang. A waitress stood behind a grey podium where a pot of pale pink tea roses rested. Walking up to the woman, Elaine asked, "Has a Ms. Fex come in yet? She has reservations for two at one this afternoon outside."

"Let me check." The waitress looked down at an unseen list from Elaine's perspective before she met Elaine's eyes again. "Well, the reservation is here, but I just got on a few moments ago, so I'm not sure if she is here. You're welcome to walk outside and see if you can find her, or I can check with the waiter that was on before me before he leaves."

"It's fine. No need to do that. I'll just go look outside. Thank you." Elaine smiled to the woman before the waitress smiled back and answered the nearby ringing phone. Moving away from the podium, Elaine walked towards the back door. When she opened it, another bell jingled. A few heads glanced her way before they returned to their own business. Well, that was the case except for one individual.

A woman stood up from her seat and indicated for Elaine to join her. Edmund had mentioned his aunt's appearance, and the woman standing fit it perfectly. Her light brown hair was tied back into a bun so that loose strands touched her shoulders and framed her face in a softer light. Blue-hazel eyes glowed with analysis and warmth. Upon her form was a white blouse that was tucked away into a loose, beige and floor-length skirt. Light brown flats covered her feet, and no make-up greeted her face, which showed a few wrinkles forming around her eyes and lips.

Distance between them closing, the older woman held out her right hand, and Elaine shook it in response. "It's a pleasure to finally meet you, Elaine. Edmund has mentioned how pleasant and beautiful you are to me." Her cheeks heated up at the compliments. Elaine parted her lips to return a compliment or two, but the older woman shook her head. "No need. I know that he has said little about me, other than I probably run a gardening business and my description."

Slightly, her lips remained parted before Elaine regained her composure. "Well yes, actually." She gave a slight chuckle and took her seat on the plush bench across from Hana.

Hana retook her seat, folded her hands over her lap and crossed her legs. "Though, I'm sure that you'd rather learn more about me through my stories about Edmund?" Elaine didn't answer verbally, but the surprise in her dark brown eyes was enough to give that away. His aunt's hands left her lap and picked up the menu in front of her. "First, though, let's order something. The drive here exhausted me." Much to Elaine's slight shock, his aunt was more energetic than she expected even if Hana just had mentioned how tired she was. She had assumed Edmund's more business-like side to stem from his aunt since she had raised him for most of his life. Then again, Hana wasn't working presently.

Switching her eyes to the menu, Elaine found the drinks section and grinned a little at the juice section. They had about every juice imaginable on the menu and combinations that she had never heard or seen of before. Talk about a selection. It almost was too overwhelming. Elaine peeked over the potted plants lining the back of the outdoor area and to the garden beyond it. Several fruits greeted her, and she made a point to order a juice that contained the fruits in the garden. Her excitement fell a little when she realized that Edmund wasn't with her.

Briefly, her eyes averted to his aunt. She couldn't compare, but Hana taking her time to come and visit her was sweet, and Elaine was appreciative of the gesture. When she glanced back to her menu, Elaine decided that she would order an apple, berry and green tea drink. Out of the corners of her eyes, though, she noted that Hana shook her head to someone. Looking up, Elaine noted that a waiter was walking away. "Is something wrong?" the younger questioned as she set down her menu after she had flipped it over to the food section.

"He had the wrong table." Elaine was certain that he hadn't been carrying anything, but she didn't press more on it. "Are you ready to order a drink? I think that our waitress should be coming out."

"Yes, though, their selection made it hard to pick something. How did you hear of this place before? I only knew about it after you had recommended it."

"Ah, I had done some digging around on garden-themed restaurants. I like to know where my food is coming from, and this place seems to be quite decent at providing that information." She took in a deep breath and exhaled. "Besides, it smells lovely out here, and the temperature is just right too." Hana smiled to her. "Do you like it?"

"I do. I had read some reviews, and they definitely had been accurate." Both of their attention diverted over to a waitress, who looked a little worried but smiled nonetheless. Elaine pushed it aside, thinking that she was putting too much thought into the situation. After Hana and she ordered their drinks, the waitress headed off. The younger faced the older again and leaned forward as if she was about to whisper incredibly vital and secret information. "But, is it okay if I ask to hear about some childhood stories of Edmund?"

Laughing, Hana nodded. "Of course, you can. I can tell you a few." She lifted up her right index finger and tapped her lips. "Just don't tell him that I told you." Hana laughed some more before she shrugged her shoulders. "He'll probably figure it out eventually, but we can keep it a secret until then."

"Definitely," Elaine agreed before she leaned back on her seat and prepared herself for whatever story was to come. Not teasing him, though, would be difficult, but she couldn't resist the urge to hear more about her fiancée.

"Well, the first that I'll tell you about was when he had been seven, and the story involves several of my rose bushes that I had been growing at the time. Guess who I had found sampling the taste of their petals?" Hana covered her mouth with her right hand and giggled, and amusement instantly decorated Elaine's dark brown eyes. Now, she had to add roses of that kind to their wedding, specifically on their cake. Hopefully, Hana would approve despite their prior agreement.

## <u>Chapter Forty Five: Dress</u>

*Chiffons, satins, cottons and many more fabrics lined the racks of the store. Accessories were sealed behind glass cases, and shoes were stacked upon glass shelves; everything seemed to sparkle.*

Elaine covered her mouth with her right hand as she tried to laugh quietly since Hana and she were in the bridal shop now, awaiting their appointment time. Lunch had been enjoyable, and Elaine had learned a series of funny stories featuring her fiancée. From the rose eating to painting his room walls with blueberry and blackberry juice, he had been quite the active child, and the many stories made it hard not to tease him when she called him next. Thankfully, though, Hana had agreed to the cake idea. Now, however, Hana just had finished telling her about how Edmund had clung to his father's pants until his father had seated him upon his lap and bounced him. That had been a phase of Edmund's since he had been two and until he had lost his parents. The younger's laughter quieted down at that remembrance.

"Hana, do you mind telling me what had happened, or what they had looked like if you don't mind of course?" Her voice was soft, and she glanced to Edmund's aunt only a little bit.

Hana's chuckling fell silent before a light sigh past her lips. "I don't mind, and you should know." She crossed her hands on her lap. "His parents had been killed in a convenience store theft. While I had been watching him, they had gone for an evening movie together, and they had stopped at a convenience store on the way back to pick up some food and treats for him since Edmund had liked the pastries at that store. A man had come in with a knife, and his father had tried to stop him. Things had taken a turn for the worst, and the clerk had managed to escape and call the police while his parents had been ... well, distracting the man." No words left Elaine, but she rested her right hand on top of Hana's left and squeezed it. An appreciative smile touched the elder's lips. Another sigh left the elder. "Edmund hadn't talked too much for the rest of that year. He also had followed me everywhere, but I hadn't minded. I had known that he hadn't wanted to lose me too."

Meeting Elaine's gaze, Hana wrapped her hands around Elaine's tightly but not uncomfortably so. "If he does seem ever like he's trying to keep you away from the world, just know that's the reason why. He's scared of losing you, and he just wants to keep you safe."

"It's fine. I understand." A smile touched the younger's lips. "And, it hasn't seemed like that. I mean he's been trusting me to stay on my own mostly while he's away." Slowly, his aunt nodded, and hesitation greeted her blue-hazel eyes briefly before it vanished. It was a peculiar response, but Elaine reassured herself that she was over-thinking.

"As for what they had looked like, Bernard had the same hair color as Edmund, but his eyes had been a dark green. My sister, Lita, had green-hazel eyes and the same hair color as me. They had cherished Edmund so much, and even as such a young child, he had picked up on that easily." Hana gave Elaine's hands another squeeze. "Again, though, just know that he's going to do his best to keep you safe. You will have nothing to worry about."

"I know. Thank you. And, he's been keeping me safe presently too and before we had started dating even. He had helped me through the death of my ex and when I had discovered that my ex had been cheating on me. Emotionally, he had kept me safe by giving me the support that I had needed then. I couldn't ask for a better fiancée, Hana."

A large smile broke out on the elder's lip. "You have no idea how happy that makes me to hear that. And, you're going to adore the surprise that he has for you."

Raising a brow, Elaine asked, "You know what it is?" Hana nodded. "Can you give me a hint?"

"No, I'm not allowed to give you even that." A childish smile met the older woman's mouth. "You'll just have to wait a little bit longer." Hana pulled her hands back and continued to smile mischievously, which only caused Elaine to want to learn the secret more.

Footsteps, however, caught both of their attentions. A petite woman, probably around five feet tall, stood before them. Her brown hair was pulled back tightly into a bun, and her medium brown eyes looked somewhat tired from the day. At the same time, she appeared genuinely excited to help them with the dress selection. "My name is Tia, and I'll be your consultant for today. Now, which one of you is Elaine?" she questioned kindly as Elaine raised her hand.

"Well, congratulations on your future wedding." Tia shook Elaine's hand before she shook the hand of Hana. "And, you're ..."

"Her fiancee's aunt."

"Well, thank you for accompanying her today." She withdrew her hand and stood back up straight. "I find that it's always nice to have someone come with the bride-to-be for her dress fitting." Tia clapped her hands lightly in front of her and folded them over her black jacket. "Now, is there anything in particular that you're looking for in a dress, Elaine?"

"Umm ..." Elaine shifted her eyes over to Hana before she felt heat touch her cheeks. "What would Edmund like? Has he hinted at anything without me knowing?" Edmund always had seemed to like what she chose for her outfits, but he never had given his opinion on what he would like to see her in for their wedding, and she didn't have any preference. As long as she loved how it looked on her, the rest didn't matter to her too much. That was how she had bought her other clothes.

"Something with flowers might do well. He does like roses." Hana and Elaine shared a look before they both quietly chuckled and looked back to Tia. The two women nodded to her, and the consultant smiled back.

"Flowers, then. We do have quite a few dresses that I think will look good on you. Please follow me." Tia faced away from them and headed back into the store. "Would you like to select a few things yourself or wait in your dressing room for me?"

Glancing over the large quantity of dresses, glass cases of accessories and shelves of shoes, Elaine felt somewhat overwhelmed. "Maybe, it would be best to see what you pick first. I think that I'd get lost otherwise." A slight chuckle left the bride-to-be, and Tia nodded in understanding.

When they reached the dressing room, Tia unlocked and opened the door for both of them. "I'll be back shortly with some dresses for you." She smiled again to them before she closed the door and headed off.

"Thank you!" Elaine called out before the door shut completely. She seated herself on the plush purple chair and leaned back to get more comfortable. "So, am I still forbidden from hearing a hint?" A nod was returned to her. Elaine slumped her shoulders and pouted. "Not even a little one?" Hana shook her head. "Well, I guess that I'll know in just two weeks." At that recollection, she sat up straight. "We forgot to tell Tia that. That'll limit the selection significantly. I should go let her know."

Already up, though, was Hana. "No, you sit and relax. I'll go tell her, and, maybe, me being there will help too. I'll be back shortly." Before Elaine could get another word in, Hana was gone. With both of the other women gone, Elaine slouched more on the chair until her eyes averted towards the mirrors in the room.

Pushing herself up, she walked over to the podium. Nearby on one of the many hooks in the room, there was a satin bathrobe for her to change into. She supposed that she might as well change while she was waiting. It didn't take her too long to switch out of her clothes and into the article of clothing. Elaine kept the tie loose around her waist since she would have it off soon, but she did wonder what dresses would be pulled. Hopefully, the selection would have some good hits given the time limit. Perhaps, she would get lucky, and the first dress that she saw would be the one.

Returning to the one chair, she made herself comfortable again just as Hana's phone started to ring. It was placed on the dresser, which was between the two chairs in the room. Elaine tried to ignore the caller ID until she noted that it was Edmund calling. Maybe, he needed something from his aunt or wanted to recommend something for the dress. Should she answer? It technically wasn't for her, but it was her fiancée calling.

Why did her stomach knot uncomfortably, though? It was as though a rush of negativity hit her before it formed itself into a ball. Just as she was about to reach out and answer since the feeling was bothering her, the phone stopped ringing, and it went to voicemail. For a second, she heard a frustrated sigh before the line went dead. Had something gone wrong with the project? The door opening, however, caught her gaze. Hana and Tia walked in, and Tia was holding three dresses. "These are the only three floral dresses that we can have ready in time for you I'm afraid." Elaine shook her head and smiled, indicating that it was understandable and fine. Besides, one instantly attracted her eyes. That had to be the one. Truly, she was lucky unless that call ... No, Hana would see his call and resolve the problem if there was one, and that thought eased her mind.

## Chapter Forty Six: Address

*Leaning back in the cushioned chair, he crossed his legs at his calves while a paper cup of coffee rested on the table. No one besides the two of them was in the room, but footsteps were on their way.*

Tapping his fingers on the steering wheel, he looked down to his phone. A smile rested on his lips. *I think that you'll love it.* Her text was short, sweet and simple, and he wished that he could see the dress presently, but he only had a few more weeks to go, less than that after the current day. Still, though, he needed to talk to his aunt, and he had been hoping to arrange a meeting time with her. Unfortunately, she hadn't answered the phone, and he had business to attend to at the moment. Later, he would call her again. He placed his phone into his right, front pocket and left his vehicle. Edmund locked the door behind him before he adjusted his black suit jacket and red tie. After he made sure that none of his white button-up was un-tucked, he looked towards the hospital. It was time to handle the matter of that nurse.

After her behavior at the department store, he had wished to have acted sooner, but he had become tied up in the project. Ultimately, that plan was more important than anything concerning the nurse. Now, though, he had some time to deal with her. Almost, she had told his beloved about how he had known about that vile man's cheating, which would've delayed and might've harmed his future plans for his treasure. Something like that simply couldn't be tolerated.

His steps across the asphalt were smooth and with purpose. A neutral expression coated his face, and an air of business hung around him. Edmund had to remain calm even if he wanted to toss the nurse over the edge of the hospital roof. Almost, a malicious smirk touched his lips at the thought of the satisfying splat. It would be like swatting a fly, only an immense feeling of relief would follow.

The sliding doors opened and granted him access. Her supervisor already was informed of his visit, so there wouldn't be any delay. He even could pass the front desk, which he did, since he knew the location. Along the way, a few glanced in his direction. Some whispers transpired too. None of them were honeyed to his ears. To Edmund, only his treasure's compliments would sway a tender look to form in his eyes.

When he noted the fourth floor staff break room, he headed for the door and pushed it aside with no issue. None of the nurses were around. Then again, the chief nurse probably had a say in that. Entering the room, it was modern, warm and inviting. Large, rectangular windows permitted a flood of light to come in, and tables and chairs were pressed to the window so that staff could view the outside world and escape the innards of the hospital for awhile. Other tables and chairs filled the room. Along the back wall were appliances as well as a counter and cupboards.

To his left sat a man upon one of the few cushioned chairs in the room. Loose brown locks framed his face, and light brown eyes stared down at a cell phone. Only one cup of coffee sat on the small round table in front of him, though; some of it already had been partaken of. How thoughtful. Edmund's steps across the grey-white tile caught the man's attention. He stopped by the empty chair across from the man. "May I take a seat?" No words left the chief nurse; he merely indicated to the chair as he put his phone away. After he was seated, Edmund crossed his legs at his calves and maintained perfect posture. "Thank you, and thank you for meeting with me, Mr. Sini."

"Sure." His response was curt, and the chief nurse looked ready to pull out his phone again. Edmund held back the urge to twitch an eyebrow. "Just call me Donald. Don for short." He shrugged his shoulders before he leaned forward and intertwined his fingers. Don rested his arms on his knees as though he was about to interrogate his guest. "So, what do you need? I'm quite busy."

"Oh yes, I'm aware of that." The nurse had been reading a text of some sort, and Edmund doubted that it had been work related. "This won't take long." Don relaxed and settled back onto his chair comfortably. "What I need you to do is simple. Remove Gina from her work here. I know that your connections here will allow you to do that. I would've spoken to them myself, but I felt that this way would be more impactful." Every syllable of the last word, he stressed. Edmund's smirk could be heard in his tone.

"And, why would I do that? She hasn't caused a problem here." Amusement crossed Don's countenance, and he pulled out his phone as though he was finished with the conversation.

"That's an awfully biased opinion." An annoyed look fell onto the nurse. Edmund rested his left cheek against his fist. "You're sleeping with her." Don lowered his phone slightly, confusion in his eyes. His lips parted, but Edmund didn't let him speak. "She's probably not a problem to you because she's fulfilling something of yours."

At that, he set down his phone on the table. "I don't know how you know about my personal relationshp with her, but that is none of your business. Our conversation is over. Leave."

"I'm entitled to twenty minutes with you. That was our agreed upon terms." Edmund sat upright again. "And, you will fire her, or I'll have you fired and her as well."

"Now, you're threatening me?" He laughed darkly. "Look buddy, you're out of line. I'm having you removed and reported." Don stood up from his chair, and Edmund tried not to laugh, though; a smile on his lips appeared. The nurse paused angrily. "Tch, just what is your problem?"

"Gina. That's why I'm here. And, your supervisor knows that I'm here too. Like I had said, I know your superiors. How do you think that Gina had started working here in the first place?" Edmund quirked a brow. "I moved her here, and she crossed me when she knew not to, so my deal with her is off." Don clenched his fists and headed for the door. Now, he couldn't help but laugh. "So, you're really going to walk out on me?"

Shifting his position, Edmund faced him while remaining seated. "I'm surprised. You're acting like you care for her. Isn't she just one of your sleeping buddies?" Edmund chuckled. "What do you have ..." He looked like he was counting in his head even though he already knew the number. "Six?" Don stiffened.

Resting his arm on the back of the chair, Edmund smirked. "Or, is it because you're frustrated that I know this information? Is your pride ruined now that someone found out about your secret?" Edmund stood up from his seat and adjusted his jacket once more with a crisp tug. "Your decision, but I will know about it. You can either save your job and your other five relationships, or lose both and still lose Gina. If you wish to tell anyone about what I've told you, be my guest, but people will have a hard time believing such a productive cheater. And, I have other arguments stored to benefit me."

Abruptly, Don turned and met Edmund's gaze. Fury danced in his eyes, but fear rested there too. "I'll talk to my supervisor. Gina has been ... slacking." His eyes broke their hold with Edmund before he breathed in deeply and exhaled. "I never want to see your d*mned face again, though."

"You're not making the requests here, Donald." The staff room door opened, and Gina stepped in. Both men looked to her, and blood drained from her face upon seeing Edmund. Her eyes met Don's, and Edmund's expression went back to a neutral one, though; he was having a laughing fit on the inside. What timing. Then again, he might've slipped in a request for Gina in the staff room to one of the whispering nurses from before.

"Wh-wh-what ..." Her eyes were wide, and her limbs trembled. Hate and terror swirled in her brown eyes. "Don, what ..." A heavy frown set on the chief nurse's lips, and he was about to leave the room. Edmund, however, stepped ahead of him.

Leaning down to the male nurse's ear, he whispered in an ill-teasing manner, "You might want to take your phone before she sees it." He stood back up and left the staff room. Gina's questions followed soon after, and Edmund could hear them well down the hall. Due to how Don had gone rigid, the male nurse most likely had been texting another one of his lovers. Things had passed perfectly. Well, he should've controlled his laughter more, but he only could hold it back so much.

Of course, he would check in with the hospital to make sure that Gina had been fired. Otherwise, Don would be punished too. If either one of them bothered him in the future, though, he would have to take into account other means of handling them. Hopefully, it wouldn't come to that. He'd rather focus his efforts now purely on his treasure, and his project was halfway completed.

A vibration occurred in his pocket, and he removed his phone from it. Hana was calling. Excellent. He answered and held the phone to his right ear. "Thank you for getting back to me. I wanted to meet with you next week to discuss everything."

"I understand. She's doing well, though, and she has no idea about what your project will be. I haven't given anything about it away either. Regardless, you're going to be at the house still?" He hummed in response. "Then, I'll meet you there when I get back from my visit with her. I should have the roses by then, and I'll transplant them based on where you would like the planter boxes. Till then." She hung up, and he did the same.

Getting into his car, he locked the door and set his phone on the seat. A grin overtook his lips. Once the roses were in place, the surprise would become even more wonderful. Oh, how she would love it because she didn't have a choice on that matter.

## Chapter Forty Seven: Discuss

*Black wrought iron sat atop adobe bricks while the smell of roses was all around. Condensation formed on the outside of glasses where fresh-pressed orange juice resided; it was something close but also distant.*

Hands in his pockets, Edmund stood at the edge of the gardens. His right side was leaning up against an oak tree, and his right leg was crossed behind his left. The morning sun was warm and inviting, though; the clouds rolling overhead promised rain later on. A delightful scent of tulips filled the air, and the slight breeze brought over the scent of roses, which were closer to the house. Mixed in with the pink tulips, there were blue and white baby's breath flowers.

Out ahead, the landscape sloped downwards, and a set of stone stairs guided a path down towards the sand-covered shore. Dark blue waters lapped up against the sand, and the sea's smell occasionally merged with the floral scent. Edmund took in a deep breath and exhaled before he smiled. Soon, very soon, she would see what he was seeing. She would be looking out over the sea from a different viewpoint, but, ultimately, it would be the same. No longer would they have to deal with that nurse either. Don had kept his word, and she had been removed from the hospital. Hopefully, neither he nor she would make an appearance again.

His green-hazel eyes glanced back when he heard soft steps upon the grass. Hana held a straw hat, with a dark brown ribbon, to her head when the wind picked up for a moment. Her hair was tied back in its loose bun. An off-white blouse, dark brown skirt and off-white flats covered her form. A tired expression hung on her countenance, but happiness did meet her eyes. "It's all finished." He pushed himself off of the tree. "The planter boxes and flowers are where you requested them to be. She'll love it."

A slight smirk met his lips. "I know. She doesn't really have a choice in the matter, though." He stepped up beside her before she turned the other way and walked with him to the brick patio. "Has she mentioned anything that I should know about, though? Any developments since we last had talked?"

"She misses you and understands that you'll keep her safe, but you already know that." Edmund chuckled a bit and pulled out a cushioned, wrought iron chair for his aunt before he took a seat across from her. She smoothed out her skirt before she rested her hands atop her lap. "And, her wedding dress," Hana smiled, "it's gorgeous on her, though; she may have difficulty walking on sand with it."

"I can change the locations. It's a quick fix."

"Won't she see the house from a higher vantage point, though? That's why you originally were having it on the beach and having her enter from another path than the stairs."

"If we take one of the mountain paths, she still won't spot it. If she does, she won't know that it belongs to me. The mountains might be better than the beach because of the stairs. If she spots the stairs, she might question why we would be on private property. I always can make up some excuse, but it might raise suspicion." He chuckled. "Or, it might not. She's completely devoted to me, so she might not become doubtful of my words at all."

"And, you're certain that you want this?" Hana adjusted her hat after another brief breeze came by. "She may not forgive you after she learns the truth of the surprise."

"It's not a question of forgiveness." Edmund sat up straight as he reached forward and poured each of them a glass of fresh-pressed orange juice. "She'll accept it because there is no other option for her."

"What if it breaks her? She might become someone else after you reveal it."

"Then, that happens. Her safety is my priority. Besides, I've arranged everything so that she'll remain comfortable, and she'll have my company. I don't intend to leave my darling wife alone, Hana. That's why the project has taken so long, and I still have a few more additions to make. Unfortunately, I, technically, won't be able to complete it fully until its unveiling."

"Edmund, it's not only about her safety. I'd like to believe that, but I know that isn't the only reason. You're tired of leaving her on her own and giving her the chance to look at another man. And, you don't want another man to stare at her either."

"And if that's the case? Are you saying that you're backing out on me, Hana?" His tone remained level, but his gaze turned to his orange juice. He swirled the drink in his glass, and a warning look crossed his eyes. Hana, however, wasn't fazed.

"No. I would never back out on you. I only worry that she may back out on you. I don't want you to lose her. I want you to be happy."

Relaxing his gaze, he smiled up to his aunt. "I'm happy. This decision makes me happy. She'll finally be able to live in my true home, and I can get rid of that apartment. The curtains on the stage finally will be able to be pulled back."

Hana couldn't help but smile back to her nephew. Her eyes scanned over their scenery, and she admired the many rose bushes surrounding the patio. There were no purple roses among them. Edmund reserved those only for Elaine. Blue-hazel eyes rested on a patch of white roses. "Should I include any other colors in her bouquet? White is a traditional color for a wedding rose."

"Perhaps. Do you think that it would match her dress better that way?" Hana nodded in response. "Then, please add a few in." He took a sip of his orange juice before he tapped his fingers against the table in a light rhythm. "I think that'll be the only other modification for the wedding. The hotel suite isn't far away, so morning travel here will be simple."

"You're not intending to take her on a honeymoon? I thought that you had been." Hana partook of some of her drink and sat a little straight on her chair. She set down her glass and held down her hat as another breeze passed. Once it was gone, she decided to remove her hat and set it on her lap since that would be easier.

"Yes, I had, but I had realized that it only means more time for something to go wrong. That horrid nurse almost had ruined things already. Something like that could happen again. I don't desire that. We'll have our wedding night, and then she can enjoy her time here."

"I understand. I would've done the same if I could go back; I would've had your mother and father stay here with you. Maybe, your parents would be alive still, and you would've never had to witness that night."

"That might be true, but that part is over. I miss them, and I never want that to happen to someone I love again. However, I'm thankful for your guidance over the years, Hana, and for your help on this project. Most would find my idea bizarre and terrible. They wouldn't see the overwhelming benefit of it." Edmund finished his drink before he stood up from his seat. "And thanks to you, I'm one step closer to finishing it. You being my gardener has been helpful in a tremendous way."

Standing up herself, Hana nodded her head. "Of course, Edmund. And, thank you. I do look forward to hearing how the ceremony goes, though; I understand if you don't tell me immediately. You're going to have your hands full with explaining yourself and your project as well as the aftermath of it."

Both of them started to walk from the table after Hana completed her drink. They didn't enter the home; rather, they followed the brick path encircling it. "Yes, I'm aware of that. I'm prepared for whatever her reaction may be even if it's an unsatisfactory one. As I've said before, she has no choice in whether she loves it or not. It's my decision, and my decision is the best option for her." Hana made no verbal comment, but she nodded her head again.

Rounding a corner, they saw a delivery truck pull up towards the home. "You had to order more?" she asked as he opened the wooden gate, which led to the front of the house. "How many?" she questioned further while she stepped forward and thanked him.

"Quite a bit. I made more than I originally had expected, but there will still be room for all of them. In fact, I think that they will make the space all the more wonderful for Elaine. There won't be a space left empty, nor should there be."

After he closed and locked the gate behind them, Edmund followed alongside his aunt to the truck. Two men left the vehicle before they moved to the back and started to unload several boxes. Neither of the workers noticed either of the residents yet, but neither of them minded. Edmund simply watched them carefully so that they didn't drop and/or ruin anything. Everything had to be perfect for his treasure. Anything less wasn't acceptable.

"Hana, do you mind opening my studio door for me?"

"Not at all. I'll set up everything for you also." He smiled and thanked her before she walked into the house after she had unlocked the front door with her own key. Edmund remained outside and wore his business smile when the two men finally noticed him. The men placed down the last box, and Edmund thanked them. Inside of those boxes were some of the final pieces to the puzzle, and he couldn't wait to open them.

## Chapter Forty Eight: Seal

*The car unlocked, and the doors opened, bringing in the smells of the sea air and mountain flora. A dirt path lied ahead, but any rocks from it had been cleared; it made it even easier.*

Hands resting upon her lap, she leaned back onto the cushioned seat of the car. She sat on the back seat on the driver's side since it allowed her a better view of the water. Driving the car was a trusted worker of Edmund's. The woman didn't speak much other than to introduce herself as Anita, but a comfortable silence existed between the two of them.

Elaine had offered to drive her own car to the location, but Edmund had insisted that a bride shouldn't be driving to her own wedding, especially when the drive was a long one. She hadn't been able to get in a word after that, so she accepted to have Anita drive her, and the drive was quite long. Already, it had been several hours. They only had stopped once so far so that both of them could stretch their legs a bit and use the restroom if they needed it.

Other than that, Elaine hadn't wanted to take a break. It had been a month since she had last seen Edmund, and she was anxious to see him again. Maybe, it would be informal for a wedding, but she wanted to run towards him and hug him. She doubted that the officiant would judge her action, and no guests would notice since none would be there. And knowing Edmund, he would be thrilled by such a greeting.

Realistically, her dress and heels might make that running jump somewhat hard, and it depended on how the terrain looked too. From the looks of it, they were going to be getting married in the mountains. A mental sweat-drop formed. Maybe, she should take her heels off. Her dress was long enough, so Edmund wouldn't notice ... at least at first.

Attention shifting to her attire, she lifted her skirt a little and peeked at her white heels, which had little fabric bows on the front. The fabric matched the sheer first layer of her dress. It was white and had small polka dots along it.

Unlike the dress, though, the shoes didn't have small pale pink and tan tea roses on it. They were placed in such a way that the roses bore a waterfall effect from her left shoulder to the skirt of the dress. Underneath the first layer was white cotton fabric, and a corseted, cotton top covered her torso while the sheer sleeves were off-shoulder.

Hopefully, he would like it, but she was sure that he would with the roses on it. If the roses were purple and white, though, it would've been better since they would've matched her bouquet more, but they matched somewhat nonetheless. Besides, the purple rose was unique for them, and that was more important to her.

Averting her eyes back to the scenery, she noticed a street, which turned left, up ahead. Tall pines lined the road and made it impossible to see where the road led off to. Curiosity would've struck her if she hadn't noticed Edmund's car up ahead. She forgot about the mysterious road and focused on the fact that the car would be parked soon.

When it was, she about leaped out of the car, heels and all. They clicked on the asphalt as she shifted in them and smoothed out her skirt once more while her bouquet rested in her right hand. "Thank you, Anita!" she called as she waved to the woman before she drove off. Once her car was seemingly gone, it was silent. Only Edmund and probably the officiant's car were in the parking lot.

Heart thumping louder in her chest, she gripped her bouquet tightly and headed off towards the only path ahead, which was dirt. All of the rocks had been removed from it, though, so that it would be a somewhat smooth walk. Thankfully, it only had a slight incline upwards, so it wouldn't be too much of a hassle.

Stepping upon it and advancing forward, the smells of the sea and mountain flora grew stronger it seemed. She took a deep breath in before she exhaled, which calmed her to a degree. As she continued to hike up, she turned to the right and then to the left. Some wind traveled through the path, and she was thankful that she had styled her hair into a simple braided updo.

Making another turn, she noticed two people up ahead. Her sepia brown painted lips broke into a smile, and she was happy that she chose not to wear a lot of light-colored eye shadow or mascara. Otherwise, it might get ruined from crying later on from pure joy.

Steps becoming quicker, she hurried towards them and lifted up the skirt of her dress a little so that she wouldn't trip. The officiant looked up and over her way while Edmund finally faced her. Her heart skipped a beat, and her legs moved faster. He smiled to her, but his smile was cut short due to her jumping a little and wrapping her arms around him. His balance wavered for a bit before he stabilized them both. A chuckle escaped his lips as he hugged her back and placed a kiss atop her head. "I'm happy to see you too, Elaine, and you look absolutely stunning, my love."

By a bit, she stepped back from him and continued to smile up at him. Her cheeks probably would hurt later, but that was a miniscule price to pay. "And, you look very handsome." She didn't even have to glance at his tan suit and vest, white button-up and pale pink tie to know that, though; it was unusual not to see him in black, but it was a nice change also. Elaine diverted her eyes to the lavender tea rose on the left side of his vest. Lightly, her right fingers brushed it petals before she moved her hands to his.

Both of them shifted their gazes over to the officiant. Elaine turned her eyes back to Edmund as the officiant started to read for the ceremony. Edmund looked to her too. When it came time for the vows, Edmund tightened his hold on her hands and brought her a bit closer to him. They had prepared their own vows, and he would speak first.

"Elaine, my treasure and my love, I'll forever seal myself to you as your loyal and loving husband. When you need me to hold you, to wipe your tears, to ease your mind, I'll be there." His left hand parted from hers, and his fingers rested under her chin tenderly. "I'll be there whenever you require me. All you have to do is ask, and I'm yours. I'll keep you safe for as long as I breathe, and I wish that I could've kept you safe from the first time that I had laid eyes upon you. Then, perhaps, I could've made this promise to you already. But, you have my word that I'll cherish and love you until death do us part. Even beyond that, I'll be connected to you and hold onto you, my dearest love."

Biting her lower lip a little, she leaned into his touch before she pressed a light kiss to the tips of his fingers. She held back tears from embarrassment and jubilation. His words pierced her heart fiercely, but she forced herself to remain composed so that she could speak her vow properly.

"Edmund, I'll eternally bond myself to you too, for you have shown me kindness and love that only someone once in a lifetime could give to me. You helped me through my darkest times and never turned away from me. You were there and have been there since. I can't think of a life without you now, and I wish that I had known you sooner. I trust you with all of me until death and beyond."

Dropping his hand back to hers, he intertwined his fingers with hers again and tugged her even closer. Her body was a few inches from his, and her heart picked up its rate even more. Elaine's eyes stared into his before they traveled down to his lips. She didn't even hear the officiant speak as Edmund answered, "I do."

Edmund's words cut into her mind, and she caught onto the officiant's question just in time. "I do." Removing both rings from his right pants pocket, Edmund handed his to her and kept hers. Both of them exchanged their gold rings, which had roses engraved into them. The officiant smiled and pronounced them as husband and wife and for Edmund to kiss her. Before she knew it, Edmund's lips were upon hers. Her hands slid up his chest before they wrapped around his neck. His hands rested gently on her hips and moved her flush against him.

"Congratulations to you both," the officiant spoke when they pulled apart from each other. He nodded his head before he bid them farewell and headed off to his own car. Edmund and Elaine didn't follow. Rather, they stayed on the large rocks that overlooked the ocean below and remained close to each other.

Resting his forehead against hers, Edmund smiled gently. "Tomorrow, you'll get to see your surprise. Do you think that you can wait for the rest of today?"

Closing her eyes, she enjoyed the feeling of him against her. "I think so. Tonight, we have plenty of surprises already." She opened her eyes as he pulled away from her and chuckled.

"Yes, we do. We have the whole night to ourselves." A smirk touched his lips slightly, and heat invaded her cheeks. She looked away from him and stared to the flowers in her hands. Another laugh parted from him before he held onto her free hand. "Of course, we have to get to the hotel first. I think that you'll like our room."

"Our luggage is in your car, right?" she asked, trying to get various mental images out of her mind.

"Yes, I have everything that we'll need. I even brought an extra outfit for you so that you can change out of your dress for dinner unless you'd prefer to wear it." She shook her head, happy to hear that news. A wedding dress would draw an awful lot of attention, and she didn't want that to happen. "In that case, I think that you'll like the change. I made sure that it matched my attire as per usual." Elaine released a light laugh and started to walk back with him to his car with a skip in her step. Like her, Edmund walked with a lighter air too. The night would be wonderful. Tomorrow, though, would start a permanent bliss for the both of them.

## Chapter Forty Nine: Comfort

*Late afternoon light poured in through the large dining area windows. Almost, the sun was ready to set, and waiters and waitresses came around to light the candles on each of the dining tables being used.*

Stepping down the stairs, she intertwined her right fingers with his left. Tan pumps covered her feet, and a pale pink, flared dress, which had a tan and white bow on its left side, decorated her form. Her hair remained in its braided updo, and those who already had seen them in the hotel knew that they just had gotten married. Thankfully, that didn't include too many people. Congratulations were nice up to a point, and then they became tiring. Admittedly, though, it was nice to know that complete strangers cared or were that polite.

Reaching the bottom of the steps, Edmund guided them to the dining area. Back in their room, which had a lovely view of the mountains, he had removed his jacket. It was odd to see him walking around in public without one, but he did have the vest on. And, she wasn't complaining that she could admire his form all the more, which led her mind elsewhere. Quickly, however, she pulled her mind out of those thoughts. There was dinner first.

When they entered the dining room, she paused momentarily. The views from the windows were similar to that in their room, though, on a grander scale. Rich, red velvet curtains outlined the glass portals, and red carpet swept across the floor. Each table was simple but elegant and had comfortable, plush chairs for the users. On each table, red roses and pink baby's breath complemented the tea lamps and standing fan-styled napkins.

"Wow, it's lovely here." She stepped forward a bit. "You chose well. This is a surprise in itself."

Guiding her further into the room, he smiled. "I tend to have a good taste." His eyes glanced to her briefly, and they met hers. A look of embarrassment crossed her countenance, but a small smile touched her lips regardless.

"Thank you," she mumbled before her eyes caught something else in the room. Among all of the other tables, there was one with a purple rose and white baby's breath. A grin now graced her lips. "I take it that's ours." Edmund nodded and pulled her chair out for her when they reached it. "And, it's even a window seat."

"Well, it's our wedding day. We should enjoy it while it lasts." A warm, gentle smile touched his lips even though his tone towards the end was ... suspicious. She furrowed her brows momentarily before she told herself that she was over-thinking again. That was a natural thing for someone to say on their wedding day.

Relaxing her expression, she nodded in agreement and picked up her drink menu. When she noted that the menu had a well-recommended pinot noir on it, she suspected she would be drinking that, not that she minded. Elaine turned the menu to face him and tapped the name of the wine. "Is this why you selected this place?" she questioned in a teasing tone.

Edmund quirked a brow and shrugged. "It's possible. You'll enjoy it, though, if you've liked the past wines I've selected for us." She shook her head in amusement and placed down the menu. "Unless you would prefer to order something else. We can order two different drinks too."

Again, she shook her head, and she smiled back to him. "No, I trust your opinion. Let's order it."

~ ~ ~ ~ ~ ~ ~ ~ ~ ~ ~

Finishing dinner and her glass of wine, Elaine leaned back on her chair and faced the gorgeous view outside. The sun was setting, and waiters and waitresses started to light the tea lamps on the tables being used. Edmund signaled that they didn't need theirs lit, and he soon stood up from his seat. He held out his left hand to her, and she took it easily as she shifted her attention onto him. After he lifted her up, he walked out of the dining area with her.

The halls were quiet, and a warm glow came off of the lights, which staff members flicked on for the evening hours. Off to their right, there was a lounge. Both of the paned glass doors were open, and soothing piano music drifted out of it. That environment would be perfect for casual conversation over a drink.

Towards the back of the hall, paned glass doors opened up onto a large balcony, which overlooked the mountains. Tables and chairs were out there, and a part of them was connected to the restaurant. Strings of lights hung overhead and flickered on as the sun finally set. Its rays swam across the hallway before they vanished.

"Should we head to our room, or would you like to stay down here for some time?" His eyes drifted over to the lounge. "They might let us dance in there."

At the thought, a soft smile graced her lips. "I know somewhere better." She tightened her hold on his hand and led him out the front of the hotel. If she was correct, there was a more private spot which was near the lounge. They should be able to hear the music from there.

Winding around the building by a bit, there was a small patch of grass, which had a cobblestone patio in the center of it and overlooked the valley of mountains below. Luckily, no one else was there. She stepped onto the patio with him and intertwined her other fingers with his. He leaned down and pecked her on the lips. "Yes, this is better."

Slowly, he started to lead her in an easy, relaxing dance. The piano music just was audible in the background, and a faint glow from the inside highlighted them. Their shoes clicked against the stone in rhythm with the music, and she hoped that they would be able to share similar moments in the future. Perhaps, future vacations would grant them such an experience again.

Liking that thought, she leaned her head against his chest and listened to his heart beat at a steady pace. She closed her eyes and allowed the music and his heartbeat to guide her next steps. His one hand slipped around her waist while hers traveled up his chest and rested on his shoulder. As the music faded out for a new song, their feet slowed too until they stopped completely.

Elaine lifted her head up as fingers glided under her chin and tilted it up more. Her eyes met his before they closed once more when his lips connected to hers. The kiss was caring and warm while those snaps of fire happened underneath it all. As the kiss deepened, her other hand left his as both of her arms now draped over his shoulders.

Soon enough, her fingers glided up and tangled in his locks gently. Both had to pull apart for air, but their lips remained close to the other. Edmund ghosted his over hers, and the invitation was understood well enough as she opened her eyes and nodded. Reluctantly, they moved farther away from the other, but their hands rejoined together. A new song played in the background, but its tune fell deaf upon their ears while they climbed the stairs when they were inside.

Picking up a little, her heartbeat increased, and she could feel heat invade her cheeks. Her gaze became downcast when they entered the hall in case anyone passed them by. Thankfully, no one did, or that would've been embarrassing. A click caught her attention, and she noted that their room door opened. Edmund led her in, and another click sounded soon after.

His hand left hers before his fingers found her chin again. She closed the distance more between them after she slipped off her shoes. Her hands pressed against his chest lightly while his other arm wrapped around her waist once more. Their lips met, and a gentle fire brewed as one stepped back and the other forward. Edmund's legs bumped into the back of the bed, but he didn't fall over. Rather, he kept his balance and continued to kiss her while his right fingers slipped up to the buttons of her dress and undid them one by one.

Dress slackening around her shoulders, it started to slip off before she shrugged it off of her arms. It hugged her hips until Edmund's hand untied the ribbon. Both the ribbon and the dress pooled around her feet. She pressed more into him due to the draft of cold air that greeted her form. Momentarily, their lips disconnected, and Edmund fell back onto the bed. His hands gripped her hips tenderly while he situated her on his lap.

It wasn't long before his lips met her again. They trailed along her jaw-line while her hands undid his tie and removed it from him. A gasp parted from her when he kissed the left side of her neck and sucked at the skin teasingly slow. Her head hung, and her hands gripped the edges of his vest before they slackened and rested on the buttons of it. Before she could unbutton the first one, a moan escaped her lips, and a pleased chuckle left him.

Trailing his lips down to her collarbone, he started on a new mark, and she forced her hands to work. One, then two buttons were undone, and her hands slipped the vest from him before his hands landed on her almost bare back. His right began to undo the latches of her white, lace corset while his left ran along the rim of her matching underwear. A warm chill traveled through her, and she had to lean her head against his shoulder in the process.

Slipping from her torso, the corset hit the ground delicately and landed atop her dress. Her chest only had a moment to adjust to the air before her back landed on the bed. Edmund parted his lips from her as a few locks broke free from his hair gel and framed his face handsomely. They shared a smile before she raised her hands and tangled her fingers in his hair. Their lips connected soon after.

## Chapter Fifty: Lock

*From almost every angle, almost every direction, she saw them. Each was crafted beautifully and portrayed the scenery to a perfect, terrifying point, and she couldn't help but collapse.*

A groan escaped lips as eyes opened gradually against the sun pouring in. She moved her face back into the pillow as a roaring headache consumed her. Elaine furrowed her brows. Last night, she hadn't drunk a lot of wine; she only had one glass. Not to mention that her mind hadn't been foggy during ... well, later on. By a little bit, heat touched her cheeks.

That was the case until her memory moved onto later in the evening. She had woken up in the middle of the night to the light hum of a driving car. Headlights had illuminated the road ahead, and the faint outlines of mountains and trees had been on either side of the car. Around her form had been her clothes she had been wearing during dinner. How she had been able to dress without waking up had been ... Wait, that couldn't be right.

She groaned into her pillow more. Last night, she had changed herself and followed Edmund to the car. He had stated that he had wanted to show her something spectacular and that they had needed to leave then to make it on time. At that time, she had been half asleep and had fallen back asleep once she had seated herself on the passenger seat.

Had they arrived at their location, and she just had forgotten in her groggy morning state? That couldn't be right either. What had happened after the second time she had woken up? Her hands gripped the edges of the pillow ... Wait, pillow? Were they back at the hotel? Why did such an idea seem odd to her? The mountains and trees passing by ... Instantly, she shot up on her hands before she gripped her head with her right hand. She stared down at the lavender-colored pillow. It hadn't been the color of their sheets at the hotel. They had been cream-colored. Her mind snapped back to the memory of last night, and her eyes widened.

When she had awoken, her eyes had drifted over to ... over to ... someone. She couldn't remember who. The car had stopped, she had asked something, she had yelled something and a hand with a cloth had covered her nose. Chloroform ...

Panic began to set in. Where Was She? Lavender pillows ... had someone been watching Edmund and her? Was he okay? Moving onto her knees, she rested her fists on them and told herself to take a few deep breaths and exhale. If she had been kidnapped, she needed to keep ... she needed to ... Why was she wearing a nightgown she had never seen?! Who had changed her?!

Forgetting about her headache, she whipped her to her right before she gripped it tightly. Another moan of discomfort left her before she sat up straight slowly. What ... What was she viewing? The wall in front of her ... She steadily glanced to all of the walls. They were on all of them.

Shock and rejection brought her to her feet. She was wobbly at first, almost falling down, but she managed to stay standing. Elaine stood closer towards the wall opposite the end of the bed. Her eyes narrowed as she read the title on one of the paintings: *Recount.* The picture displayed her curled on her bed back at her old apartment. All of the sheets were off of her and wrinkled beneath her. That had been the night that she had been thinking about Edmund asking her out to *The Fox's Garden.*

"H-how ..." Sentences couldn't form in her mind. Her eyes darted to other pictures. If she started with the pictures closest to the door and looked clockwise around the room, they played a story. The story of how she had become closer to Edmund. How could someone know all of that, let alone paint all of it? Ed-Edmund ... No. No. NO! "He isn't like that. This doesn't make sense," she muttered to herself.

Legs failing her, she collapsed to the floor. The lavender lace nightgown pooled around her form, and she shook her head delicately so that it wouldn't hurt too much. Tears started to form at the corners of her eyes as she tried to process what she was viewing. Maybe, it was all a horrible nightmare. She closed and opened her eyes, but she remained in the horrible room.

Eventually, her eyes landed on the door. She had to get out. With any luck, whoever had done all of this had forgotten to lock it. Her mind told her who it was, but she denied its words. "I can't believe that." Barely, her words were audible. As she was about to stand up, the doorknob turned.

Once again, panic struck at her veins. She surveyed the room, but her action sent another wave of pain through her head. There was nowhere to hide but under the bed. Wait! Her eyes landed on another door. That had to be the bathroom or closet. It was obvious, but it wasn't under the bed at least. It was too late, however. A click resonated throughout the space, and the door opened. The voice she didn't want to hear met her ears.

"Elaine, what are you doing on the floor? It has been cleaned, but there is a bed for a reason if you wish to rest." His tone was casual, painfully so. Edmund stepped more into the room and closed the door behind him, locking it too.

"I ... I ..."

"Yes, you're probably surprised, confused and possibly angry or happy. I'd prefer you to be happy. All of these paintings had taken a month." Her lips parted as more of the pieces fell into place. "While you're thinking on how I accomplished all of this, don't return to that assumption that I had killed that ex of yours. I can assure you that I had no part in his accident or death. Things simply had worked out for me."

"How ... How long?" she spoke, not able to meet his eyes. Her mind was breaking at the seams, and the words out of his mouth seemed like those in a far-off world.

Stopping in front of her, he asked, "How long what? How long had I known you, been in love with you?" She nodded her head before she recoiled at his second phrase. "Since I had seen you in that bakery with your ex. I had paid for your two's meal since he only had a credit card." A saddened smile coated his lips. "Unfortunately, you hadn't paid much attention to me." His smile morphed into a pleased one. "Clearly, though, that worked out in the long run."

"Why?"

"You know the answer." He grabbed her hands, but she didn't intertwine her fingers with his. Edmund sighed and tugged on her wrists before she was on her feet again. "I love you, and I want to keep you safe." She froze. His aunt's words ...

"Your aunt ..." He nodded. She pulled her wrists from him and took a few steps back. More tears began to form. "Wh-what else a-are y-you kee-keeping from m-me?"

"Do you need to know? You're here now in your new room, new home. You're safe, and you have my company." Edmund walked past her and stood by the window. "I even provided you with a view similar to that picture you had liked back in the magazine. Hana did an excellent job of planting identical flowers in the garden." A smile continued to coat his lips. With the motion of his head, he indicated for her to come over. "Don't you want to see what I've created for you?" His tone was more of a demand than a question.

"No. No," she mumbled mainly to herself. She created distance between the two of them; she needed a break from the room, from him. Her mind needed time away from it all. Everything she had done with him was crashing around her, and the rings on her left ring finger only caused her more turmoil.

"I even had willingly married you, had ... had sex with you ..." Edmund finally faced her, and he looked pained. He had no right to look like that. All along, he had been watching her before they even had dated. The matching clothes, where he had shown up, all of it made sense now. And, the fact that she had been so stupid to brush facts aside or trust his carefully framed words made her present reality all the worse since part of the blame fell on her for foolishly letting him get so close.

"You played me. All for," her hands weakly gestured to around her, "for this. No wonder you knocked me out! You knew that I wouldn't willingly come into this room or that I would fight you!" Anger started to control her as tears continued to fall down her cheeks, and she forced her headache away momentarily.

Past his lips, a long, drawn-out sigh escaped. He placed his hands in pants' pockets. "I assumed so. Your reaction is living up to that." Edmund seated himself on the window seal. "I really hoped that you would accept it, but I suppose that was too ideal. Just please know that I'm only doing this out of my desire to keep you safe. You're my only love, and I can't lose you. This is for the best."

"No, it's not!" Her hands curled into fists at her sides. "This is too far! You're locking me away; you're taking away my freedom! That's not something you do to someone you claim to love." She uncurled her hands and reached for her rings.

In seconds, he was by her, and his hands gripped her wrists. "Don't. You're married to me. Keep them on." She tried to remove her wrists from him, but his grip was iron. He tugged her closer. "Please, calm down. Look at the pictures. See how much care I put into them. They're all for you."

"Liar." Her tone was harsh, cold and rang of misfortune. "They're for you, only you. You locked me in this cage so that I only can think of you, of your time with me."

"I do want you to think only of me, to depend only on me. That'll keep you safe because I can keep you safe best. Even if it hurts right now, it'll get better. I'm your husband. I'll make it better."

Managing to rip her wrists away from him, she shook her head before she winced. "Wrong. You've already made this a nightmare." She sucked in a breath before she exhaled again. "Just let me out." Her weaker side was taking over again. The prospect of staying in the horrible room for the rest of her life frightened her. "Please. You can correct this."

"Liar." He returned the word back to her, but his tone was only saddened. "You wouldn't let me change what I've done even if I did accept your offer. You'd get rid of me as soon as you could one way or another." Edmund walked past her, and she spun to round a punch on him. He tried to dodge, and she hit him in one of his ribs.

A wince touched his face before he grabbed her wrists again and backed her towards the bed. She struggled and cried out, hoping that maybe someone would help. Even if someone did hear her, though, she doubted that they would do much since anyone else in the home probably already had known of his scheme. Edmund pushed her onto the bed gently and removed her rings. "I'll hold onto these while I'm not in the room with you. You could injure yourself."

Covering her countenance was a sharp glare. "Didn't you just tell me to keep them on?"

"Yes but when I'm in here with you. Otherwise, you could hurt yourself. I'm not taking any chances." He started to walk away from her. "I'll be nearby so that if you need me, I'll be here quickly." She scowled at the suggestion. "A staff member of mine will wait outside your door. Tell them what you need, and they'll come get me." Another hurt smile graced his lips. "I'll check on you later, my love."

Facing away from her fully, he headed towards the door. Hurriedly, she got off of the bed, only for her head to act up again, but she recovered and continued after him. "Take another step forward, and I'll have to restrain you to the bed in the meantime." She stopped. His tone was dead serious, and fear crept into her again.

Before she could give anymore protest, the door opened and closed behind him. The lock clicked once more. Her energy drained from her, and she collapsed again to the floor. Tears continued to stream down her cheeks and hit the carpet below as her gaze stayed pinned on the locked door. She had been so foolish, and her broken mind couldn't comprehend how to regain its composure.

No comfort greeted her when her mind tried to think of something else. The past weeks only had been filled with thoughts of Edmund, and he was now her main source of pain. Elaine lied down on the floor, curled up into a ball and closed her eyes. Never should she have let him in. Now, she couldn't get rid of him, and her prison constantly reminded her of that painful truth.

## Epilogue:

Pushing back the curtains, she stared out at the scenery she had seen for months on end now. Ocean waves lapped up against the shore below. Bright pink tulips and blue baby's breath were bright and swayed in the slight morning breeze. Roses were many and well taken care of by Hana, who she only saw on rare occasions. Mountains stood tall in the background, and only the sky really seemed to change on a day-to-day basis. Right now, it was overcast.

During the evening, however, she would always have a bright blue sky greeting her, like in that painting from the magazine. The same scene was painted onto her curtains, and roses were still present to her eyes. Purple ones grew in planter boxes around the perimeter of the room.

To spite Edmund and even his aunt in the beginning, she had destroyed some of them. When Edmund had seen their state ... A chill ran up her spine at the memory, being restrained to the bed for days, only to be let up for the restroom and a shower. And when she showered, her wrists had been restrained, and he had washed her from head to toe. Each day of that, she had changed back into the same lavender nightgown. The experience had been humiliating.

Even presently, there was no lock on the inside of the bathroom door. It was locked on the outside too unless someone opened it for her, and they would stand outside until she was finished in case she tried anything. Once she did try to steal the keys off of one of Edmund's assistants, but that had ended up with a similar result to that of when she had destroyed the flowers.

Despite all of this, Edmund had insisted throughout it all that he only was protecting her. Maybe, he truly believed that, but she couldn't accept that; however, she was forced to go along with it. She had been following the rules for so long, and the memories of her breaking them were so terrible, that she couldn't snap out of the cycle of obedience even if her mind told her to.

Her hands dropped from the curtains, and her fingertips touched the hem of her cream-colored, silk nightgown. She wanted to shower and change, but Edmund was still fast asleep. And when he was asleep, that was better. Glancing back to his form, her eyes trailed over his exposed upper half, which she used to find attractive. Some part of her still did, but it was small, and she could push it aside easily. Now, it was hard to look past him being merely her delusional captor. Even the rings on her fingers, which she only wore when he was awake and in the room, did little to remind her that he was her husband.

Shifting her eyes over to her pillow and back to him, her mind told her that it would be so easy. He would be gone like that, but she'd probably be thrown into another prison unless she managed a way to escape, but he didn't keep the keys on him when he spent the night with her. No, like her, he would have to knock on the door and ask for them to be slid under the door. It was a risk, but he wouldn't take the larger risk of her stealing the keys when he was asleep, and he insisted on spending the nights with her occasionally.

A sigh parted from her lips, and she forced her eyes from the pillow before they averted over to the last two paintings on the wall behind the bed. The night they had spent at that hotel restaurant and the day when she had discovered the horrid fate he had in store for her. How she wished that she could tear them apart, but that would have the same effect as the roses, and he would replace them. He had paintings on standby in case she attempted such a thing; he had told her himself.

Feeling dejected, she seated herself on the floor by the bed and leaned her back against the mattress. Her dark brown, curly locks were in disarray and her face barren. She folded her hands on her lap and stretched her legs. Rarely, did she doll herself up like in the past. Now, she only did so when Edmund requested, well demanded, "kindly," that she do so.

Part of her wished to break down and cry, but her tears were too dried up, and her whole body ached already. She simply was happy that she didn't have a mirror at the moment to spot all of the bruises on her skin, and she'd probably cover the bathroom mirror with a towel later on. Her eyes diverted over to the window.

The possibility of shattering the glass and breaking free tickled her mind, but it was hopeless. That glass was incredibly strong, and she had tried throwing a planter box at it when she had destroyed some of the roses back then; the metal planter box had bounced back and almost had knocked her over. Some of the roses then had flown out of the planter box, and if the thorns hadn't been removed, she would've received a few cuts.

Hands resting on her shoulders made her jump out of her thoughts. A light kiss was pressed to the left side of her head, and she knew better than to move away from it. "Good morning, my treasure." He chuckled lightly. "You shouldn't be sitting on the floor. Come join me on the bed."

"I ..." Another kiss was pressed to her cheek, and she went silent. His hands slipped from her shoulders, and she reluctantly stood up. Edmund's fingers intertwined with her right ones before he pulled her onto the bed with him. She landed on his lap, and her hands pressed against his chest while her legs straddled his hips.

Tilting her chin up, he smiled to her and pecked her gently on the lips before he pulled back. His fingers trailed from her chin to her hair, and he brushed some of the locks back as he smoothed some of her hair back into place. Edmund shifted his eyes over to her neck, and his fingers touched a few of the marks there. She winced slightly, but she didn't speak; she tried to ignore his supposedly affectionate gazes.

Moving her eyes off of him, they trailed back to the paintings on the wall. Each one framed to perfection so that their beauty could mock her endlessly, so that his deceptive nature could live on forever. Lips pressed against one of the marks, and she closed her eyes in slight pain from the soreness, but even the darkness couldn't save her from his well-crafted, framed deception.